PRAISE FOR PAPERLESS

"A fascinating novel written in the shadow of Dambudzo Marechere, about Africans, and South Africans, hating and loving Oxford." – Imraan Coovadia, author of *The Wedding* and *Tales of the Metric System*

"*Paperless* is a voyeuristic journey through the lives of an eclectic ensemble of unforgettable characters. Siwisa skillfully interweaves their poignant stories through evocative images peppered with comical wit. With precision, he probes the politics of being African, black, undocumented and displaced in the lily-white streets of Oxford. A sensual novel that provokes all your sensibilities." – Sue Nyathi, author of *A Family Affair* and *An Angel's Demise*

The financial assistance of the National Institute for the Humanities and Social Sciences (NIHSS) towards this publication is hereby acknowledged. Opinions expressed and those arrived at are those of the author and are not necessarily attributed to the NIHSS.

First published by Jacana Media Pty (Ltd) in 2023

10 Orange Street
Sunnyside
Auckland Park 2092
South Africa
+2711 628 3200
www.jacana.co.za

© Buntu Siwisa, 2023

All rights reserved.

ISBN 978-1-4314-3401-5

Cover design by The Curators
Editing by Lynn Taylor and Sean Fraser
Proofreading by Linda Da Nova
Set in Sabon 12/15pt
Printed by Inside Data
Job no. 004081

See a complete list of Jacana titles at www.jacana.co.za

PAPERLESS

A NOVEL

BUNTU SIWISA

In loving memory of Dr Ding Col Dau Ding (21 November 1975 – 28 October 2015), my dearest friend in Oxford

To my grandparents, Dennis Didiza and Nomalinge Augusta Siwisa, who gave me life

To my uncle, Thandisizwe 'My Broer' Siwisa, who taught me literally everything

ACKNOWLEDGEMENTS

This is the novel of my youth. But it has come to pass well into my maturity. I wrote its very first draft between 2000 and 2005 in Oxford, while I laboured on my doctoral thesis work. In pursuit of work and life between 2005 and 2008, I carried it in my suitcase from Oxford to Pretoria, Gqeberha, Accra and back to Pretoria. And throughout this time, the manuscript refused to bend. To any of my rigorous edits and extensive rewrites, it refused to move. I chipped, chiselled, swerved and carved away at it, and it still refused to yield. And then, in 2008, I abandoned it to smother in dust, moving away from it to live, love, work, party and read.

During this hiatus, I recall receiving a profound critique of the manuscript from an old dear friend, Khwezi Mngqibisa, on one Saturday afternoon. At our local Dros in Waterkloof Ridge, Pretoria, many years ago, over many things, we discussed the novel, then titled, *The Party's Over, Mate!* He pointed out that the biggest flaw of the manuscript was that it went on and on about a whole lot of things. He advised me instead to focus on a core theme, and delve deeply into it. I took his advice to heart, to focus on the experiences of immigrants, their paperlessness. The subject was an onion, which I peeled, finding substance with each layer.

On revisiting *The Party's Over, Mate!* it finally bent to submission under the weight of maturity. This is how it morphed into *Paperless*. When I fetched the manuscript from the dust many years later, I was pleasantly baffled as to why this story had not yet been told. It had patiently waited for me to tell the world of its sorrows and burdens, pains and shocks, beauty and glory, wonders and history. And I can only thank God for assigning me this task.

There are numerous people who helped me bring *Paperless* to life. Bridget Impey and Maggie Davey of Jacana Media had an unflappable faith in the beauty and the originality of the novel. I thank them for pinning their commitment to publishing *Paperless*. I remember chatting with Maggie on how she was moved both by some characters in the novel, and by the style of writing. I am equally grateful to Jacana staffers – Kelly-Ann Mawa, Shay Heydenrych – for putting together all the logistics that go into preparing and publishing a novel. And I thank the National Institute for the Humanities and Social Sciences for its financial support in the production of this book.

I underwent a rigorous and wonderful structural and line editing process with Lynn Taylor of Oxford, UK. Through Lynn, I learnt the finer lessons of editing that I had never picked up before. These have empowered me for future editorial work. Sean Fraser did a superb job in the second line editing, which was just as rigorous and wonderful. Through his efforts, the manuscript came out a much finer and flowing read. Linda Da Nova smoothed out all the remaining creases in the proofreading editorial swipe. I thank Lara Jacob, Megan Mance and Lucille Koch, all of Jacana Media, for all your contributions in putting together this manuscript and turning it into this wonderful novel.

The small network of South African writers and academics I have access to helped me in various ways. Thank you Imraan Coovadia and Sue Nyathi for taking precious time out of your very busy schedules to sit down, read my manuscript and write shouts for it. Thanks also to Siphiwo Mahala, Bongani Ngqulunga and Masande Ntshanga for your support and help in various ways.

On a personal front, I have so much pleasure in expressing my gratitude to a small group of friends who read my manuscript and offered criticism. Cordelia Masalethulini, you have been there from the beginning, offering me insightful analysis, criticism and support all the way from Harare. Mlungisi Mfeketho, you have read all my fiction, and gave me holds unbarred criticism, which at times was slightly difficult to swallow. However, I know that it was done in full support, to enable me to develop my craft. And I thank Keneilwe Mmusinyane and her two sons for reading my manuscript, and for their support.

In closing, I want to express my profound appreciation to my mother, Lulu Pemba, who continually reminds me of my value as an intellectual, a creative and a person when I deeply doubt it. To my daughter, Sintu Mbatha, for your tireless cheerleading through my literary endeavours. To my eleven-year-old niece, Lilanga Siwisa, who has been my supporter in this writing enterprise from the beginning. And lastly, I am equally grateful to Siyabulela Ntutela, Jimmy Lekgoathi and William Maphosa, for your assuring, resilient and reliable companionship which silently propped me up and kept me steady in the eerie loneliness of writing.

Buntu Siwisa
22 August 2023
Johannesburg, South Africa

ONE

I WAS ON MY WAY TO SEE Ian Smith. For twenty pounds, I was going to see the last white prime minister of Zimbabwe. His name had been sizzling under my breath the whole day. And I couldn't decide whether I was excited or uneasy or nervous or appalled – or pretending to feel some or all of these things. But why? Was it that I was about to come face to face with the man who had vowed that "not in a thousand years" would Zimbabweans rule themselves? Or was it that for once – for once, that night – Africa was not going to jive on the outskirts of Oxford? That Africa was not going to be relegated to Area Studies? Why did I care anyway?

And why was I there? I had asked myself that two years back, rolling my luggage out of Heathrow Terminal One to catch a seventy-minute bus ride to Oxford. Taking my first step on English soil, I had looked around and wondered: Do I really need to be here? For this? For this long? Do I need to be here in order to write a doctoral thesis about the politics of a South Africa I had left behind? What was it that this England could offer me that South Africa couldn't? And now I had paid twenty pounds – two tenners, or four fivers – to meet my neighbour almost eleven hours by plane, far away from our homes.

Why did it matter that we all had to be there? Were we summoned by some absent father? I could not let go of that feeling of a child acting, hopping about in theatrical bounds. That child, tugging at the jacket of his father, gasping for his attention, of a father looking elsewhere. Or perhaps I had long stopped caring about the properness of these things. "Solsbrry, not Salisbheri!" Long ago, Mama – my grandmother – had jumped at how I had bastardised the whole affair of pronouncing the name of the capital city of a Rhodesia dead for a long time even then.

And for twenty quid, at the Oxford Union, I was going to watch Ian Smith stand before us, debating: Do African leaders govern for, or against the interests of their people? But we all quietly knew that the Oxford Union was gunning for the old boogeyman RG: *Gushungo, Karigamombe*, Comrade, First Secretary, Commander-in-Chief, His Excellency President Robert Gabriel Mugabe. Even lashing out at the back of the shadow of the Big Bad Wolf serenely sipping on tea with his dearest Grace down in Harare was going to suffice. That was all there was to it.

Anyway, all the black people in Oxford – the whole lot of them – were coming to see Ian Smith. We had been talking about this for the entire Michaelmas term, all through autumn. It was strange that we had said very little, and knew almost nothing about the rest of the Zimbabwean delegation – Margaret Dongo and other celebrated opposition leaders. Ian Smith. That old, fragile Ian Smith – I imagined him.

"Ian Smith." I tossed out his name in a hissing lungful. Perched on my blue mountain bike on Magdalen Street, his name did a roundabout zing through my helmet. Zimbabwe had been on my mind a lot those past few weeks. But I wanted her gone. I wanted to stop thinking about Zimbabwe, about my father, who had been exiled from there. I had just managed to push aside flashbacks of a horseshoe-shaped library fast catching fire when my mother broke the news. "Double pneumonia." My mother's voice did not break over the phone three weeks back. It had not been sad. It had not been happy. The man was dead.

The man died, my mother had said. "The man died" – that telegram had come to Wole Soyinka. Cryptically, it told him of what had happened to the disappeared fellow inmate he had enquired of shortly after his release from prison. *The Man Died*. In reading Soyinka's prison writings, I recalled weighing the many deaths, dying small and vanishing big. And I had measured my father's death – how little I had died, the vastness of my death. I turned my mind off from dying men. I forced myself to stop mourning for a man I had only seen once in my entire life following his return from exile.

I waited for the traffic lights to change. Riding past the blue Borders bookshop and opposite the three-storey brownstone Waterstones bookshop, I made a mental note to buy Miles Davis's biography. Traffic lights flipped colours to the spell of rush-hour traffic. Looking across, the crowd milled and crunched and galloped around the NatWest building on the corner of George and Cornmarket streets. Tourists – Americans, Russians, Chinese – and Eastern European students streamed in and out of the long red-and-orange and blue-and-green-and-yellow musical touristy Cornmarket. It was a pedestrians' and cyclists' street, edged by small department stores, music shops, nightclubs down alleys, fast-food joints, cellphone and computer shops.

With the traffic lights in my favour, I pedalled on, turning right onto George Street. Slicing through the frenzied crowd, I passed the double-storey Debenhams department store. I had been there a few times last summer, to buy myself some discounted Levi jeans, shirts and shoes. Then came the large glass-adorned Bella Pasta and the orange-and-black New Orleans restaurant. I rode on the pavement, avoiding a black cab slowly chewing through the traffic.

Cycling through the traffic, the "brilliant but impatient" Kwame Apollo-Gyamfi hurried his way into my mind. He was an Oxford Ghanaian student character in Kenyan Professor Ali Mazrui's weak (and only) novel, *The Trial of Christopher Okigbo,* fatally run over by a car while cycling through Oxford's traffic. Then he went to heaven to litigate in the trial of the legendary Nigerian poet who died fighting in the Biafra War.

A lanky blond wino in dirty, faded blue jeans and a black jacket, holding on to an opened can of Stella Artois, staggered in front of me outside the NatWest building. I rang my bicycle bell, and the crink-crink-crink petered out in a furious staccato.

"Shut up, you wanker!" the wino yelled as I zigzagged past him. And I watched him grabbing his crotch, mimicking pitiless masturbation.

"The madness of George Street." The words spaced themselves out through the gap in my pair of upper front teeth. I felt my dimples sharply gorging inside my cheeks, listening to my words doing the rounds inside my helmet.

"Every soul on George Street is a scintillating novel gagging to be penned." I listened to the stabs of laughter wriggling inside me and then tumbling out. My body jerked, almost trembling to a short spark of joy. I looked to my left and right, and behind, searching for that spark of joy. It had vanished as fast as it had turned up, mingling and disappearing in the grinding crowds.

I hadn't laughed for over two months. First it was Mama, who had longed to see me graduate with my doctorate in Politics and International Relations. A chunk of my innocence had gone down with her as I watched the earth taking in her casket. Then it was my father, a man I had hoped to see for a second time, maybe even a third. And again and again, the way sons see their fathers to a ripe old age. Then another publisher rejected *Ours*, my manuscript. And it had not been long since Amanda from Iowa had dumped me.

I pedalled on slowly, and stopped next to the pavement across from a small newsagent. A Lebanese flag was hoisted above the shop door, next to a lottery advert.

"Yebo!" I yelled at Dela Owusu – slim and tall, dressed in a well-cut charcoal suit and a navy turtleneck sweater. A black scarf swirled around his neck. His long black jacket flapped gently at his sides. He continued up George Street, holding on to a fresh ten-packet of Marlboro Lights. Under his arm dangled a folded copy of *The Guardian*.

"Yebo!" I shouted again.

Dela walked on.

"Dela." I hurled out his name.

He stopped, looking back.

"Luzuko." Dela called out my name in his trademark snapping jolt. It was as if he'd caught me in the middle of mischief-making. He shifted his loose round spectacles farther up the bridge of his wide, flat nose, then took them off and chewed on them. The vein on his forehead gently thickened below his shaved head – a round plume of smoke from the Hiroshima atomic bomb. No longer hiding behind spectacles, his face threw out his large brown eyes, his eyelids half drooped.

"You're back from Brixton." My voice came out sprightly. "How was it?" I lifted my bike and settled it on the pavement, its nose pointing towards the coffee shop.

"I ... I ..." Dela looked away, chewing, his left thumb tapping slowly but firmly on his thigh – pacing, timing and walking his stutter. "I ... kind of ... had the mi-mi-misfortune of running into Os-Os-Osman. Gosh." I waited for him to finish. It took just as long as I had waited for him to say 'woman' a month ago at the Late Bar. 'Gosh' came out in his trademark way – a lamer, domesticated exclamation. He stopped chewing, put on his spectacles, pushing them farther up the bridge of his nose. His lips stood pouted, their natural pose. And his smooth skin stretched firm. It was taut skin on which I had never seen a single bead of sweat.

"Oh, no." I pushed out a sigh.

"I told him," his voice bolted out. "Os-Os-Osman, kind of ... I'm busy, mmh? I'm stateless. I'm busy. I am. I am ... writing gr-gr-ground-groundbreaking chapters of my doc-doc-doctoral thesis, mmh? Groundbreaking! Kind of, yes!" His 'yes' spiked out in a high falsetto screech. "And I'm also writing a column, mmh? Yes!" Stretching out his hands, he spread his fingers, his wrist flipped up. And I saw that gash, the shape of a thick rope around it – full, deep, round, gorged. It was an outline similar to the one holding onto his right ankle – one wrist, one ankle.

I had seen them before, on nights when we had late-night red-wine sessions at his flat sitting atop Morrell Avenue. Away from the city centre and the massive college buildings, over the river, away from the Plain, with its roundabout of routes out of the city, the avenue stretched up from St Clement's alongside the park. A long pull of terraced suburban houses, leafy and old, wound up to the brow of the hill where Dela's apartment was perched among houses with low-hanging garden walls, home to professors, postgraduate students and professionals. Dela's flat stood right across from the Warneford psychiatric hospital. Looking across to the hospital, I had remembered how Dambudzo Marechera, the self-professed "*doppelgänger* of African Literature", following his disciplinary hearing for attempting to torch a New College dormitory in the seventies, had opted for expulsion from Oxford rather than be sectioned at Warneford for bipolar disorder.

With Miles Davis or Thelonius Monk, Fela Kuti or Hugh Masekela, Ray Phiri and Oliver Mtukudzi moving among us in his flat, Dela had stared into blankness, into a nothingness in front of him. It was the music of our fiction writing, of our politics, our Africa; of laughter and merriment; of aching for sex with imagined voluptuous women, harvesting moistness from their inner thighs; the luxury of our future. The stutter vanished when he talked about his scars. Then came the slow, measured words loyal only to a chill in his blow-by-blow telling of what had happened.

The notes had clung and swirled around us: the rusty muted trumpet and the dumped and donging piano chords. Then I had seen in Dela's still eyes the disbelief over a madness that had nearly come. I smelled a fading hate, but one that never went away. And I saw a searing longing for the love of a home still loved, but with much caution. In all that, I let go and hung on to the swaying of the returning and the staying, to his old home, to an exile not so new.

He had pretended he had not wiped away tears, brandishing a smile when Charlie Mingus came on with 'Horas Decubitus', his trumpet high and skipping as it swung and bleated. And then he had raised his glass to Chet Baker's 'I May Be Wrong', so purposefully and steadily happy. "We've got to live, no matter how many skies have fallen." Dela had searched the roof and drew down from its barrenness these words of encouragement from *Lady Chatterley's Lover*. Gulping the last swig, I listened to the croaking of his throat taking it all in. And I watched him watching the skinny legs of the red wine running inside his glass.

Dela's high falsetto ramblings brought me back to him, standing in front of me on the pavement, going on and on about his groundbreaking doctoral thesis and Osman.

"Every ... every chapter of my doc-doctoral thesis is gr-groundbreaking, mmh?" Dela went on, scolding an Osman long since gone, his one hand sweeping fast on his left thigh. "My thesis will outdo Mahmood Mamdani. Kind of, yes! So please, please leave me alone, Os-Osman. I ... I kind of ... don't have time for your non ... your non-nonsense. I'm sorry! I'm sorry! I'm sorry, Osman. I ... I ... don't want to know who or what ate your doc-doctoral thesis in 19

... kind of ... 1987, mmh? I'm busy. I'm stateless. Kind of, yes!" He yelped out another high falsetto soprano "yes". Mumbling under his breath, he chewed on. Two sharp lines coursed on the sides of his mouth.

I had bumped into Osman many times at Queen Elizabeth House, at Rhodes House, and at St Antony's College. A gangly figure bearing short, curly black hair sitting on a small head and a well-groomed jet-black moustache, he always dressed in a suit and tie. I had seen him at lectures and seminars on African and southern African politics, history and sociology. Sometimes I would spot him seats away at the Examination Hall on High Street, when politicians, state officials and diplomats came to deliver lectures. And I made sure I walked the other way when I had been fortunate enough on the street to spot him first.

Osman was Nigerian, a former doctoral candidate in history at St Antony's College. He was writing a thesis on the comparative study of pre-colonial nineteenth-century Nigerian caliphates. And then, somewhere towards confirming his doctoral status, he lost his thesis. If it was not the story of the disappearance in 1987 of the floppy disk holding his thesis, it was about him writing another journal paper that never saw publication. Since that year, he had been living on the dole in Oxford, and had never found or rewritten his thesis.

Like that army officer in Rushdie's *Midnight's Children*, who had fallen in love with a "local floozy" and chose to remain behind with her when his army left town, Osman had become less than whole, belonging half to one world and half to another. Osman forced his presence on us. When he stopped us, we chatted with him as we hurried past him. Or we chose not to see him at all.

"By the way," I changed the subject, "I bumped into your woman outside the School of Geography thirty minutes ago. She ..."

"Hey!" Dela took off his glasses, rashly rallying his tongue around his lips. He quietly wiped the lenses of his spectacles with his scarf, his eyes sticking out red and small. Twirling his spectacles in one hand, he launched out. "Mark fff-fff ... kind of fff ..." Pausing, he breathed in, biting down hard on his lower lip. Carefully returning his spectacles to the bridge of his nose, he drummed his thumb on his lap, pacing and taking his stutter for another walk. Sucking in fresh breath, he threw himself out there. "Mark took Catherine to bed." It all tumbled out loud and fast, landing with a thud.

I looked around, hoping he hadn't brought any attention to us.

"Who is Mark?" my voice crawled out.

"Mark is ... is ... a spy," he shouted, splaying his fingers. "MI6, the French DGSE, or a combination of this ... this ... and that or something, man. Gosh." His voice came down fast, his sleepy eyes looking away. He quickly pushed his spectacles up his face.

"Who?" my voice slunk, trying not to excite him.

"Mark is my spy."

"Really, Dela?"

"It's a pol-pol-i-tical strategy meant to throw me off my pol-pol-itical work." The stutter had slowly crept back.

"Man, are you sure?"

"I ... am ... am ... never wrong." He yelled, his eyes protruding, wet and bloodshot. "I am never wrong! Don't you know that by now? Mmh? Gosh." He turned away again, mumbling and chewing and flailing his hands.

A silence nestled between us. I caressed my bike handlebars, looking away.

"They are coming back for me, Luzuko." Dela broke the awkwardness. Then his eyes bulged. "The goons are coming for me again."

TWO

"Who do they think they are?" Bongani hissed, grinding his teeth. Slowly opening the bedroom window, he hauled in Oxford's crisp and wintry December air. His eyes strayed to his bed. On the bedside drawers squatted a digital clock announcing: 5 December 2003, 02:45. The icy wind seared his nose to numbness. His jaws jutted out and clenched. Through the opened window, he watched the gathering of Cowley Road's sights and sounds, the nightclubs and bars having closed. Squeezed in at the mouth of Cowley Road where it joins the roundabout at the Plain, a small Polish restaurant nursed the last five drinkers.

Shrieks of laughter stretched from alleys and street corners. Four yobs swaggered about in uniformly striped white-and-black tracksuits. Jamming their hands inside their crotches, they spat about, kicking rubbish bins, searching for yet another scuffle with the police. Tipsy undergraduates crossed back to the High Street, leaving the 'townie' side behind at the roundabout. And police sirens raked after the disorder, dashing alongside cruising black cabs issuing restful Eastern music.

Bongani's eyes lingered on the world outside his window. Located on the bus route to Blackbird Leys, his house was a couple of streets from Tesco supermarket. A couple of Indian and Bangladeshi stores and a horse-betting drop lined the way. At the corner of Cowley Road and Randolph Street, the thick night curtain hugged flickering street lights that poured a rustic orange over the dots of drunks bobbing and swaying up and down the pavement.

A line had formed outside the Mahmood's Kebabs van. It was run by an old Sudanese man who fumed and cussed, insisting that he was from Turkey. And when he cursed, his nose ran with dribbles of snot and sweat. The droning of the van's generator chugged and heaved on, drowning out the long drunken laughs, the honest and hearty swearing.

Just behind the van, Bongani watched a white Toyota Corolla pull up, a big dog-eared sticker reading 'Oxford Brookes University' loosely plastered on the driver's door. A chubby, bespectacled man in his early twenties bundled himself out of the front passenger seat. He walked around the car, and opened the rear door. From the back seat, a skinny young man leaked one foot out.

"Goodnight," Chubby said, smiling, holding open the rear door.

"Mate," Skinny strained his voice, burping, "first say to me, 'You're a bit of a cunt now, aren't you?' And then, I promise you, I'll climb out of the car."

Chubby's face twisted, sliding up and swinging sideways.

"No, no, no." Laughing, Skinny flapped his hands about. "I'm not fighting with you, mate. Don't you worry. First, you just say to me, 'You're a bit of a cunt now, aren't you?' Then I'll quietly come out of the car and go to my room to sleep, won't I?"

Chubby sighed, just as the driver, a tall and slim young woman, came to stand next to him.

"Don't worry, mate." Skinny went on, his smile swiftly disappearing. His voice suddenly rising, he continued. "I said, first call me a cunt." His rapid breathing slowed down again. "Then I'll leave you in peace and go to my room now, won't I?" His lips quivered and his eyes narrowed as he plastered his palms flat on the seat.

Bongani's eyes quickly shifted to the Jamaican bar and restaurant farther up Cowley Road. The place throbbed and heaved and jammed with dancehall reggae. Its name stood out in vibrant orange on the wooden plaque below the roof. The only place openly selling alcohol and food after two in the morning, a throng waited at the door facing a tall and beefy Jamaican on door duty. His thumb rested on the round, shiny metallic head counter. The swarm outside the door tightly hugged itself from the cold, waiting for the magical 'one-out-one-in' click from his counter that would let them in.

They dared to pay for the priciest drinks and the expensive, tiny portions of Jamaican-style spicy goat meat, rice, potatoes, pumpkin and vegetables served on enamel plates. Outside, a group of West Indian youths hung around two black Mercedes-Benz sedans. They rapped to the jumping ragga music of their own. In a corner, one young man bragged that he had spotted Mark Morrison of the hit song 'Return of the Mack' somewhere in Oxfordshire that afternoon.

"Dun lin un da table mon, da table fell!" Bongani recalled the reprimand from the old man one night. The restaurant owner had yelled at Bongani, right in his face, when he was there for drinks with his friend. And before that, he had been stunned when the old Jamaican had moaned to him, "You sold us to slavery, you wanking Africans!"

"Come again?" Bongani had asked, leaning closer to the old Jamaican. His matronly English wife behind him had looked bored. Bongani had strained his ear, edging closer to the old man. Hovering over Bongani with his grey beard and dreadlocked mane of piled grey, the Jamaican had yelled above the boundless din of reggae and chatter and the croaking of the rickety wooden floor, "I said, dun lin un da table mon, da table fell!" Cassidy, Bongani's Scottish friend, had deciphered: Do not lean on the table with only three firm legs, lest it caved in and fell over.

Bongani had stared at the old man's trembling eyes, knowing that another "Come again?", another "Pardon me?" could mean a rapid spewing out of sweat and blood and spit and police. And then the papers. The papers. It was surely to come. It had come to Chinodakufa Madamombe. When he got into that fray with some Afro-Caribbean bouncer at a nightclub in the city centre six months back, it had come.

The enormous bouncer had condemned Chinodakufa's Africa with filth, starvation, shit, flies and wars. Chino had urged the bouncer to keep quiet if he had never been to Africa. The bouncer hadn't taken it well at all that a puny, short, raw native African had had the gall to talk back to him. And then he had huffed and puffed, throwing his toys, the bathtub, water and the baby. Soon the police came, in that haze of swishing and walkie-talkies. And then the papers. Chino had been bundled off to the Cowley Police Station, and then to Campsfield House Removal Centre in Kidlington, just outside Oxford. Five days later, he had called Bongani from Harare. And Bongani had never gone back to the restaurant or the club again.

"Who do they think they are?" Bongani's voice tensed, gazing out of the window. Frowning, he fished out a Marlboro red from the back pocket of his baggy jeans.

"Noni." He whispered her name. Fishing the yellow lighter from his back pocket, he lit the cigarette dangling between his lips. Noni, that "fit" South African he worked with on the assembly line of the motor plant, had disappeared right under his nose at The Bridge nightclub. He had warned his friends on the third hip-hop floor not to mess with her, because he had already "pulled that fit bird". And his friends had cheered him on; the "original nigger" they had called him. But Noni had walked off with a muscular Americanised Nigerian. Half dressed, his sweaty shirt tossed over his mountain of a shoulder and his arm wound around her waist, the Nigerian had hustled Noni out of the club right under Bongani's nose.

"Fuck alpha males!" Bongani balled his fingers into a fist, saliva splattering his face. "Fuck alpha niggers and their muscles and six-packs and height and shit!" His eyes stuck out with rage, as did the long, bony muscle running up his neck. "Bloody hoovers! Who do they think they are? Dammit!" He drew in a long and fast breath. "*La makwerekwere*, these African foreigners are finishing our girls in this country." He caught his breath. "But she didn't say no to my money, those bloody cocktails, and my cigarettes now, did she?" he shouted, flinging the cigarette out of the window. The last trail of smoke snaked indolently from his nostrils.

Running his hands through the mop of uncombed spikes of his short new dreadlocks, he toyed with the stud pierced underneath his thick lower lip. He wiped his rough-looking angular face, with its protruding ears and thick, flattened nose. He shuffled towards the bed, his slim, mid-height stature barely making a sound. The walls were hung with posters of Tupac Shakur, Snoop Doggy Dogg, The Notorious BIG, Nas, Jay-Z, and a massive nude of Janet Jackson barely covered in a silky lilac sheet. At the door to his bedroom, a huge poster read:

MANAGEMENT WILL NOT BE HELD RESPONSIBLE FOR THE LOSS OF VIRGINITY WITHIN THESE PREMISES.

Emergency thoughts rummaged through his mind. He

thought of Nomzamo, his overweight, fellow South African tenant. *Indlala inamanyala* – "Hunger can make one do shameful things," he murmured, idly unzipping his pants. He knew that Nomzamo was twenty-two years older than him, a quiet single parent and an ex-primary-school teacher back in South Africa, now working at the motor-assembly plant.

Bongani leapt over the bed, to the basin on the other side. From the toiletry cabinet beneath the mirror, he took a small bottle of baby oil. It landed with a thud on the bedside drawers. He stared at his reflection in the mirror, his brows knitted into a knot of rage. He rinsed a navy facecloth and slapped it next to the bottle of baby oil. Then he headed over to the rusty white refrigerator on the other side of the bed, opened it and pulled out a six-pack of chilled Foster's Lager.

Back at the bed, he unbuckled his belt and slipped off his jeans. The sound of the metal can being cracked open soothed his nerves. With the foam hissing from the can beside him, he slowly took off his socks. He lay back on the bed, heaving out a long sigh.

Click. Click. Khassshhh ... khassshhh! Bongani watched the flashing bright blue pulsing through the slits of his bedroom door. Heavy footsteps creaked on the landing, two voices murmuring far down the passage. Click, click, swisssh, khassshhh ... Still the blue, green and red lights streamed through the slats of his bedroom door.

THREE

Nomusa piled herself into the far end of the black cab. Prising open a wider gap between herself and her mother, she leaned a corner of her forehead against the window. The glass threw back at her the delicacy of her eyes. Her eyes welled up, threatening to swamp her face – long, the shape of a pear, smooth – her reflection receding and then returning to focus. Her face was a much younger face, belying her twenty-five years. One that dared not reveal anything of what had just shifted inside her. The cab queued outside the fish-and-chips shop, its signboard neon yellow, green and orange. The smell of frying oil, vinegar and the sea wafted towards her. Blinking, the outline of her face emerged, sharp against the gush of lights and dimness of the early night.

Grace, Nomusa's mother, cooed and talked gibberish to eighteen-month-old Baby Angelina. Nomusa stole a corner-eye glance at them, trying to ignore the slow gongs of a new, hot headache.

"Sodom, six." A tap snapped on the window, and Tata Linda held up six fingers outside the cab. A sharp lisp came from him, his voice halting and jumping. Nomusa blew out a jilted sigh. Beyond the window, Tata Linda kept his six fingers held up, the red, yellow and bottle-green Oxford Tube jacket draped over his shoulder.

"Mmh?" Opening the window halfway, Nomusa struggled to hide the sneer.

"Sodom. Sodom," Tata Linda whispered sharply. "Come. Tomorrow. Six. Come." He scratched at his stiff, dry, uncombed hair. Nomusa watched his mouth moving, wondering how the teeth of a man in his late fifties could hold onto that strong, glimmering white.

"Okay," Nomusa whispered, showing a thumbs-up through the window. Tata Linda walked off, his shuffle slowly gaining pace to a nimble stride to catch up with his fellow driver on the way to the bus on George Street at the end of their shift.

But Nomusa was not going to Sodom. "A place of iniquity" – a languid pleasure had nestled on Tata Linda's smile when he said so. He had shifted his tongue, spaced the words about, and then pushed out a huffing laugh. Sodom was where Original Fitness lived, his mistress, a former Soweto beauty queen. There the homies huddled, cooked pap, braaied meat with Aromat, ate biltong, and listened to the latest kwaito and Afro-jazz hits from home. At times, they cooked sheep and pigs' heads, if someone had managed to pick them up from Thursday's open market in the city centre just behind the Old Fire Station.

And there, when the homies had come together, Nomusa knew there was always a moment when she had to make a delicate sizing up, balancing a measure of drunkenness and bile. When it came to it – and it always came to it – it would spill over. The brawls tumbled out in the small hours of the night, followed by frantic scampering when the police crept out of the woodwork. Then, in bunched corners, there would be the hushed morning-after sniffing for rumours of who among them had called the police in order to send who home for how much.

Aggie, Tata Linda's wife, a nurse at the John Radcliffe Hospital in Headington, had asked Nomusa many times and in many ways about Sodom – where exactly it was in Blackbird Leys. "*Qhaqha*" – it was in the way the clicks soared out of her that startled Nomusa. Aggie folded each *q* separately. That flying *h* emboldening each *q* delivering thudding clicks with a punch that floored Nomusa. "*Qhaqha*" – the evil of it all went against Aggie's breathtakingly smooth hazel face. Out of that loveliness came death in *qhaqha*. And all the minion words rolling along with *qhaqha* said it all – to strip, take apart, tear asunder the bottom of that woman, and then fling it away.

"Who's that?" whispered Grace, faintly panting as she swayed the baby.

"Doesn't matter, Ma," Nomusa barked. "What matters is this thing you're telling me now."

"Don't you dare raise your voice at me!"

"Mama, Mama, we agreed. You come, you stay here for two months, you take Baby Angelina back home. That's it. This, this ..."

She returned her eyes to the foggy window, as the cab slowly drifted from the fish-and-chips shop. Indicating to the left, it glided onto George Street past St Peter's College on the corner with New Inn Hall Street. Soon the road opened onto a small square set on a cobbled street, the Odeon cinema on the left.

Nomusa noticed the unassuming grey building on the left behind St Peter's. She used to clean there, polishing a sign for politics-and-international-something-or-other, a university department. Her first cleaning job when she had arrived in Oxford from London. But then they had started whispering about contracts and signed papers with stamps and signatures and that other paper from some other London office and the South African consulate. It was why she had run away from London in the first place. And before that, the same whisperings had chased her away from Manchester.

"Mama, Mama, you have a visitor's visa. You can't work here."

"You talk as if you yourself have papers. And don't you talk to me like a child."

The cab ambled on, the stealth of its glide soon gathering tempo. In the next block crouched an Italian restaurant, its white marquee slung over the pavement, the name writ over it in large cursive. And the smell of Joe and the theft of that morning almost two years back slid inside Nomusa.

After feeding her well, and plying her with sweet drinks at the nearby bar, he had stolen her. In the stillness of an early-morning unfurling in an alley where a homeless man slept with his Jack Russell, Joe had stolen her. With a swoosh of his hot breath, his baritone jumped onto her ear, telling her that he was stealing her. She had felt his chest muscles plastered firmly to her back. And then her skirt had gone up, the panties down to her thighs.

He had taken her from behind, his hands working through jagged breaths. He had pulled her in, nestling her waist inside him. Huffing and heaving, his voice hung at pained peaks, he had mumbled that he was stealing her. Stealing her. She had gasped in his woody fragrance, her mind trying to work out the traffic – the rush of edgy breaths, the nimble moves of his fingers, the sway and flap of her skirt, the snap of the panty's elastic band. And then Joe had vanished as fast as he had appeared.

"Mama, sooner or later, they will catch you and send you home."

"Believe in me, Nomusa."

"Believe what, Ma? Believe in what?"

"Don't shout at me! I'm not your child."

"Mama, once your six-month visitor's visa expires and you're still in England, you're illegal. That's it. There's no other way of looking at it. Sooner or later, you will be sent home. You can't disappear here. We are all written down on paper. You can't disappear from paper."

"And how have you disappeared from paper?"

"We play hide and seek here. All of us. I cannot watch you play cat and mouse with these people. It's rough. This whole running around takes everything from you. It strips you apart. You are my mother. I cannot let these people turn you into a mouse. They will catch you, Mama. They are going to catch you. Even if you learn the system, know the system, sooner or later, they will catch you."

Another pause wedged itself between them. Nomusa cupped her chin with her hand, watching the buildings appear and fade away as they approached High Street.

"Mama, I'm working on a plan. I'm not planning on living here forever."

"Jacob ..." Grace almost whispered, cradling the baby in her arms.

"Dad is not a god, Ma." She felt a long, slim plume of breath streaming from her mouth.

The cab drifted slowly along High Street until the expansive grey and stony Magdalen College came up on the left. In that building, Nomusa recalled the Algerian Bilal's bearded face. In his green overall jacket, he hovered over her as she scrubbed a stained corner of the floor on her knees. She had thrown an eye over him, taking in his short curly hair, his almond skin. And then he had jabbered on and on: he was an Arab, not African; he'd lived in London and Liverpool and Birmingham for twelve years with his parents, so he was British, he said; black Africans should not be pitied – they came in droves, draining the British dole.

And then, one afternoon, old Marlon, the security guard from Trinidad who had lived in Oxford forever, had taken her by her hand, rushing, and stashed her in the storeroom. Bilal had called the police on her. Nomusa had heard the police barking on and on about an illegal as she had remained tucked away inside the storeroom. Marlon had insisted to the police that he knew nothing about an illegal.

Cowley Road seemed so far away – the blue, orange, red and yellow lights dancing amid the many kebab houses, the Indian, Thai and Chinese restaurants, lone Polish, Jamaican and Japanese eateries dotted among them. Nomusa wiped her nose. The melody of Wagner's 'The Valkyrie' scurried to and fro on her phone. She stared at the screen of her flip-top silver Samsung. *NOMZAMO* flashed on the screen.

"*Yebo*," Nomusa answered.

"Where are you?" Nomzamo panted on the other end of the line.

"In a cab."

"Let's meet now. Please?" Nomzamo sobbed.

"Why?"

"Let's meet now. At *Endodeni*?"

The cab edged into a queue at the Plain roundabout, an Oxford Tube bus heading back to London grinding slowly along in front of them. The cab driver cursed in Urdu, roughly stroking his long white beard. Nomusa asked him to pull up a block before Tesco on Cowley Road, across from the Somali shop that sold international phone cards. *Endodeni*, an Nguni word meaning "at the man's place" – she and her friends gave it that name on account of a Somali young man who stood outside the shop door in summer in his bony naked torso. Customers had to pass by him with their purchase orders of international phone cards.

The cab pulled up outside *Endodeni*. The Somali leaned against the door, dressed now in a puffer jacket and a black-and-white scarf. Nomzamo stood on the pavement, her eyes darting left and right, rubbing her palms against her thighs in tight faded jeans. In a maroon turtleneck and black coat, her fair-complexioned face with bursting lips stood out against her ponytailed hair. Nomzamo rushed towards the cab, clutching her black purse and three bulging black plastic bags.

"They have Bongani." Breathless, Nomzamo climbed into the back seat. Panting, she dropped the three plastic bags to the floor.

"What?" Nomusa's eyes lit up.

"This morning." Nomzamo swallowed a breath in between the panting, her eyes large and protruding. "They took in BB."

A blue-, yellow- and white-coloured Thames Valley police sedan appeared from nowhere behind them.

"Tell him to go," Nomzamo shouted.

"What?"

"Nomusa," Nomzamo flapped her fingers wildly. "Tell the driver to go, now."

The cab lurched forward, heading down Cowley Road, but the Thames Valley vehicle latched onto its tail, *Reducing crime, disorder and fear* plastered in blue cursive on its doors.

"Oh, *nkosi yam*, my God," Nomzamo sobbed, throwing her fingers about. "I'm going home now." She cried. "*Bayangigodusa manje*. They're taking me home now." Her Adam's apple moved up, then settled. The cab rolled on gently, Thames Valley trotting behind them.

"But why are you taking us home with you?" Nomusa yelled, leaning in to Nomzamo's face. Baby Angelina suddenly wailed.

The cab stopped at the traffic lights opposite the narrow entrance to Leopold Street. Two imams in flowing white walked about doling out pamphlets. In the kebab house across the street stood a tall Middle-Eastern-looking young man with a clean-shaven face and shiny ponytailed hair. The smoothness of his skin, the smile on his round face, which widened his thin lips, gave him the look of a teenaged girl. He stood over a grill, turning and basting doner kebabs in a muscle-hugging, long-sleeved passion-pink sweater. A pair of tight black leather trousers gripped his waist. He tilted his head, gently tossing back his ponytail.

A middle-aged white man climbed out of a sporty Mercedes-Benz parked outside the kebab shop. In a black leather jacket, and also in tight black leather pants, he sported a blond ponytail and large earrings. The man strode into the kebab shop, with its *Strictly halaal* signage in large Arabic script embraced by the crescent of Islam. He and the young man behind the grill smiled. The middle-aged man tossed back his ponytail, then drew his face closer over the counter. The young man moved closer and, sweeping his own ponytail away, the tips of their noses nearly touched.

The traffic lights turned green, and the cab driver pressed on. Thames Valley continued behind them. The cab driver picked up speed, passing a grey wall spraypainted with *BLACK POWER, MARCUS GARVEY, MALCOLM X, HAILE SELASSIE.* The cab indicated right and then turned swiftly into Between Towns Road, passing the old Macmillan Publishers offices, the faint-yellow Swan Lake pub now behind them. Still Thames Valley moved steadily behind them. Piercing blue, yellow and white now flashed straight into the cab's interior. The officer in the passenger seat stuck his arm out the window, pointing to the cab, stabbing out four firm fingers.

FOUR

"Antoine?" I didn't feel the goon's name tumbling off my tongue. Slippery, its nakedness had simply slithered out of me. In silence, we stared at the oaf standing on the pavement. And that slick, wavy sensation of a gossipmonger's goosebumps overcame me. I had crossed the line. Antoine was the name of anguish, and I had no right to awaken Dela's agony. He had to summon it first. It was his agony, and his alone. I had been ahead of myself. Dela looked away. And I thought I spotted a shine in his eyes. A wetness. Perhaps it was water coming with the wind that bandied about us.

"We ... we ..." Dela coughed, not turning to look at me. "We met, kind of there, you know?" His eyes searched far ahead, across the road, at the wide space joining St Giles and Banbury Road. To my left stood the orange and blue of Sainsbury's supermarket. Ahead of it, on the same block, lay the red and navy-blue of the Oxford Tube stop. The road stretched to meet the yellow- and white-walled Ponana nightclub. A few steps from it, on a grey pavement strewn with an empty pack of cigarettes here, a spent pack of crisps and an out-of-luck lotto ticket there, a pavement that might have been a cobbled street a few centuries ago, stood St Cross College with its heavy wooden gates.

In the ever-pressing whirl of Oxford traffic, Dela's eyes might have been wandering to all manner of meeting places. Farther up, four students carrying backpacks walked out of the Queen Elizabeth House yard. And I imagined the all-too-familiar crunch of lime pebbles crushed and squashed beneath their feet.

He could have been staring across at The Lamb & Flag pub. He could not have met him in the small cemetery in remembrance of fallen soldiers of the First World War, calm in the space that divides Woodstock Road and Banbury Road heading north out of the city. Dela spat at the relics of European history. He spat at the statue of King Charles I centred in the yard of the Bodleian Library. He turned his head, a sneer on his face, when I went on about how I admired Oliver Cromwell, the man who had beheaded King Charles I during the English Civil War.

At those low-hung gates of the cemetery park was exactly where, two days fresh in Oxford, I had spotted a mad black man. Watching him from afar outside Sainsbury's, I had wondered: What on earth is this man doing in Oxford? Frothing at the mouth and talking to the wind, he had scratched his face. With dirty, matted dreadlocks and bloodshot eyes, he had flailed his hands about in swinging speed. What was he doing here in the centre of Oxford outside a cemetery of white soldiers? That could not be where Dela and Antoine had met. Not there.

They could not have met at St Cross College. Dela did not have anything to do with St Cross. Anna Mwangi had been there, a Llewellyn Scholar undertaking her doctoral studies in Cultural Anthropology, but Dela and Anna were not close. And they could not have met at Brown's, the small swanky restaurant where Anna's girlfriend worked as a grill chef. Brown's was too expensive. It could not have been there. I kept my guessing to myself.

"We had a pint there." His head tilted towards the throng of traffic far ahead across the road. "L-lamb and ... and ... kind of ... Flag, you know?" He coughed, lashing out a smile. "That goon still fancies seeing himself as a student of St John's College, you know? He insisted we meet there for a pint, because St John's owns the pub. Ridiculous. Gosh." That lame howl came out with a low laugh.

Swinging my bike firmly to the pavement, an ease settled on my shoulders. The last time I had drunk there was three months back. I had had three pints following a big African seminar on decoloniality. As per custom following African seminars at Queen Elizabeth House, we had poured out into the neighbouring pub. I remembered tagging along with Dela and Bafana, aka 'Slimy', a post-doctoral fellow and my good friend from Soweto. I had to pull a drunken Bafana away from hitting on a bespectacled married Somali woman wearing a full *hijab*.

"And then?" I asked.

"Then I had a pint with Antoine." He spat out his name.

"How is he?"

"His left hand does not work."

"Mmh?"

"Kind of dead. Gosh." I found his eyes staring far ahead across the road.

"What happened?"

"A stroke."

"A stroke?"

"Mmm ..." Dela moaned. "Perhaps. I don't know. I didn't ask. I don't care." His eyes remained fixed on the traffic up ahead.

"That's terrible."

"All I know is that he remains Eyadéma's goon." I strained my ears to his mumbling about a hand working or not working.

"You mean a goon of Eyadéma, the son?" I asked.

"A son of a goat is a goat." He licked his lower lip. "Eyadéma the father, Eyadéma the son. It's the same goons. It's the same sick Togo."

"Do they still want to kill you?"

"They want to kill my voice. Muffle it first, and then rip it out of my throat."

A silence came between us. I picked at and brushed off unseen specks on my bike's handlebars. Dela looked far away in the direction of the traffic swarm.

"After doing a pint, we took a cab to my place," Dela went on. "He refused to take the bus, 'Because … because … it is … it's … beneath the weight of my office, of Director-General Antoine.'" Mimicking Antoine's gravelly bass, the 'Director-General Antoine' part staggered out of Dela, leaving him out of breath.

"Oh! So he's Director-General now?"

"Who cares?"

"Of which department?"

"Of … of … kind of … a goon's office."

"So, what did he want?"

"Eyadéma's chief goon," Dela went on, "the smart, stra-stra-strategic goon. He wasn't the smart, stra-stra-strategic goon the last time I met him in Lomé, m-m-many years ago."

I had no idea why the stutter had returned. Another quiet settled between us.

"He still … still goes on and on and on about Ox-Ox-Oxford, you know? About his lost op-op-opportunity of coming up to St John's. About how The Lamb & Flag would have been his drinking hole. He fff-fff-fancies himself as some kind of inte-inte-intellectual heir to Léopold Sédar Senghor in French and African poetry and literature, mmh? Gosh."

Another silence came. And I wondered about Dela and Antoine. I wondered about what a former tortured could say to his former torturer over a pint of lager. Then I remembered reading a book about the strange intimacy that develops between tortured and torturer in the military regimes of South America. How, in that two-way street, in hurried breaths, in anguished panting, the torturer wipes away the tortured's tears and wets his parched throat, in how personal information, gestures, are passed on between the two, and an intimacy mushrooms.

"But power, violence and blood are sexier than scholarship." Dela bit hard on his lower lip.

"So, what did he want?"

"To stop me from writing my co-co-column, in exchange for fff ... kind of fff-fifteen thousand pounds, cash."

"What?"

"And another fff-fifteen thousand in two months."

"Wow."

"I saw it. The whole loot in a b-b-briefcase, on my b-b-bed."

"Really?"

"All of it, for me, there and then. Gosh."

"And then?"

"Don't you know me by now, Luzuko?"

Another silence fell flat between us.

"I have a du-du-duty to my generation." Looking heavenwards, he blinked, and started rambling, quoting Frantz Fanon.

"Listen, Dela," I cut in, studying my digital wristwatch. "I have to rush for supper in college." Silence. "And there's Oxford Union after that," I went on. "Perhaps we can finish this conversation later?"

Returning his eyes from the heavens, he said, "Oh, yes. Ian Smith." Dela's eyes brightened.

"Let's do a pint after the debate, mmh?" I mounted my bike. "At the Oxford Union bar, mmh?"

"Good," Dela said, shoving his hands into his jacket pockets. "I have to go home now and write my co-co-

column." He started walking fast, vanishing around the corner of Cornmarket Street, to take a Cowley and Blackbird Leys bus back towards Morrell Avenue.

I walked my bicycle to my college. At the back gate, I took my small e-mos key from the pocket of my leather jacket and inserted it into the gadget. The steel black gate issued a creaky ring as I pushed it open, steering my bike into the college grounds. My college looked like a massive two-storey green-grey house.

The modestly sized but well-stocked library on the top floor looked down onto the street below and, farther down, to the long-established Indian restaurant on the corner. I spent a lot of time in that library, working on the literature review for my thesis. It held a lot of valuable material on anti-neoliberal social movements, social citizenship, and urbanisation in the global South. My doctoral thesis focused on municipal service delivery in the face of the growing tide of privatisation and private-public partnerships when it came to public services, like water and electricity. It also looked at the opposition of the anti-neoliberal social movements of public-private partnerships. There was, though, a choice of libraries to work in, so when I had grown tired of working at the college library, I would start to write titbits of my novel there. "Are you a d-doc-doctoral candidate, or a novelist?" Dela had asked me one Friday afternoon, as I scribbled notes for a chapter of my novel.

Parking and locking my bike among many others in the bicycle parking lot, it crossed my mind that Dela had had three of his bikes stolen within two and a half years. One had been stolen right here, the second from the yard of the Politics Department behind our college. His third bike had been taken outside his apartment on Morrell Avenue. That bike theft was rife was one of the first things we were warned about when we came up to Oxford. Behind the parking lot stood the two-storey grey dining hall. Fellows and the college master dined on the ground floor, in the dim and elegantly small Senior Common Room, the SCR. Students ate upstairs.

Opposite the dining hall stood a face-brick, housing undergraduate students. It was a standard-built, two-storey building, and one of the only two modern structures at the college. Opposite was the Middle Common Room, the MCR, for postgraduate students, which boasted a lounge, bar and TV room. The kitchen doubled up as a bar, the 'honesty bar'. This meant you were trusted well enough to jot down next to your name in a book on the counter whatever alcohol, soft drinks, chocolate bars or crisps you took, to go into your battels for payment at the end of the month. Battels was the account for termly accommodation, food and other student expenses. The Junior Common Room, the JCR, for undergraduates was located at the other end of the college grounds, next to the college bar. I had never been there. I had no reason to.

I turned and headed for the dining hall, walking up the six wooden steps. I was relieved that there was no queue. I hated the pretentious and superficial conversations in the queue. I took off my jacket and black beanie and hung them next to the first of the two flights of steps leading to the dining hall. The dining area was usually noisy, reminding me of my boarding-school days back home. It was massive, with five rows of hard beige tables pointing to High Table, reserved for the college master, the fellows and the Bursar.

High Table stood just one step up from the floor where everyone else ate. It took its 'highness' from just that, that one pedestal elevating it from the floor. Each student had a certain number of High Table dinners allocated per term. High Table suppers were preceded by grace in Latin, and we wore graduate gowns, longer than the undergraduate gowns, all hung up on a wall outside the dining hall. And so I ticked next to my name on the list held by one of the cooks, and that I had not brought a guest. At times I brought Dela, especially for High Table dinner, since he had not signed and paid for college meals.

I grabbed my warmed-up plate and walked to the servers, all in white cooks' uniforms. They were lined up in front of the different dishes. I went for the baby potatoes, carrots, cauliflower and a boiled chicken thigh. Taking my plate and cutlery, I scouted for familiar and friendly faces. There were many loud undergraduate American students, so I looked for an un-American spot. I made my way up to the middle row and sat down. Looking around, I realised that I was the only black student in the hall that night. We numbered eight out of a total of about two hundred and fifty college students – Dela, Josh, Maud, François, Chantelle, Nneka, Lydia and me.

Dela was a stateless doctoral candidate in Politics and International Relations from Togo. We shared a thesis supervisor. He had been a journalist in Lomé, Togo, in the early nineties. Agitating against Étienne Gnassingbé Eyadéma's regime in his pro-democracy newspaper and magazines, he had been caught and tortured by his soldiers. Late one afternoon, a British journalist abruptly took him from a popular bar in Lomé to the British Embassy. The soldiers had been out and about in the city with an order to shoot and kill Dela Owusu on the spot. He eventually left Togo for England with only the clothes on his back. And had never been back since.

Josh, a doctoral candidate in Neuropsychiatry, had already graduated with a medical degree from Bristol University. He had briefly practised medicine before enrolling for his MSc, and then DPhil in Neuropsychiatry at Oxford University. As part of the requirements for his doctoral thesis, he was allotted practical sessions at Warneford psychiatric hospital.

Josh was a muscular, six-feet-two, British South-Sudanese Dinka. Once or twice, hovering over me, he had rested his triceps on my head, laughing, catching me unaware. Born in England, he had never been to South Sudan. He was from

Newcastle, where his father was a chemistry professor who had taught for some time at Yale University. His mother was a civil engineer. When he talked about South Sudan – a South Sudan he had never seen – it was with a love rushed headlong. I saw it in the way he talked about the peace accord between the Sudanese People's Liberation Movement of John Garang and the Sudanese government of Omar al-Bashir. I had never seen so much love for one's country as in Josh for his South Sudan. While Dela's love for his Togo was of the only lover he had ever known, a lover he had no choice but to love, Josh's love for his South Sudan was blind, flaming, all consuming. And my love for my South Africa was hopeful, scarred, wary, expectant.

Maud, from Botswana, was a full-figured woman in her mid-twenties. A Llewellyn Scholar like me, she was a doctoral candidate in Physics. I could not stomach her strict Catholic ways, and her incessant stories about her doting father. "I have to go now and take beer," I once announced, stunned at how bravely those words escaped from me, freeing me from the constant repetition.

I had nervously counted on my wristwatch the two hours I had left before pubs closed. It was going to take me about ten minutes to power-walk up to Que Pasa farther up the street, and a couple of blocks before Cornmarket Street. The place sat huddled right across Oxford's municipality offices, a bright red-and-blue electric-coloured joint steaming with upbeat hip-hop. Josh sternly refused to go there. "Immigrants, mate. Immigrants." And then I would watch his face – bored, tired, every time.

François, a doctoral student in Physiology, was from Montpellier, that caricatured wine and cheese connoisseur, an Old World gentleman. With a pipe dangling between his lips, cufflinks, a chain linking his undercoat to his trousers, a 1950s' hair parting, he thrice told us at MCR bops, "I'm three-quarters white." But all I ever saw in him was a typical mixed-race man – one who went darker in summer, and lighter in winter. Nothing out of the ordinary. And he relished the back-and-forth banter with the British students about the French-British wars of the sixteenth to nineteenth centuries. Often, they waved their Union Jacks and French flags around, laughing and hugging and slapping each other's shoulders.

I could not figure out what a three-quarters white-black man was supposed to look like. All those degrees of skin colour and tones amused me. They reminded me of how CLR James, in his magisterial *The Black Jacobins*, carefully relayed the laws of and obsessions with skin-colour grades among the black and *métis* population of French colonial Haiti. Without any shame, François had told us that his only link to Africa, to blackness, was his late grandfather. He had been a Guinean journalist who had settled in France after the Second World War, and had married his French grandmother.

Chantelle was Jamaican, an undergraduate student in French, Italian and Spanish. She was beautiful, slender and athletic, with a crop of short natural hair and a small round head. She moved in an all-white cast all the time, mostly white undergraduate boys. And she changed her white boyfriends almost every term. She did not socialise with us at all, the black crowd in college. And I had never seen her with any black person outside college. Even at college bops, she did not mix with us beyond exchanging soulless pleasantries from a distance.

Nneka, a master's student in Development Studies, was Nigerian-Dutch. She had been born in the Netherlands, and had moved to England with her parents when she was in her early teens. Her parents had separated soon after their move to England and her Dutch father had then relocated to The Hague a few years after their divorce. Nneka huffed up a casual matter-of-fact connection with the Netherlands, as if it was a sin to belong to the land of her whiteness. And she had a blind excitement when it came to a Nigeria she had briefly seen only twice, as if she would never see Heaven if she did not identify solely with the country of her blackness. And yet I had caught in her a natural connection with the Netherlands that she quickly dismissed. And there was a surprised fondness to her voice for the England of her youth.

I fancied Nneka. A lot. There was the bounce of her smile, the spark of her dimples, the sight of her supple breasts. But I could never find a way to talk to her in that way. We had become quite friendly. Anyway, she dated my friend, an African-American Llewellyn Scholar.

"Does her boyfriend have ... have ... kind of ... nine heads? Mmh?" Dela had once egged me to steal her from him anyway. But I did not follow his advice. It was the same daring attitude he had displayed even when I had revealed to him at one MCR bop that the woman he lusted after, a Japanese doctoral student in Archaeology working on her thesis on Swaziland, was in fact living with her British boyfriend. "And so?" With profound annoyance registered in his eyes, Dela had paused from taking a sip from his Guinness.

And then there was Lydia, a doctoral student in Mathematics. Small and quiet, she was a black British student from Brighton, Sussex, and kept to herself most of the time. But I saw her free and chatty side when she was with Josh. They were both black British. Black British, black, Afro-Caribbean, West Indian – it was a fascination that I grappled with. At what point was one not one of these? They were talked about as though there were grades of relations to being and not being British. At what point did one stop being one and move on to become the other? They made these differences among themselves. Sometimes I thought I understood them. And then, again, I would lose the sense of it all.

In all the conversations I had with Lydia, she showed no interest in Africa or the Caribbean. Everything about her was English and British. And she didn't feel guilty about being disconnected from Africa and Africanness. I don't think it was something she even thought of. It didn't seem to bother her at all. In fact, she found it strange when I subtly suggested that perhaps she needed some black connection from outside. And I had to learn that there was nothing wrong with her not associating with Africa or the blackness I was familiar and comfortable with. It did not make any sense to her. Her reaction to any outlandish new African cultural fact she learnt was purely as an anthropological curiosity, as it presumably would be to any average British person. She had this silent confidence, an easiness within herself that didn't latch on to anything outside England. She was just Lydia from Brighton, Sussex.

I had noticed, too, that Josh became different, became British, and completely cut off from me when he talked about football with his British friends. Or when he reminisced about high school or discussed some peculiar British economic or social issue. He left me out. And I was not sure if he was sensitive to that, or that it was just natural to him. Yet he came rushing back to me, to cry on my shoulder about how he had felt left out as a black person in British history and society. And I could see it in his eyes when we African students talked casually about some common African social or cultural custom or practice – it was as if he was watching us on a TV screen.

Josh, whose benchmark was 'tell it like it is, there and then', could barely stomach the often undiplomatic Dela. And Dela never understood why Josh never dated black women. Josh had never showed any interest in black women at all. He did not even talk about them in romantic or sexual ways. And I found it strange that we had never talked about it either. Dela, on the other hand, had vowed a long time ago he had stopped going out with white women. "For political reasons," he had often said. "A matter of life and death." They would only compromise his political work, he said. And Josh hated anyone telling him how he had to live his life. Only his family (his extended family in England and the US), South Sudan, his studies, his Estonian girlfriend, football, the gym and hip-hop mattered to him, in that order. But I liked Josh a lot. We hit it off very well, and often went clubbing together.

Dela had a way of reaching out to Maud that I did not quite understand. He was soft, understanding, and yet rough with her sometimes. Once, bursting her Catholic innocence, he told her in his usual matter-of-fact way that on several occasions he had bought the services of the ladies of the night at hotels in Lomé. This left the innocent Catholic daddy's girl gobsmacked.

Josh and Maud had no relationship whatsoever. I had never seen them chatting. As far as I was aware, there wasn't any particular reason why they did not get along in any meaningful way. And Josh and François only ever exchanged staid, simple pleasantries. Josh intensely despised François' white and Old World bourgeois airs, but François did not pick up on this resentment, and kept going about in his ever-cheerful mood.

Nneka, however, was on good terms with everyone in the black college crowd. She had even found a way of reaching out to Chantelle. Maud and François were good buddies who often enjoyed tea sessions together in the MCR. They had long chats about European paintings, art and culture, and visiting Nice. And it was very rare that all eight of us black students were at college at the same time.

Dela loved profound, investigative conversations with François and had a way of tapping deep into his psyche. It was a Dela talent – connecting with an adversary. Even when it came to outright racist right-wing students, he found a way of getting them to open up to him. I guess it was his old journalistic skills that worked their way into enemy territories. Naturally, François felt completely comfortable with Dela. I also enjoyed conversations with François. His white French ways did not offend me at all, but rather amused me.

I looked at the sea of whiteness around me in the dining hall. It reminded me of Dambudzo Marechera in his short story, 'Black Skin, What Mask?' He found his black skin always drawing attention in Oxford. I forked out a baby potato, puffing out a silent laugh at the thought. Across from me sat two undergraduates, one American and the other a freckled German with curly red hair. I sliced a piece of chicken and chewed on.

"You know," the German undergraduate started. "In Africa, there's this other tribe."

"Where in Africa?" the American asked, playing with his carrots.

"Can't remember," the German went on. "When they count, they go: one, two, three, more, many."

"Fascinating," the American snorted.

I stood up, took up my plate, and walked out.

FIVE

BONGANI PULLED HIS hoodie down over his face. Looking up from the pavement to the opened window of his bedroom, he wondered how he had managed to climb down so far and so fast. In the distance were the white, blue, red and yellow flashes of the police. The colours mixed, whirled and shifted shape in front of him, generating a loud throbbing in his head.

He walked steadily, turning right onto Randolph Street, his eyes following the pavement. He glanced back at his place. Three policemen and a policewoman stood at the opened front door. Two other officers filed inside. If he ran or just walked faster, he thought, it would beckon the attention of the police. Listening to his feet pounding the pavement, he flinched, waiting for an 'Oi!' from a policeman.

The corner leading up to Cowley Road looked far off. Stooping to tie his shoelaces, again he stole a look behind him. Two police officers still stood outside. One of the policemen watched him, his arms crossed. Bongani, tightening his already tied laces, thought back to that moment three years ago, back to his clammy palms.

⋯•⋯

He grabbed the suitcase firmly, and hoisted his black-and-white Adidas gym bag from the ground, and slung it over his right shoulder. Taking off his woollen yellow Bafana Bafana beanie, he folded it neatly and shoved it into the back pocket of his baggy jeans. Tilting slightly up and down, his head counted the number of people queuing in front of him. The immigration official stood behind a podium, flipping back and forth through a mound of papers. Stopping, he fidgeted with the round spectacles on his freckled face, scratched his sandy hair, and then flipped the pages back and forth again. And then he punched the passport with a stamp, nodding for the next person to come through.

Bongani's eyes moved over to the lounge. The rejected sat there, waiting patiently. His hands buoyed behind him, a lean young black man led by a burly policeman in a scotch jacket crossed through at the end of the queue. A tall African gentleman dressed in a long, white priestly robe walked gently in small circles around the lounge. A large-headed man in a dark suit and a light pink tie stood studying the queue.

Another African gentleman, middle aged and in a suit, sat cross-legged in the lounge reading *The Sun*. A clean-shaven youngster argued feverishly in Arabic with a well-dressed Arab-British immigration official with a black ponytail. Another female official stood patiently behind them with a big camera. Eventually, the young man stood, leaning languidly against the white wall. The ponytailed immigration lady snapped the camera. The youngster slowly walked away, pushing his feet, to take the nearest seat among the rejected.

With a quiet nod, Freckles turned to Bongani, an assortment of A4-sized brown and white envelopes and a bundle of papers under his arm. Bongani dropped his bags at his feet.

"Hi," Bongani greeted.

"Good morning, sir. Your passport and documents, please," Freckles gently asked.

Bongani handed the passport over. The assortment of envelopes and the sheaf of papers spilt, sprawling across the floor.

"Sorry, sir." Bongani stooped down to collect them. And down there, as he tried to scoop up the papers, he noticed a beautiful young black woman with thick make-up and painted eyebrows standing behind Freckles. *Angel Njoroge*, Bongani quickly read the badge on her chest.

"There we are, sir." Bongani neatly placed all the documents and the envelopes on the podium. Freckles silently flicked through them, carefully opening each of the envelopes and decking all the documents on the podium.

"These people …" Angel Njoroge hissed to another immigration official who suddenly appeared next to her. "These people," she went on, her steely eyes sifting through them in the lounge of the rejected. "They think they can enter this country willy-nilly." The priestly gentleman continued to pace the lounge in small circles. "You know," Angel continued in her painstakingly measured British-Kenyan accent, "there's a flight to Lagos scheduled to leave in three hours." Her colleague stared silently at her.

"Angel," Freckles called out, stepping away from the podium. "Please take over here," He had already walked away. "Here we go again," Angel murmured under her breath, taking to the podium. Beads of sweat squeezed through Bongani's forehead. Flipping through Bongani's papers, she shoved some to the side, giving the rejected area another quick eye swipe.

"So," Angel began, staring at Bongani, "you're coming here on a two-year working visa?"

"Yes, ma'am."

"The letter here, this letter from the person who is going to accommodate you, it is not certified."

"That letter is from my cousin, Connor Zungu. He—"

"It is not certified."

"But—"

"When you came to England, when you applied for a two-year working visa, it was clearly stipulated that all your documents need to be certified."

"Look—"

"And I have questions about your employment here in the UK."

"There is a letter there from the ABC Call Centre stating that I already have a position. That letter also states that I should report for duty on 1 August 2000. Today is Friday, 29 July."

"But this letter is not original."

"That is a letter I received – a copy. They sent it already certified and stamped, and signed by the Director of Personnel."

"But this could be a fake letter, and this could be a fake stamp, and a fake signature."

"That is what I have received. This is what was sent to me."

"We need an original copy, on a letterhead."

"That is on a letterhead. There it is. It is original. Why don't you call them?"

"At seven in the morning?"

"That letter is certified, ma'am. Look at the stamp of the Commissioner of Oaths. It is authentic."

"Here's another problem." Angel lifted the page with the tip of her long, polished nails. "We need a comprehensive bank statement."

"But that bank statement is complete. It has been signed by the bank's branch manager in London."

"It is not comprehensive."

"What do you mean?" Bongani swallowed the saliva that

had built up in his throat.

"Your documents don't add up, mister. All your documents, they don't add up. Everything here is dodgy. Your story does not add up."

"Dodgy?" Bongani swallowed again.

Angel walked over to the next podium. She stopped to whisper to her colleague, and then quickly walked off. Her colleague then gestured to Bongani to take a seat in the rejected area.

"Please, sir, take a seat. We'll attend to you as soon as we can."

Bongani gathered up his luggage again and collected his documents from the podium. Sitting next to the cross-legged gentleman reading *The Sun*, he felt warm tears flowing down his cheeks.

"Welcome to England," the gentleman said over the corner of his newspaper. "It happens to the best of us, my brother. If they can do this to Wole Soyinka, they can do it to any of us." Then he flipped to the next page of *The Sun*. Bongani stared at him, a fresh well of tears ready to fall. He wondered who Wole Soyinka was.

•••

Bongani sat on the edge of the bed, staring at the *No Smoking* sign on the wall. *Heathrow Terminal 1*, a small sign next to it stared back at him. A thin stream of tears flowed down his cheeks, reaching the moustached corners of his lips. His eyes were swollen, bloodshot, itchy. The doorknob suddenly turned.

"Oh, pardon my manners, please, sir." A rotund middle-aged British immigration official stood in the doorway. "Sir, we are now moving you to another detention room. I'll take your suitcase and your bag. You hold on to your documents and passport. Your flight back to Johannesburg is, finally, scheduled to depart at nine this evening. It is nearly midday now. Your lunch should be ready in twenty minutes."

Click ... click ... shush ... shush ... The official attended to the walkie-talkie.

"Mr Shezi, I'll lock the room now," he said. "I have to attend to an emergency right away. I will leave you to make your way to your allocated detention room. You go straight, take a left, and then head straight. Turn right, and you're there. You'll find an immigration official waiting for you there. I'm sorry that I have to leave you." He closed the door behind them and then locked it. "Oh, and please accept my apology, on behalf of the Heathrow Immigration Authority, for having kept you here for three days. We experienced some problems trying to get you a seat on a flight back to Johannesburg. But I hope we treated you well." He smiled.

Silence.

"Have a safe flight." He scurried away, talking hurriedly on the walkie-talkie.

Bongani followed. The official then took a swift left turn and walked away. Alone, Bongani continued towards the escalator. And then he simply carried on walking and walking until he found himself at the exit of Terminal One. The doors opened automatically. Drawing in a deep breath, he took his first step on English soil. And he walked on, not wanting to look back, lest he turn into a pillar of salt.

SIX

"It's headed back to Cowley Police Station." Nomusa tossed back her head, and let out a long sigh. Her eyes trailed the police car as it swerved into the next lane. She watched the two policemen who had settled into a deep conversation and followed the *Reducing crime, fear and disorder* wording on their car becoming smaller and smaller ahead of her as it picked up speed and then vanished.

The cab continued straight, towards the shopping centre. Nomusa leaned over to massage Nomzamo's shoulders as she burrowed her head deeper between her thighs. She listened to Nomzamo sniffing, and for a moment fixed her eyes on the cab driver. His slim, frail fingers trailed slowly through the long strands of his long and silky white beard. Nomusa watched Grace rocking Baby Angelina back and forth in her arms.

"I was there, Nomusa," Nomzamo echoed from inside her thighs.

"When?"

"When they came to pick up Bongani."

"When?"

"This morning. Early this morning, at about three."

"Oh, my God ..." Nomusa turned her eyes to the window.

"I was already in bed when they came." Nomzamo slowly raised her head from between her thighs. "I heard a loud bang on the door. I woke up immediately, thinking it was BB," she said, wiping tears from her cheeks. "I thought Bongani was drunk and had lost his house keys again. When I opened the door ..." She swept her hand across her left cheek. "... They were there, right in front of me."

Baby Angelina let out a wail, so Grace shuffled around, swaying the baby back and forth. At a loud announcement in Urdu from the radio, the cab driver turned down the volume, muttering softly. And, still in Urdu, followed short tremors of curled words. The driver's fingers jabbed at the air, the wrinkles of his hands stretching out flat.

"There were so many of them," Nomzamo continued. "About ten or more, with their loud walkie-talkies." She dabbed at the tears on her cheek with her index finger. "They demanded to come inside. Then they went straight upstairs, to BB's room. I was so shocked. So confused. I didn't know what to do. A tall policeman remained behind when the rest went upstairs. He asked me a whole lot of questions about Bongani. And then he, too, went upstairs to join the other officers. Oh, my God." The cab stopped outside a terraced white house with a low wall sporting a decent crack down the middle of it.

"Barns Road," the cab driver announced. "And that will be five pounds and sixty p, ma'am." The *p* came out thin and naked. His fingers dug back into his beard. They clambered out of the cab, dragging suitcases, handbags and plastic bags behind them, and made their way through the shabby, white-painted wooden gate. Nomusa fished the house keys from her back pocket and unlocked the door. Down the narrow, carpeted passageway, they walked straight into the spacious living room. Dumping the luggage on the floor, they threw themselves on the black leather sofas.

"When they went up to Bongani's room," Nomzamo heaved out a sigh, "my mind kept saying, 'Get dressed – there's the window.' And so I got dressed, and pulled on these clothes you see me wearing now. I packed these black bags you see now. I took my purse, my passport and identity document, all my cards and papers, and dashed for the window. I managed to wiggle through it, and fell so hard on the lawn. And, Nomusa, I ran! I ran! I ran, and ran, and ran up Cowley Road. I didn't know where I was going. I just ran. I've left behind a lot of clothes and other things in that house. Please, help me, *sisi*. Just to hide my head for a few days until I figure out what to do. Who's going to take care of my children if they take me home now? I can't go back home. What's there for me back home? Not now." Nomzamo sniffed again, her voice quivering, and plunged her head back between her thighs.

"Nomzamo." Nomusa's voice was strained.

"Mmh."

"Go back to the time the police came to your house this morning."

"*Ja*." Nomzamo narrowed her eyes.

"You know that some of my mail goes to your house, because I only moved out of that house four months ago."

"Yes, I know."

"Did you see any of my mail there?"

Silence.

"Yes," Nomzamo replied.

"What?" Nomusa stood up.

"I've been meaning to tell you to pick up your mail. But I kept forgetting, what with my shifts and …"

"What mail, Nomzamo? What mail?"

Nomzamo coughed.

"Oh, my God …" Nomusa whispered, her eyes gawking

at the nothingness in front of her. She slid to the wooden floor.

"You know how it is," Nomusa almost whispered. "One is caught, and ten follow. You know how it goes."

Nomusa covered her face with both hands, her eyes closed trying to shut off the baby's piercing cries. Do I need to move, again? she wondered. Oxford had been her home for the past three years. Bongani's arrest will set in motion a chain of arrests, she thought. It happened before, in London, in Manchester. You get one illegal South African, and you net five more. That's how it has always worked. I can't move again. I'm tired of moving.

Oxford had been good to her. She had, long ago, decided that Oxford was hers. Oxford was for keeps. She let out slivers of a long sigh through the slits between her slim fingers. Not again. Not another move, so close to my nine-pounds-an-hour job. Nine pounds an hour, eight hours a day, five days a week. Much better than the six pounds fifty at the motor-assembly plant. I can't leave Oxford. I can't move cities. Not again. Not with my dream nursing job just in reach. No more running, no. Damn, Bongani! She felt the heat of her thoughts threatening to spill over.

Nine pounds an hour washing and wiping the buttocks and mucus of grand oldies up in a Summertown retirement home would take her where she wanted to be. It would place her far above the others, ahead of teachers and principals and nurses back home in Durban. All those people back home had written her off, a disappointment, never to amount to anything. Now, with nine pounds an hour, she was going to be far above them. And then she would finally return home to take her place over them all. The buttocks and the mucus, after five years, would buy her a townhouse in the suburbs, or a big double-storey house in her township, and a nice, comfortable second-hand sedan with a reasonably low mileage. It would shut the mouths of everyone who had written her off. Bongani's arrest is not going to spoil my plans, she decided.

"I let him in." Nomusa suddenly thought back to Mavis, back to her scratchy voice that day. The steam from her cup of coffee had snaked lazily up. She had looked straight into Mavis's eyes, watching the tears collecting in the bags under her eyes. "For your job, Nomusa, I let him in. For a job. Just a job." Her voice had quickened to a rustled whisper, leaving the ends of her lips wobbling.

Glen, Mavis's elderly supervisor at the retirement home in Summertown, had been drooling over her large hips and buttocks. "Smooth sliding, I tell you now, if you ask me?" he would say, the cracks in his chapped lips splintering. The crookedness of his smile spread across his face. Mavis had held back his acned hand from reaching her hips. For a couple of years, Mavis and Nomusa had laughed at Glen's stories. They had laughed at how his hand accidentally caressed her hips, how it somehow found itself planted firmly on her buttocks.

"What have we become, Nomusa? What have we become in this country, Nomusa?" Glen had agreed to hire Nomusa as a nurse, to start in two months. And at the promise of a nine pounds an hour, eight hours a day, five days a week job for the next five years, Mavis had let him in. And Nomusa could no longer see the high-school teacher Mavis had been back in Durban. She had become just another woman wiping the buttocks and mucus of grand oldies in England. She was the Mavis she had first met in London three years back, cleaning toilets at a hospital.

"Whichever way you look at it, Nomusa, it's just a job." Mavis had bitten into her lower lip. "What have we become in this country, my sister? How did we become these things? When did we turn into these things? When exactly? For nine pounds an hour?"

But what can we do about it now, Nomusa had wondered, slurping on her hot coffee. "What else is there to do, my sister?" Nomusa had said, turning her eyes from Mavis.

"What else is there to do, Mavis?" The question came out almost a whisper. "Going back home poor and praying for wealthy men to take us in with our bundles? Men who are going to use us and chew us and spit us out, anyway? Or do we rather duck and dive Thames Valley now for a good life? Either way, you are eaten. Either way, you lose yourself," Nomusa had said, clasping her cup of coffee with both hands, feeling her fingers wanting to slip away.

Nomusa returned to Nomzamo, her mother and Baby Angelina in the living room.

"What are we going to do now, Nomusa?" Nomzamo cleared her throat.

"Not 'we'." Nomusa strained her voice.

"What the hell are you talking about?"

If only he had told me the truth, Nomusa thought back, looking away. If only he had told me the truth six months back that his real name was Philani, not Desmond. If he had told her that he ran with two names – one name for real, and another for Oxford, she would have been able to cover for him. Nomusa stared at the wall in front of her. And everything of that night six months ago flooded back to her – the flashing lights of the police. The rush of two police cars, one in front and the second behind them.

Desmond had picked up Nomusa from her place on Randolph Street after work. They had planned to have dinner at the home of a South African couple who had just relocated from Birmingham. Desmond, with his pleasant round face, had picked her up in his blue Toyota Corolla. He was a charming, generous, polite and orderly man who smiled and laughed often. He had been working with Nomusa and Bongani at the motor-assembly plant in Cowley for the past year.

In the car that Wednesday night, Nomusa had found Sis' Zuki in the front passenger seat. An elegant woman in her mid-thirties with a spotlessly beautiful face, Sis' Zuki rode on every word Mkhize said, laughing out loud. Mkhize, an ex-policeman from Durban, hunched in the back seat, gossiping loudly, his lithe body and small face betraying his over-the-top crassness. They drove off as the loud banter and laughs from Mkhize scaled even higher.

"*Nabo* – here they are," Sis' Zuki had shouted, her eyes wide. Desmond's mouth parted. Nomzamo had covered her face with both hands. And Nomusa had fidgeted in the back seat, her hands plastered underneath her thighs. Three policemen. One stood at the driver's window, the second at the front passenger's seat, and the third policeman had posted himself at the back window where Nomusa sat. Nomusa couldn't pick up what the policeman was saying to Desmond, who had rolled down the window. Soon, they were all being questioned separately.

The one with Nomusa told her they would all be released soon. They only wanted to verify Desmond's car insurance. Nomusa then confirmed his name to the policeman: Desmond. And then they took Desmond and his car away, leaving the others on the side of the road. They had left in such a rush that they had neglected to check the status of the three they left behind. A week and a half later, Desmond/Philani had called Sis' Zuki from Middelburg, Mpumalanga.

"There's no 'we', Nomzamo." Nomusa looked straight into Nomzamo's eyes. "I'm not going anywhere. I'm not moving again. I'm staying put – right here in Oxford." Nomusa listened to the soft whispers of Baby Angelina's sighs. I would rather play this cat-and-mouse game for the next five years than leave this job. Nomusa bit on her lower lip.

SEVEN

Keep off the lawn. The sacred warning on a blue noticeboard was staked deep into the ground on the edge of the sprawled-out, immaculately kept lawn. Every college lawn boasted one. And Trinity College had one of the most expansive and most beautiful spreads of lawn. I walked on, straight into the small passageway, through an open glass door, and then the green wooden one leading to the porter's lodge – a small, square, well-lit room.

The porter, Jack the Mighty Atom, scooted around the back of the lodge, dipping in and out of his office. A little man with boundless energy, Mighty Atom was built not far from the ground. And, in his hurried display of the activity of an atom, he often muttered in Geordie, an accent that mangled words and ate them as soon as they were uttered. Often, out of those mutilated words came a pungent distaste for New Labour, and his constant warning of the bitter deceit that lay behind Prime Minister Tony Blair's bright grin-smile.

An outbreak of students fluttered around the porter's lodge. Some stood chatting, others checking their pigeonholes. Another neat cropping was dotted here and there, discussing their essays, tutorials and theses with their supervisors. Next to the porter's lodge, on the right, was the college fellows' mail and administration office. Across the passage leading to the glass exit stood a small green door to a computer room for postgraduates, with twelve desktop computers. I checked my e-mails, and sometimes worked on my thesis research work in the evenings there. Upstairs was the two-storey, well-stocked college library.

I moved through the rowdy lot, heading for my pigeonhole. The cabinet filled the entire wall space. I was not inclined to befriend undergraduate students. Many of us postgrads had come to the same arrangement – that we didn't forge relations with undergraduates unnecessarily.

I spotted Chantelle next to the college fellows' mail and administration office. She held hands with one tall, curly-haired and good-looking undergraduate. I guessed that was Chantelle's new boyfriend, the youngest son of a wealthy investment banker from North London. Dela had been going on and on about them. I took the mail from my pigeonhole, marked *L Goba*, shared with an S Gopal. I had bumped into Shiva Gopal several times as we poked into our pigeonhole – a pleasant, slight-figured medical student from Kolkata.

I had three letters. The first contained my battels. Shoving it into the breast pocket of my jacket, I flipped to the second. A brochure from the Royal Shakespeare Society. I scanned it for a mention of the play to be staged that Michaelmas term, then folded it and squashed it into the outside pocket of my jacket. I fished out the third letter, giving the pigeonhole one last check. I wanted to see whether my supervisor had left a review of chapter four of my thesis. I had been eagerly awaiting my supervisor's comments since the previous week – my first foray into a write-up on the empirical findings and analysis of my fieldwork research. The second and third chapters were theoretical foundations. Of course, I planned to write the introduction last, after I had finished the conclusion. As a PRS – probationer research student – preparing to transfer status to a doctoral student, to DPhil, I spent an enormous amount of time on theory.

And once I had transferred status and undertook my fieldwork research, I started writing up my empirical findings. This was in preparation for the confirmation of my doctoral student status. Dela had confirmed his DPhil status two months back, towards the end of the last Trinity term in June. Having begun his write-up during the summer holidays, soon after the end of Trinity term, he was well into writing his "gr-gr-groundbreaking chapters".

Confirming one's doctoral status was a deadlier affair than simply transferring status. Before transferring status, to officially place a student, we had to matriculate – a largely ceremonial function officially assigning a student to his or her college. It was marked by a long walk of students, *en masse*, who had been admitted that term, from one's college to the Bodleian Library, in full *subfusc*: gown, mortar board, black suit, white shirt and white bow tie. It was the easiest of steps, embracing both matriculant and PRS status.

Confirmation was an official go-ahead, a nod to continue writing one's thesis as a DPhil student. There were stories of not making it – sincerely frightful nightmares. Failing to confirm status meant either being demoted to a master's degree, or being sent down altogether. To be demoted from DPhil to MA or MPhil or MLitt was a truly unspeakable atrocity. And no one could ever, ever, recover from that. What use was it pocketing a second master's degree following demotion, whether from Oxford or elsewhere? An additional master's degree was awarded to you because you were deemed "not doctoral material". And some students with mean, intolerant supervisors, were demoted to master's status far ahead of transferring status, right in the midst of PRS status.

Even if you managed to get a PhD from some other university some other time, you could never recover from that injury. It remained a gaping wound, and even an ant trying to cross it would find itself drowning in its blood. There was never any hope after that. Even if you managed to obtain another doctoral degree from elsewhere in the world, it would never be a DPhil. It would be a PhD, never a DPhil. And, anyway, what was it that Josh used to insist on with combative pride? You obtain a DPhil only from Oxford and Cambridge, and a PhD from any other university in the world. But, to me, it was just semantics.

I often thought of Brandon Pillay, a DPhil Pharmacology student from Pietermaritzburg who had returned home following a demotion to MPhil status. He simply couldn't get his act together when his wife back home filed for divorce. He had floundered about, drinking and weeping and shrivelling away for an entire Trinity term and the following summer holidays. And at the beginning of Michaelmas term, in October, when he had to submit material for confirmation of status – three thesis chapters and a methodology research proposal – it proved far too slim and flimsy.

I had vowed to confirm my DPhil status, then write the rest of my thesis, and defend it at an oral *viva voce* – a three-hour formal affair in full *subfusc*. Josh and I often sat on the three-seater couch in his small living room-*cum*-bedroom in the graduate apartment block on Wellington Square – a garden square with university administration offices. The central garden came to life in the long summer evenings and his apartment block reminded me of a long passenger train, moving from one section to another.

In Josh's bedroom, with the bright yellow of his small study lamp pouring over us, we dreamt of that instant after the long *viva voce*. It was that exact moment when the external and the internal examiner announced to you that you had passed with minor corrections. Downing a bottle of Stolichnaya with orange juice and ice, we shut our eyes, listening to R Kelly's 'The Storm is Over Now.' And when R Kelly circled on a spot, wanting to lift off, with a falsetto soprano 'Whoo!', Josh and I leapt off the couch, arms spread, and those small vodka glasses hoisted.

The third letter from my pigeonhole was from South Publishers in Johannesburg, its blue emblem an eagle with outstretched talons. The black letters stood out clearly. And I froze. I tried to calm myself down, my eyes stuck on the 'Johannesburg' of the stamp. I felt my heart pounding. I read the time on my wristwatch. I had just twenty-five minutes to get to the Oxford Union. If I opened the envelope now, it might spoil my entire evening, if not the entire week.

I had been waiting for that letter for nearly four months. Enclosed was the fate of my first novel, *Ours*. I had only just recovered from two publishers' rejections. The last rejection letter had rambled on about storylines, themes and characters not gelling. And then it had gone on about editorial swipes required to beat the manuscript into submission.

Drawing in a deep breath, I slid my pinkie through the ear of the envelope, tearing it. I ran my index finger along the coarseness of the page. The fragrance of fresh print wafted through my nostrils. Checking my wristwatch again, I quickly skipped through the mound of a minced second paragraph, landing on the last line just above "Yours sincerely". *Rewrite, rewrite, rewrite.* They stared at me, those three words, fed up, not knowing what more to say about a dishevelled three-hundred-and-four-page manuscript.

I wasn't getting anything right. I did not write right. In the previous Hilary term, in preparation for my transfer of status, my supervisor's notes on my theory chapters read more like a wrenching demand for sweaty labour of all manner of rewrites, additional references, lively rejoinders, more rigorous intertextual deliberations and even further rewrites. I was just not writing right. And Amanda, my then girlfriend from Iowa, dumped me. She said that she had warned me often enough about my piggish chauvinistic ways. The straw that had apparently finally broken the camel's back happened one night in the MCR. As I chatted with a handful of college mates, I saw her through the window, standing outside. I gestured to her with my index finger to come inside. And she dumped me the following day for my "irredeemable patriarchal ways".

I also did not get anywhere in that Commonwealth students' short-story competition in which Dela's story had won second place. So, no, I was not writing well. I was not getting anything right.

"Mr Goba." I felt a sticky cognac breath carried by a slight wind of steamed chicken floating over my back. Turning around, I encountered his stained upper rabbit teeth simpering over me. "I've been looking for you." Chaplain Andrew Primrose tottered over me in a black suit, white priest's collar, black jacket and black coat.

"Yes, Chaplain." All I could see in front of was: *Rewrite, rewrite, rewrite*.

"Can we have a brief chat? I'm afraid I have some rather disturbing news to discuss with you concerning your rather ... how shall I put it ... sordid misbehaviour last week."

"Sordid?" I repeated after him, almost whispering, listening to my heart skipping three fast beats.

"And *sordid* is perhaps an understatement, if I may say so."

"Oh?"

"Repugnant. Irredeemable. That's more like it."

Silence fell between us.

"This won't take long, Mr Goba," Chaplain Primrose coughed.

"I'm in a hurry," I huffed. "I'm on my way to see Ian Smith."

"Barney," the chaplain coughed again, this time into his fist, "our maintenance chap, has laid a complaint against you."

"Barney?" I frowned, trying my best to conjure up a Barney.

"He said that last Thursday afternoon you threatened to kick down the ladder he was on top of while he fixed the church roof."

"Oh, that Barney, Chaplain."

"He said that you said, I quote, 'Repeat what you've just said, and I'll kick this ladder off from under you.'"

"Oh, yes." I felt a wave of relief wading through my chest. "I remember that."

"And you called him a fat *F* word."

I stared at the chaplain, watching a frown quickly creeping up on him.

"That's awful, Mr Goba." Chaplain Primrose's voice was strained.

"Did he tell you why I threatened to kick the ladder from under him?"

"That doesn't matter now, does it? You could have killed him, or hospitalised him."

"It matters, Chaplain." I felt my voice firming up. "Otherwise I wouldn't have threatened him. So, yes, it matters."

Primrose panted a heavy warm breath through his hairy nostrils.

"While he was fixing the church roof," I started, "I walked under his ladder. On my way from the dining room, I naturally passed the church, walking under the ladder, because I didn't want to walk on the lawn. You've seen those signs. He told me that I needed to kill my cigarette because I was passing through a church. I told him that I was not in church, but passing through, and far from the church door. Then he said that this was not Africa, where I could walk about anywhere without regard for sacred ground. I told him that was not sacred ground, and I was fairly distant from the church building. Then he kept on referring to me as 'you people'. That is when I threatened to kick the ladder from under him if he continued with his racist comments."

"Racist?"

"Yes, Chaplain."

"Oh, Mr Goba, you have such a chip on your shoulder."

I wondered if I also had a chip on my shoulder when some student, riding his bicycle one night last month across the High Street in the opposite direction to Magdalen College, had shouted at me "Where your lights, nigger?" Had that also been a chip on my shoulder?

"If you continue with such misbehaviour, Mr Goba, college authorities may need to take disciplinary measures against you."

I stared down at his coat, feeling the heat of the chaplain's breath.

"For years, Chaplain, years …" I saw my finger going up.

"I said you stop with your behaviour forthwith, or you will have to contend with stern disciplinary measures. Whatever happened does not require taking a man's life, or hospitalising him."

"I did not take anyone's life. And I did not injure anyone."

"I'm warning you, Goba."

"Chaplain, I may have been off balance." I finally let out a breath, staring straight into his blue eyes. "My father, whom I have only seen once in my entire life when he returned from exile, had just been buried while I was here in Oxford."

And then he appeared to me, my father. He stepped from of a roll of film hewed and chiselled in my mind, passed down to me over many years. My father sat me on his lap, his balaclava pulled tight over his head. A combination of the distinctive smell of his favourite Malawian weed mixed with the Wilson's XXX mints wafting from his mouth. And then his smile opened up, and he delicately enveloped my little chest in his big hands.

'I'm leaving now,' he said, smiling with his meaty lips, much like my own thick lips, moving closer to a spot on my head, wanting to kiss it. I kept my silence, staring him in the eyes.

'What should I get for you when I return?'

'A tricycle.'

'Sure. Okay. I'll get you a tricycle when I return.'

My father put me down gently, pulling his balaclava back down. He walked out of the kitchen, stealing a look around him, searching for anyone who may have been a police informant. And then he speed-walked to the red, left-hand-drive Valiant parked outside the gate. The driver, his friend, pulled down his own balaclava. My father took one last look at me and, shutting the rear car door behind him, lay low on the back seat, as his friend drove away.

"These are our people, Goba," the chaplain yelled. "We take care of them. Our people." Then he stalked off, out through the door and down the narrow passageway, turning to the right.

I walked out of the college trying not to think about the chaplain's rant. Next to the college sat the small Methodist Church. A bald, middle-aged homeless man sat outside the church with his wet poodle. He held a white plastic bowl between his legs, a blue blanket draped over his head and shoulders. I took a right turn towards St Michael's Street, a narrow passage running parallel to George Street. Next to Chutney's – a small, pricey Indian restaurant housed in a small white building – just around the corner and across from the Oxford Union, stood a homeless shelter, a building whose white paint was flaking away. On some evenings, it was turned into a working-class gay nightclub, different from the middle-class Coven club on the other side of Oxford. From its steamy dark hall, men came out for air and leaned against the wall. They smoked and laughed that brisk laugh one emits in the nakedness of a cold, icy winter.

Across from the shelter stood the Oxford Union building. Its formality stood quietly facing the homeless shelter-*cum*-working-class nightclub. Only the modest-sized plaque announced its grandiosity, and then only in name – *OXFORD UNION* – a massive, sprawled-out Victorian house on a modest lawn. Brown engulfed everything: the colour of the house, the roof tiles, barren trees and autumn leaves. At the gate stood two bald men in elegant black coats. Without a word, I handed my invitation card to one of them. Snatching it, he gave it a thorough look, and signalled me through the main gate.

I made my way slowly across the gravel of small greyish pebbles, through the crowd of students and dons. The entrance to the building was walled with black-and-white photographs of old and distinguished members of the Oxford Union and its guest speakers. I did not recognise anyone on the wall except Barry White. There was the usual crowd: cocky student politicians, a handful of thoroughly Anglicised Indian and Pakistani students whose fathers and grandfathers had come down from Oxford and Cambridge, a gaggle of rich and drunk undergraduates and their equally drunk girlfriends, and cranky, old, past-their-time wannabe-Oxford dons in odd-coloured bow ties.

Finally, I headed out the rear door, through the back yard and into the main hall, with groups clustered in small circles. Quickening my pace, I found myself at the entrance of the debating chamber. My eyes swept the place, looking for familiar faces. Then I went up the stairs. On the seventh landing, I stopped and sat on the chair next to a Jamaican politics lecturer from Harris Manchester College. I took off my jacket, preparing to sit next to her. I had instantly recognised her. She and another senior Nigerian lecturer in Politics and International Relations from Wadham College had been my oral examiners for my transfer of status last Hilary term.

"There's the old bastard," the Jamaican lecturer whispered to me. I turned to the assembly of speakers.

"Ian Smith." She spat out his name, her finger resolutely pointing to a sturdy, grey-suited old man.

"Ooh." I felt my lips opening up. There, in front of me, stood Ian Smith, the embodiment of "the last white hope" of a dead Rhodesia. He just stood there in a grey light-bluish suit, white shirt and blue tie. Like in the photographs, his thin lips were tightly pursed, reining in a slight wobble, I noticed. He stood there, quiet, unperturbed, careful, sure of himself in a rather polite way. And I had paid twenty pounds to see him.

∴

"Ladies and gentlemen," Smith started, "I put it to you, in this House, that African leaders do not put their interests before their people." Rustles and murmurs followed. I shifted slightly on my seat. My mind stood still. I caressed my balding head. I should have figured out that they were going to launder him, cleanse him, slotting him in on the challenging side of the debate.

"We acknowledge that there are a few leaders in Africa who have a tendency of spoiling the reputation of Africa and her people," Smith went on, looking straight into the eyes of his opponents. They sat across him, the maverick Labour MP George Galloway; Margaret Dongo, another independent Zimbabwean opposition MP, vibrant and flamboyant; and two lesser-known opposition MPs.

"I am a Zimbabwean," Smith continued. "And I have always been an African. The late Josiah Tongogara was my dear friend. You know, weeks before he was killed by his own ZANU-PF comrades, he confided in me, saying, 'You know, Ian, I fear for my life.' And he was killed by the rotten apples in our African leadership. These are the people who have given Africa, our continent, a bad name. But, generally, I put it to this august House that African leaders do not put their interests before those of their own people." The Adam's apple shifted in Smith's throat.

"This man should not be allowed to go to his grave exonerated." Galloway had rushed up to the podium, pointing a rolled-up paper at Smith. I stood to my feet, clapping, joining the majority of black students in the chamber.

"Order! Order!" the Speaker of the House shouted, hammering on the table. "We are not here to condemn Mr Smith." I remembered hearing from a few British students that the Speaker of the House was a white Zimbabwean. Although his parents had relocated to Sussex a long time ago, he had spent his childhood in Zimbabwe, and they still owned a couple of farms in the Midlands province of Zimbabwe.

"What are we here for then?" Donald Dudzai, a bulky Zimbabwean Theology undergraduate student at Balliol College in the front row, shouted. Dudzai always had these swollen, wet blood-shot eyes I found strange in a Theology student. The Speaker shot him a hawkish glance.

"Ladies and gentlemen," Galloway yelled, "this is the man who proudly proclaimed in the sixties that Rhodesia was the last white hope. I say, this man should never be allowed to die forgiven …"

"Order! Order!" the Speaker interrupted again. Margaret Dongo leapt forward, prancing about in her colourful dress, spewing a tirade against President Robert Mugabe. The two lesser-known opposition politicians pumped the crowd with chunks of anti-Mugabe statements lifted from British and South African newspapers.

The debate was over, and I slowly began to make my way through the uproar, the Jamaican lecturer following. The rest walked out haphazardly through the two doors. For some reason, the Speaker had not explained the voting procedure: you vote by walking through either the 'yeah' door or the 'nay' door. Many black people, unknowingly, walked through the 'yeah' door, voting: 'Yes, African leaders put their interests before their people.' And so the 'yeahs' carried the vote.

EIGHT

Bongani stooped over his shoelaces, his knee joints shaky. Giant dots of police colours from further down on Randolph Street flashed on his back. Their torches were some distance away, but not fading. Sharp edges of his breath cut faster. The whirling in his stomach churned ever faster. Hauling himself from his shoelaces, he eyed the corner of Randolph and Cowley far ahead. Sliding the hood down to his eyes, he strode up the street – neither leisurely, nor at a run. In between. Fast enough to pick up speed for a run, but slow enough to deny he had been running away should it come to that. That was how it was done. A trick he had learnt a long time ago.

Midway on Randolph, a gaunt, pock-faced middle-aged man lay on his back at his doorstep. His hand hung limply mid-air, stretching to reach for the low-hanging doorknob. Saliva dribbled down his cheeks. With eyes half closed, his fingers twitched and twiddled, fiddling at the doorknob.

Outside the house, beyond its low brick wall and wooden gate, a three-series black BMW was parked. Three young black men and two blonde women sat inside, listening and singing along to loud rap music.

Bongani looked behind him. The left fork behind his house was a road that weaved between terraced houses with flaky paintwork and knee-high, gateless walls. It snaked past the only grassy patch on Cowley Road, teeming with hooded hip-hop youths and yobs in tracksuits. A bewildered-looking middle-aged woman with tousled, dirty-blonde hair, wearing a Mexican-style shawl, dragged rope-stringed cans along the pavement behind her. Small, stuffed-to-the-brim Indian and Bangladeshi grocery stores dotted the full length of Cowley Road. And then there was that one 'get-what-you-won't-find-anywhere' Pakistani butcher. Stashed here and there all the way to the end of the road were greasy back-yard mechanics' garages.

Caroline stood outside a betting shop on the corner of Cowley Road and Randolph Street. Her shoulders stiffened, waving to a man across the street. In her mid-twenties and with her hair matted and knotted, she puffed on a roll-up. Her other hand played up and down with the zip of her navy bomber jacket. Against her pretty pear-shaped face, her blue-green eyes looked alarmed. She quickly dropped the roll-up, blew out the last trail of smoke, and hugged herself. Steadying the shiver, she hugged herself tighter. Moving nimbly in circles, she watched Bongani emerging from Randolph, pulling behind him that rainbow of police colours. Hurriedly, she crossed the street, quickening her steps before finally hurling herself in the after-club Cowley crowd.

Caroline was a tenner-a-session girl. And Bongani had shared marijuana rolls with her on her regular spot. On Friday and Saturday mornings, as the nightclubs shut down, she shared her spot with a number of other tenner girls. And, one Saturday morning, she had sold out to Bongani and

Rankitseng: a tenner for each bloke. It was like something straight out of a movie. "Quality stuff, mate! Quality!" she had said, splashing a smile, sizing them up and down. Bongani had taken the head, with Rankitseng coming from behind. But somehow it had swiftly turned out a slappy-slop. Quiet for a minute, then followed by abrupt, twitchy bam-bams, slips, slaps, sloshes, the session had petered out as soon as it had begun.

Bongani watched the shuffle of his feet, sliding the hood farther down over his eyes. He knew the drill far too well – the *godusa* drill, the 'take them home' drill. They had all been marched out of Oxford that way in the past two years. All of them: Thabo, Rankitseng, Sipho, Gideon, Thulani, Susan, Theodora, Nozuko, Nolusapho, Tshepo, Joan, Mihloti, Kwame, Segun, Zoleka, Dikeledi, Sam, Nolubabalo, Tsitsi, Simbarashe, Itai, John, Zama, Khumbo, Mandla, Ahmed, Nyumbane, Mildred, Morena, Letsoalo, Ntsoaki, Sizwe, Sivuyile, Monde, Vusi, Awethu and Chinodakufa. All of them.

On a Friday evening, at the end of a hard day's work, he had hung out with Rankitseng, eating and drinking and smoking in his room. And he learnt the following Tuesday that Thames Valley had taken him away that Sunday. He had had a very lucky sultry evening with an upset and elusive Mildred one Monday night. And Thames Valley took her away on Thursday, back to Johannesburg. He had sensed that Segun had been lying all along when he claimed to be a student at Oxford Brookes University. He had last seen him walking outside Commonwealth House in the city centre, where he lived. And then, soon after, he disappeared back to Nigeria.

Walking on, still following the shuffle of his own feet, Bongani felt a net of emptiness, a sadness sagging him down.

They had all been taken back to their homes, back to South Africa, to Zimbabwe, Zambia, Malawi, Botswana, Lesotho, Swaziland, Uganda, Kenya, Tanzania, Cameroon,

Nigeria, Ghana. Homes they did not want to get back to, not then, and – for some – not ever. He knew them all. He had been friends with some of them, most of them, and had gotten drunk many times with the others. He had slept with some. And he had lent money to some. Others had swindled him. He had corrupted some, and had helped others. He had partied with many. He had shared marijuana with some. He had run away from the law many times, both in London and Manchester, with them. And he had worked with them at the motor-assembly plant, at the post office, in hotel and restaurant kitchens, at factories in London, Manchester and Oxford. They had all been his friends, a part of his life, his Oxford, his England.

Oxford had been theirs also – a pretty, wholesome girlfriend. But she had no idea that she was theirs. Oxford would have spat a gob of phlegm on their faces and thrown a vicious tantrum if she had found out that she was also their girl. This Oxford, the girl of African men, of Pakistani and Bangladeshi men. And so they kept mum about their claim of love for this beauty.

Did he take her against her will? In all those years, did he force himself on her? Bongani had asked himself over and over again. He had turned the question inside out. It was a matter of consent, of not forcing oneself on a girl. At times, consent – or its sudden, rude withdrawal – was loud. "We greet in this country!" That skinny old customer at the newsagent in Summertown, where Bongani had once worked as a cashier, had barked at him. His stained yellow teeth had stuck out in a snarl. Then the skinny customer had plastered a magazine with nude pictures of grossly oversized women and a chocolate bar on the counter in front of the till. Bongani had smiled at him, customarily asking if he had needed a plastic bag to go with his stash. The teeth and scowl of the skinny customer still hung over him.

The consent, the withdrawal – they were in all the gorges and nooks of all the alleys of Oxford. You had to read it well. It was there in the soft, pliant movement of her face. In the smile that swiftly turned into a cringe. And then there was the dullness in her eyes, the spasm you felt as she took herself back from you, her muscles becoming taut. It was in the twitch of her arm, the feeling of her blood gushing warm, calling on you to pour yourself inside her. You had to read it well all the time. Because it changed all the time, and suddenly, whichever way it fancied.

But she was his girl, this Oxford, this England. Everything about her had been his, theirs. She was his woman also. It was here that he had received his first haircut from a blonde woman at a barbershop on Cowley Road. That was something that never happened, in the past or in the present, in the South Africa he came from. Wanting to pull back, he had asked her if she was sure of what she was about to do. Fingering her own silky blonde hair, she had stared at him with a foolish smile.

She was his, this crazy Oxford of outbursts from Muslim men. His old friend and former tenant from Mthatha, Sir Khaps, had one Friday afternoon bought a pig's head for ninety-nine pence in Reading on his way back from work. In a house owned by a Pakistani and shared with other Pakistanis, Sir Khaps had stashed the raw pig's head in the refrigerator that they all shared. He had planned to cook it the following day, to go down well with his anticipated hangover. It was as if the Pakistanis were going to stake his head there and then when they encountered the pig's head, with its flapped, pointed ears and fat snout, in the refrigerator. She was theirs, this Oxford of African and Pakistani men. How could she not know that she was their girl?

She was the Oxford of the Bullingdon Arms on Cowley Road, the dark pub his rock-music-mad Anna raved about. It was the Oxford of JD Wetherspoon's on the way to Blackbird Leys, a gathering spot Africans loved for its half-priced food and drink. Kenyans, Ugandans and Tanzanians huddled next to the entrance. They hollered about soccer and 'Fagason', 'Ferguson' beaten into submission under their Kenyan tongues. Burundians had their two large tables next to them. Hunched together, they drank, their eyes puffed up with a frightened guardedness. Across sat the West African table: the Nigerians loud, the Ghanaians quiet, the Sierra Leoneans and Liberians stuffing their mouths with mounds of rice and things oily and fried. Right across the bar, closer to the toilets, the South Africans, Basothos, Batswana and Swati sat at tables strewn with beer bottles. Behind them, Zimbabweans swelled on their own.

It was the Oxford of his pound sterling, a wonderful big money that had turned him from a haggard boy-man into a confident man. She had given him his first proper job, a decency he never hoped to get back home. And, for the first time, he could be seen. He had become a man. A man with a fat wallet, a thick wallet that took him to London or Manchester or Nottingham or Edinburgh at a whim, anytime he fancied. Oxford had made him a man. But Thames Valley had caught up with him, vowing to take him back to a place that promised to turn him back to that sunken boy-man.

She was his girl also, his Oxford of the drunken May Day rallies in the wee hours of the morning. It was a long, hearty and colourful march on High Street, knocking down chilled Foster's Lager back to back in a chomping crowd. In the crowd they drank, passing by Magdalen and Queen's colleges. She was the Oxford of the covered market, the delicacy of skinned rabbits hanging over the heads of proud butchers. She was his Oxford of low, thin slices of snow that thawed and dissipated quickly in December. That was the only time, around Christmas, that Oxford was quiet and almost emptied of Thames Valley – the only time he had taken Oxford's face closer to his. Then it felt like he had Oxford all to himself.

And there he had walked down to the Christ Church Meadows behind Corpus Christi College. He had turned off the High Street, onto St Aldate's, winding down to the

Thames Valley Police Station just past the Job Centre with its orange-and-blue signboard. Across from Corpus Christi College and the entrance to Christ Church Meadows stood the 'Alice in Wonderland' gift shop. It made no sense to him that an entire shop would be dedicated to a storybook character.

There were the sprawling green lawns of Christ Church Meadows, the wet and lightly snow-capped trees and shrubs, the squeaky silence of the squirrels. And there he had brooded about how his new family with Anna was coming together. It had warmed him, how what had once been so elusive was now wonderfully coming together. She was his Oxford, where he had planned to grow old with Anna. And perhaps, in time, they would move together to her neighbourhood in Liverpool and settle down. Anna had promised to sort out his papers. It was going to fade away, the problem of papers, Anna had promised him. No more Thames Valley on his back.

Then their baby had slipped out of her. For two weeks, Anna had cried muffled cries. Sometimes she wailed. There was no baby. All of a sudden, there was no baby. Then there was no Anna. No Liverpool. No papers. And then no Oxford? *Baya wamfony' amaphepha* – 'They keep their papers crumpled under their armpits.' Sis' Zuki had thrown her hands about, stomping her feet, cursing Jimmy, her Jamaican-British boyfriend who had suddenly disappeared after he had promised to marry her. And Anna had vanished with papers crumpled under her armpits. *Baya wamfony' amaphepha*.

And he continued the in-between walk, neither leisurely, nor a run.

NINE

It can only be Thandi, Bongani mused, crossing the roundabout towards the High Street. It can only be that jealous, bloody woman! Hot steam leaked out of his nostrils. What more could I have done? I apologised to her now, didn't I? Several times, I apologised to her. What more could I have done? I had to move on. Bongani felt the red mist of anger rising.

He had dumped Thandi eight months back, just after Thandi miscarried their baby and as his relationship with Anna was picking up. He already had a baby on the way with Anna. He had never loved Thandi. Nothing stood out with her. Everything about her was bland – her looks, her body, her intellect, her personality, her sex, her manners. She was more into him than he into her. When she lost the baby, Bongani felt sad for her, but he had to get out. He just could not stay any longer and create yet another permanent link with her.

They worked at the motor-assembly plant, all three of them. It was her sense of herself, not shaped by any need of attaching herself to anyone that attracted him to Anna. It was take it or leave it with Anna – her love for hard rock music, her appreciation of abstract art, her leftist British politics that Bongani barely understood, her love for her working-class community. And soon after he had started dating her, he had made her pregnant. And all this happened under Thandi's nose.

One Friday night, Bongani had decided to take Anna to Sodom. There was the usual crowd, and a crew of South African girls who were visiting from Manchester and Birmingham that weekend. The party had already started to warm up a bit when Sis' Nomfundo had turned up at the kitchen door with three massive black plastic bags. An ex-high-school teacher from Mthatha, Sis' Nomfundo was in her late forties. She was a kind and warm-hearted woman who always sought to help others in the South African immigrant community. And yet she was fiery in the face of any disrespect directed at her or her loved ones.

Thames Valley had come looking for her that morning while she was at work. Many in the crowd had begun to suspect the usual inside sniff: Big Mavis. She and Big Mavis had had rough fights over some rich Ghanaian-British doctor from London. And Big Mavis's threat to South African women who had dared cross her path was her old chorus: "*Ngizokugodusa ma ungena ngqondo!*" – "I'll get you sent home if you're stupid."

Sis' Nomfundo had poured into the kitchen as people were still flowing in. Some men braaied meat on the stoep outside the kitchen. One kwaito hit after another played loud in the living room. Panting and huffing, she had dumped the three black bags in the kitchen and then bolted, muttering something about seeing someone on night duty at the Jude the Obscure bar in Jericho. But before she had left, she had vowed to give Big Mavis hell the next time she saw her.

Nomusa had quietly watched the entire scene unfold. She stopped Bongani and Anna on their way to the living room, but Anna had quickly walked away, joining the rest of the crowd.

"This was not such a good idea," Nomusa had almost whispered, caressing Bongani's left shoulder.

"What?" Bongani had taken a can of Foster's Lager from a bag.

"Thandi. She's coming over."

"And so?" He took a gulp of his beer.

"You want to dangle your new pregnant British girlfriend in front of her?"

"We've broken up, *mos*."

"You dumped her just after she lost your baby. Now you come here with another woman in your arms so soon after? And this woman is pregnant with your child. How insensitive can you be?"

"Thandi just has to deal with it."

"No, BB, you need to put yourself in her shoes."

"I'm not going to do that, Nomusa. Life goes on."

"Just don't dangle your pregnant girlfriend here. Not now. Not here."

"No, Nomusa."

"*Mfowethu*, my brother, please go home now. Go home, or take her home and come back on your own. You know how Thandi is. We don't want to have to take anyone to hospital. And you don't want to cause a scene. You know Thames Valley. They come very fast when a neighbour complains about a scuffle among foreigners. And a lot of people will be removed. You don't want that on your hands, BB."

"Nomusa, we're not going anywhere." Bongani kept drinking as he spoke.

MaDlamini, Sis' Nomfundo's aunt, stood in the kitchen, arms folded tightly under her breasts. A full-faced and matronly woman in a long maroon dress, woollen stockings and a black bomber jacket, it was the first time she had attended any of the South African parties. At sixty years of age, she had come to England through her niece. A retired high-school teacher, MaDlamini now cleaned at some college, and also worked the cash till in a mid-sized supermarket in Blackbird Leys. At one time, she had worked in Reading, taking the bus as early as five every morning in the bitterly freezing winter. Bongani had wondered how she had managed, with fingers brittle, crawling inside with arthritis. She had said that this was her last shot, working to add to her pension, paying her bonded house and maintaining her five granddaughters. With her husband long gone, and all three daughters unemployed and high-school dropouts, she had been forced to come over to England. Working paperless for at least the next five years, she did not attend South African parties in Sodom, because she lay low. But she had to come to Sodom that night. Her niece faced removal, and she was to meet her there to take her belongings as she went into hiding. She could not meet her at her niece's place. The police might be there looking for her, even waiting for her.

The party boomed with tunes from Ringo Madlingozi's latest album. Then there was the favourite hit song from Mafikizolo, a lively lament of a woman over her man's incessant drunkenness.

..

"Wait, man, wait." Tata Linda had almost screamed, his face twisted and knobbed, carrying a tall glass of gin and tonic with two lemon slices. He had suddenly stopped dancing, wagging a finger at the young South African student from Oxford Brookes University. The graphic design student had beamed at Tata Linda. He had told him that, having taken an elective course in African History, he was keen to hear his adventure stories as a guerrilla fighter in Umkhonto we Sizwe in Angola.

"Stop taxing my brains, man," Tata Linda had yelled,

swirling his drink, the ice swaggering cloppedy-clop. "Take it easy, okay? This is a party." Tata Linda had shuffled his feet to the rhythm, dancing behind the woman jiving vigorously in front of him.

"How does one enter this woman?" he had giggled, showing his gleaming, bright white teeth. "That is the question you should rather be asking, not these stories about guerrillas and bush wars." Taking a sip from his glass, he had gone on, loosely grinding against her buttocks. Caressing her hips and whispering silliness into her ear, she had thrown her head back, giving out a plentiful laugh.

"Have you ever eaten a white woman before, *mfowethu*?" Khumalo, a former taxi driver from Ulundi in KwaZulu-Natal, had moved closer to the student, carrying a can of Stella Artois. "I mean original white, *mfowethu*. Original."

"*Mfowethu*." Khumalo had bobbed his head unsteadily. "I hear they are *lastig*, hey. *Baaie stout*. Naughty girls. I'm not leaving this country until I eat a white woman." And then he had arched his head back, taking a long gulp of his lager.

"Guys," Tata Linda had suddenly stopped dancing, looking around him. "I'm warning you again about this Khumalo guy." He stared at Bongani and the student, wagging a finger at Khumalo.

"This guy is drunk all the time. Every day, he's drunk. This is not a taxi rank or the township, going around drunk as you please. He'll get you all deported. When Thames Valley catches him on the streets one day, he'll sing on all of you. Khumalo, I've told you time and again, when police stop and ask you where you work, you say you don't work. But I know you won't do that, because you're drunk all the time. And Thames Valley is intimidating. I don't trust you. I don't trust you at all. You're going to tell the truth, that you have a job." Then he turned to Bongani. "And when they ask him about other South Africans working here, he's gonna sing on all of you." Tata Linda took another sip. "Don't say that I didn't warn you, guys. Mark my words. Keep this guy on a leash. I'm worried about you guys. Me, I have papers. I have papers, me." Tata Linda pounded his hand on his chest.

"He didn't come to England with me, Tata Linda," Bongani had said. "He came with Mkhize. Talk to Mkhize."

Tata Linda had then shuffled back to the vigorously jiving woman, once again plastering his groins against her buttocks. Original Fitness, his former Miss Soweto beauty-queen mistress, ambled over, bringing his refill. Tata Linda had shown her that his glass was full, and then went back to the dance floor. Original Fitness danced her way back to the kitchen to the tunes of Mafikizolo.

A huge guy then swaggered in from the living room, bouncing to the music, holding tight to his can. He had mumbled something, his flabby paunch reminding Bongani of the Teletubbies and Fimbles. In his mid-thirties, everyone called him Major General, on account of his uncanny resemblance to Major General Bantu Holomisa. Smiling, he walked over to the student. The student had yanked Major General away by his hand, pulling him from Khumalo's reach.

Mkhize, a married former policeman who worked shifts at the motor-assembly plant, limped on through life. Frail now, he had a spongy face with a few large black spots on his neck.

"Please, my sister," Mkhize said, carrying a glass of whisky, "just touch me here once again. Please?" He had taken a sip, pointing to his groin area with the other hand. "Please, touch me again, my sister, like the last time. Please, for the last time, just touch me here again, and then I'll leave you and will never bother you again." Mkhize blasted out a wet cough.

"That Mkhize," a middle-aged woman chatting to Nomzamo had whispered, showing three fingers in the air.

"But he goes around as if he's not sick," Nomzamo had said. "You know, last month, he approached me. And I told him off. I put him where he belonged, shame. I told him straight, 'First explain these big black spots on your neck.' And he kept quiet. I don't want to be one of them, shame! I don't want to be a statistic. I hear he's injured and all that ..."

"Mmh?"

"He's injured. He's burdened," Nomzamo had giggled. "These girls who love pleasure, they tell me he's injured, that he has a heavy burden. But still, shame, I'll never go there, no matter how big a burden he has. I know him back from Durban. He's left a trail of lifeless bodies behind."

The two women sipped their drinks, watching dancers grouping in a circle.

"These people back home have to see that I earn pounds here," Nomzamo had said, slapping her chest. "British pounds. Not rand. British pound sterling, my sister. British sterling."

"You see," the other one had begun. "My children, when they walk around the township, everyone has to see that their mother earns pounds in England." And then she had released a long laughter.

"Don't you know?" Mkhize had suddenly appeared, standing over them. "You found the pound here, and you will leave it here." He let out another wet cough, and then sucked on his beer.

Luke from Zwide Township in Port Elizabeth stood hanging on the door that separated the living room from the kitchen. He was in his late twenties and good looking in a feminine Milli Vanilli kind of way, and had spotted a head of cornrows. Leaning against the wall, he clasped a can of Stella Artois. Luke's expression changed to a frown, immediately turning away, dashing into the living room when he saw the Oxford Brookes student heading his way.

Luke was annoyed by the student's academic fascination with him. It had come to the student's attention that Luke – obsessed with all things Jewish, frequenting the synagogue and attending small exclusive Jewish club gatherings and seminars at Pembroke College – wanted to convert to Judaism. He had also noticed that, apart from his Jewish ambitions, Luke was also a closet gay. Luke had been seen on many nights at the Coven nightclub. And his drunken girlfriend from East London, Nana, told anyone who cared to listen about how sparse their sex life was. And the student found the entire combination of Judaism and closet homosexuality in an isiXhosa-speaking young man who grew up in a township and had lived in England for nearly ten years way too fascinating.

Just across the room, next to the DJ, sat two girls, both from KwaZulu-Natal and in their mid-twenties. One kept pointing at a bulky guy with dreadlocks on the dance floor.

"He says he's from Jo'burg, and yet everyone knows that he's Zimbabwean," said one.

"He thinks he's made it," the other went on, holding up her bottle of cider, "because he lives with his British fiancée."

"Really?"

"Have you seen her, this British fiancée?" She looked away, her lips turned inside out. "She's so …" She pumped up her cheeks and opened her arms wide.

"For papers, nhe?"

"For papers."

"I hate *la makwerekwere*!" the second one said. "They will do anything to get papers here."

"But these old British women love throwing themselves at young black muscles?"

"Desperate, shame. Desperate."

Anna stood next to Bongani, talking to a group of people around the dance circle. Bongani felt a plaster of a heavy slap across his cheek. As he turned around, he reeled from Thandi's punch on the nose. And then she had rained in on him with a rush of slaps and fists, all landing squarely on his face. Before long, there was a rush to separate the two.

Thandi then turned and lunged at Anna as Bongani tried to come between them. Another of Thandi's punches landed on Bongani's right cheek. Bongani had pushed Thandi away, and she, stepping back, had slipped and fell on her back. Bongani immediately grabbed Anna's hands and dragged her into the kitchen. When Thandi stood up, there were shards of shattered glass splattered all over the floor.

"You've hurt me so much, you dog!" Thandi had yelled, watching Bongani and Anna slipping out through the kitchen door. "You've hurt me so much! And you're going to pay for this, you dog." Her wailing had centred the house.

TEN

Through the window, Nomusa watched Nomzamo walk away, promising to return. It was a touch-and-go grind against the gravel, a swash-crash-crush beneath her trainers. Nomzamo paused midway to the gate. Nomusa shut her eyes. A Thames Valley eased past Barns Road. Nomzamo shuffled faster, her trainers still tossing away small stones as she picked up her pace. Fiddling with the gate, she looked sideways, scanning left and right, and clicked open the gate, vanishing in the distance, past the bus stop.

Nomusa headed back to the sofa and sat facing her mother. Grace sipped tea, and then put the cup back on the tray. Nomusa let out a full breath.

"Ma, please."
"I'm staying."
"But you should—"
"I'm getting a job here."
"Ma, I'm saying—"

"I'm staying."

"Ma, please …"

"Whatever you want to call it. A lie. A betrayal. Deceit. I'm sorry. But I'm here now, and I'm not going anywhere."

"If … *when* they deport you, Ma, they will also take me."

"I am not going back to Jacob. I'm not going back to that world."

"Dad is not a god, Ma. I told you."

"So you can run away, and I can't?"

"Ma, you can always—"

"You run away from your past, Nomusa, and I can't run away from my present?"

"Ma, we're not going there, okay?"

"I can't run away? After thirty years, I get out of that windowless cave, and you tell me to go back?"

"You chose it, Ma. You knew how he was before you married him. You knew how he was from the get-go."

"And, *wena*, you? Didn't you know? You didn't know? Didn't you know that nuns who open their legs get into trouble?"

Nomusa leapt to her feet and, with her left hand, flipped the table into the air, throwing it fast and far to the wall. As it came crashing down, one leg caved and broke, another falling off entirely. Grace made a dash for it. The box of milk had tumbled to the floor and lay there, steadily gushing out milk. A teacup had wobbled, then fell onto its side. The teapot had landed with a thud on the wool carpet, the tea spilling out fast. Baby Angelina opened her eyes and let out a screech. Balling her fingers into fists, she squeezed her eyes shut, latching on to yet another scream.

"You had to go there?"

"So you're going to punch me now?"

"After five years, you had to go back there?"

"You're fighting me now?"

"One mistake! I make one mistake!"

"And I live with your mistake every day, Nomusa. It's

not going away. It's not going anywhere. All this time, since you've left home, I've lived with it every day. I've faced it every day."

"That shame is gone!"

"I knew for sure then, for the first time, Nomusa, that you were going to get me out of that windowless cave."

"You take yourself out of your cave! It's your bloody cave. Not mine."

"When the church—"

"Shut up, Ma! Shut up, Grace!" Nomusa stood, her brows knotted together, her fists balled up hard, and slowly walked away from her mother.

ELEVEN

STANDING BETWEEN THE 'YEAH' and the 'nay' door, I sifted Wilson from the rest of the crowd. In the centre of the Oxford Union Hall, he stood among three women. I cringed at the sight of his shirt buttons stretched to their limits. Hanging by their last breath, they held on fast against the tight might of his paunch. In him I always saw the man who abandoned salt on his bacon at the New Orleans. Twitching the mound of moustache on his puffy round face, he would pour out one past political adventure after another. Dela and I would listen to how he broke some scandalous political story in Kampala. Or how he ran away with so-and-so, fleeing the grasps of Museveni's police or the military security branch.

And then, rounding up, he would bounce his thesis off us. He would squeeze in this or that theory to best fit some hypothesis for his doctoral thesis on the pro-democracy struggles in Uganda. Now, squealing in a high-pitched soprano, he was telling the three women how he was a tribesman. I never understood what he meant by that. Even over pints of lager at his college bar, I never understood what he meant by 'tribesman'. Sometimes I pretended to get along with him. But I just didn't – although I tried not to show it. It just wasn't worth it. It was only Dela who brought us together really.

I saw, from the way he threw his hands about, that he was in too far into whatever he was telling those women to notice me pass. So I shoved my hands deep into my trouser pockets and walked briskly past. I headed out of the hall and straight into the Oxford Union bar.

Soon I was soaking up the din of measured, feverish talk, the sound that carried many Oxford bars in our 'gownie' part of the city. It was different from townie Oxford, where music – 'a good number', as Josh had it – carried their bars. "You know there are black folks inside when you hear a good tune," he would say. I made my way through the maze of students who were becoming more and more sozzled. The few Anglicised Indian students, standing with their British and European friends against those black-and-white portraits on the wall, had become noticeably louder.

Dela sat at the corner of the bar, against the wall. Like many of those bourgeois African nationalist leaders with side hair partings who had founded our independence I had seen posing in black-and-white photos, his body swung sideways to his crossed legs. That day's edition of *The Guardian* lay spread on his knees. Smoothly wiggling the newspaper, smoke issued slothfully from his pipe. He had on that night a black tweed jacket, a black turtleneck and brown corduroys. Slowly removing the pipe, he tasted his lips, and then shoved the pipe back into his mouth again. Smoking contentedly, I watched his forehead moving with the lines of words on the paper. More often, he smoked Marlboro Lights. And it was always a pack of ten, never a twenty, as if he was preparing to quit.

Dela already had under his belt a well-received book on

democratic struggles in post-colonial Togo. Sometimes, after a small pint session at the Rosie O'Grady Irish pub across Tidmarsh Lane, we would return to college. He would then check on how his book was selling. "See, it is ... it is ... selling like h-h-hot cakes, kind of yes! Mmh?" he would shout through giggles in the college graduate computer room, his finger firmly pointing at the Amazon website. It was a feat of a success, along with some of his short stories published in various magazines. And he had just been placed second in the Commonwealth Short Story Prize. The prize-giving ceremony had been held at Jesus College at the end of the previous Trinity term. And he was now on the verge of completing both his doctoral thesis and his debut novel.

"My guy." I stood over him, then quickly nestled on a chair across from him. I remembered that spot where he was sitting. It was where we had sat for breakfast one Saturday morning last summer, next to the huge bay window. Dela had invited his friend, a wiry, politely violent half African-American, half Afro-Caribbean fellow I knew nothing about. At that breakfast, their conversation had swiftly gone south. And then the half-half fellow had quietly requested that Dela step outside and sort out their problem. Dela had looked intently at the front door at the end of the corridor. "Or we can go through this window if that's too far," his friend had said, pointing to the bay window next to Dela. Dela had looked away, quietly ignoring the man, until the request to step outside died down.

"Mmh." I saw a thin smile emerge through the smoke, as he rested his pipe on the bar counter.

"Excuse me, gentlemen." A bald bouncer hung over us. "Are you supposed to be here?" His closed and steely face wanted to reach closer to us. I looked behind him, and saw an old man sitting on a stool at the far end of the bar. I had noticed the man in a brown suit and polka-dot bow tie staring at us with a frown.

"Say w-w-wha-a ... what?" Dela stuttered, his face twisted.

"We have just attended the Oxford Union debate," I cut ahead of Dela.

"I see." The bouncer turned and quickly walked away.

"You ... you ... you ..." Dela stuttered at the bouncer walking away.

"A pint of Guinness, mmh?" I turned towards Dela.

"It amazes me ..." Dela tried to take it up again.

"I'll get you a pint of your Guinness," I said. "I'm parched, man. I wouldn't mind a pint of Kronenbourg 1664."

I was relieved that I had managed to cut off the bouncer's messing airs. Dela and I had much to talk about. I placed my orders and stared again at the old black-and-white photos on the wall, taking in the malty steaminess of ale and lager, the damp of roll-up tobacco, the woody fragrance of the bar counter and the creaky buoyancy of the wood floor. I did not know whether I wanted the photos to mean anything to me. Sometimes I wanted them to. And then, often, I didn't. Or I didn't think about them. I felt apart from everything around here. And yet, sometimes, I badly wanted to be part of all this, to make this my home, certainly for the time I was meant to be here. People loved South Africa. And South Africa was Mandela. But it was a South Africa in the news they loved, the voice of Mandela in the air far away.

I wanted to feel that I was part of everything in Oxford, like many of the West Africans and East Africans and Central Africans who were so happy to be in England. They yearned to remain in England, a certain craving lighting their eyes. But I couldn't. I always dreamt of the day, a week after successfully defending my thesis, when I would board the first flight out to Johannesburg and leave this place for good. The last lines of that short poem or recitation flying around the township that Mama taught me when I was six years old always came back to me: "*Andiyi ndawo, ndofel' eAfrika / Andiyi ndawo, ndofel' eAfrika*" – "I am not going anywhere, I will die in Africa / I am not going anywhere, I will die in Africa."

Up the stairs, at the end of the bar, was a smaller hall, two of its walls lined with more portraits. Oxford Union parties were held there. I had attended one such party the previous year, invited by a German undergraduate.

When the barman came back with my orders, I balanced the pints, along with two packets of Lay's salt-and-vinegar crisps, and a packet of pork scratchings in my hands and, walking stealthily, placed them all at the centre of the table at which Dela was now seated.

"How wa-wa-was ... the debate?" His voice came out soft, a little tired, as he slipped his spectacles from his face.

"Exciting. Confusing," I began. Dela switched sides and crossed the other leg. "You see," I went on, "they put Ian Smith on the challenging side of the debate, which stated that African leaders do not put their interests before their people. I had expected Smith to lambast Mugabe's regime. He did. But then he made vast exceptions. He went on, time and again, proclaiming that he was Zimbabwean and an African. And then when Labour's George Galloway took to the podium, slashing Smith, the Speaker of the House protected Smith. And so many British and European students – members of the Oxford Union – protected Smith. The Speaker said Smith did not come to the Oxford Union to be reminded of his past. Can you believe that?" I whirled my arms.

"Yes," Dela began, "I ... I ... can believe that." I stared at him, puzzled.

"How so?" Dela tore open a packet of crisps, launching two petals, then gently crunching them. I took a liberal swig from my pint. I was always a faster drinker than Dela. He took a slow slug from his Guinness. I poked around in my jacket pocket and came out with a wrapped twenty pack of Marlboro red filters.

"This is ... is ... what is referred to as the moral and cultural rehabilitation of imp-imperialism," Dela went on, resting both arms on the table. I noticed that his stutter was wiggling off him. It tended to slacken in the presence of his three faithful lovers: beer, politics and literature. When the presence of a woman was added to the mix, the stutter seemed to vanish completely.

"There is continuity here," Dela went on. "The West, the Western nations that colonised Africa, that colonised Asia, that colonised Latin America and the Caribbean islands have never, and will never, completely acknowledge their roles as colonial masters. If, or when they do, they say the past is 'complicated'. Like when they talk about the history of Cecil John Rhodes, they say his history is 'complicated'. It is not brutal. It is not savage. It is not colonialist. It is complicated. But then they readily paint King Shaka Zulu as a bloodthirsty, warmongering savage. Yes!"

"Remember that time last year during the summer holidays when I tutored history classes to high-school students from London's disadvantaged backgrounds?" I went on, putting a cigarette to my lips.

"Yes, yes."

"None of the students knew anything about British colonialism in India."

"See."

Dela lifted a pork scratching, and crunched it up. I took off my glasses and put them on the table.

"I received another rejection letter." It came out fast.

As I gently caressed the little hair remaining on my head, I spotted the old man with the polka-dot bow tie. For the first time, I noticed his wrinkled skin, puffy eye bags and yellow-greyish teeth. A smirk crowded his face, talking under his breath to that bouncer. I turned back to Dela.

"Wait," Dela began, brushing my left hand as it rested on the table. "Whatever they said, remain assured that you are a disciplined writer. The fact that you are completing a doctoral thesis on a Llewellyn Scholarship, and managed to write a novel at the same time, is a success on its own. Very few people manage to do that. It is a journey, Luzuko. This writing business is a long journey that never arrives. If they turned your novel down, and again they will, remain assured that you are destined to be published in the fullness of time. You and I are going to write books. Trust me. You and I are going to write big books. And, remember, I am never wrong." He swallowed a long, neat mouthful of Guinness, smiling.

"Gentlemen," the bouncer boomed over us, "are you members of the Oxford Union?"

"You … you … you!" Dela wagged his finger at the man.

"Man," I intervened, "we are Oxford students. Do you want to see our student cards?"

"I'm afraid you are not allowed here," the bouncer went on. "Only Oxford Union membership cards are acceptable here."

"Listen here, man …" I continued, standing and facing the burly man, my hands and lips trembling. "We are here on account of tonight's debate. A lot of people in this bar are here because of tonight's debate. Have you asked all these people to produce their Oxford Union cards?"

"Gentle—" the bouncer went on.

"No, you … you …" Dela interrupted.

"No, you haven't asked them." I raised my voice. "Tell me I'm lying."

"Gentlemen." I saw the man clench his teeth, his jaw tightening.

"We are graduate students. We can produce our student cards right here, right now, if you'd prefer that."

"I don't care who you are. If you are not members of the Oxford Union, and you don't have membership cards to produce, please leave."

"You see!" I shouted into Dela's face, and then turned to face the bouncer. "You are chucking us out of this bar because that old man in a polka-dot bow tie said you should chuck us out, because we are black."

The bouncer stretched out his hand to reach for my shoulder.

I moved back – only to find another goon behind me, clearly stepping up as the mood began to tense up. Some patrons at the bar had gone quiet. Some giggled, pointing at our table. Others stared, confused. A number of them smiled on. And the rest carried on drinking as if nothing had gone amiss.

Dela trailed behind me, and we slowly and quietly walked out of the Oxford Union. The two bouncers followed closely behind. Again, I listened to the crunching pebbles under my feet all the way to the main gate.

TWELVE

STRINGS OF SALTY WATER were welling up in my eyes. We walked out of the Oxford Union at pace with the two burly bodyguards tailing us. Then they closed the gate behind us. We strolled quietly now, turning right into St Michael's Street. The Village People's 'In the Navy' thronged from inside the homeless shelter, which had that night turned into a working-class gay soirée. Two young men leaned into the wall, eating plumes of cigarette smoke from each other's mouths. One sloped against the wall, almost sliding down, his eyes shut. A thick ball of laughter bouncing up from the floor of his belly came staggering out of him. Abandoning himself to laughter, he reminded me of how Jack Kerouac, in *On the Road*, had gone on and on about some black character's talented laughter. I hadn't laughed like that in a long time. And I had no idea until then how much I had missed losing myself in such a simple joy. Just for a day. Maybe a day and its night. I would give anything to laugh like that again.

We walked in silence to the end of St Michael's Street, past Ben & Jerry's ice-cream shop on the corner. We hadn't said anything to each other since we had been thrown out of the Union. It was all in the eyes, we knew that. We didn't want to catch each other's eye. We didn't want to see what we had become, yet again. Ours was a stark nakedness in the shape of shame. It was in the newness of the pain when it had just been skinned out of you. No matter how many times it happened, the pain never aged. It was in the eyes. And no black man wanted to see it in the eyes of another black man. His was the same as yours. You knew how it felt, but you dared not see the form of it. In the eyes of another black man. So we refused to catch each other's eye, lest we saw how naked we had become. And if you braved to see it, it would swallow you, never to come out of it quite sane again. So we walked on quietly. Blindly.

As we turned towards Cornmarket Street, I took another cigarette from my pack. Cornmarket was well lit, noisy, fun. And I imagined Marechera, in his short dreadlocks, staggering drunk. Russian, Eastern European and Chinese students had staked out Burger King as theirs. There they chatted until late, fiddling on their fancy mobile phones as if they'd never seen fancy mobile phones before. On the pavement opposite, a busker sat hunched on the ground, strumming an acoustic guitar. His notes came out lilting, unhurried. A small crowd knotted around him, listening closely. His black Lenin Kango hat sat gingerly on his head, above a clean-shaven, thin, angular face.

We turned left, towards George Street, and Dela stopped at the first kebab van he saw: Jamal's Wonderful Kebabs, outside Mood.

"Nothing like a hot meal at this time of the night." He rubbed his hands together. Although I was a bigger eater than he, I found it senseless to talk so elaborately about food like he always did.

"A meal?" He called whatever he ate a "meal".

"No, thanks, man." I shook my head.

"You sure?"

"Yes. Sure," I said, leaning against the wall next to an ATM. "I'd rather we go to the Late Bar." I gestured, my head pointing ahead towards St Antony's College.

"And we are going to drink seriously there, mmh?" Dela smiled at me. I knew his "drink seriously" meant no more than a pint and a half, maybe two. A different "drink seriously" to that of Bafana, aka Slimy, or Josh.

"I heard that your deputy ambassador to Russia is here," Dela said.

"Wonderful." But it came out flatly. The sadness of the last hour's episode hadn't yet left me.

The kebab man handed Dela his doner kebab wrapped in a naan bun, with salad, ketchup and mayonnaise. We resumed our walk, picking up our pace along Magdalen Road, past Sainsbury's, and on past St Cross College, the Oxfam bookshop, Borders and Ponana.

"Three months ago," I started, "I read *If Beale Street Could Talk*." I listened to Dela munching his kebab. Holding it closely to his mouth, the mayonnaise and ketchup slid all over his lips. "Are you a doctoral ca-ca-candidate or a struggling, unpublished no-novelist?" He continued chewing the slice of tomato between a burst of laughter, slowly licking the ketchup and mayonnaise off his lips.

"Come on, man." I dismissed him. "After reading *If Beale Street Could Talk*, I had such a sense of joy in the midst of all this racism. There was so much love, warmth and humanity in that story. I have never read a fictional text filled with such warmth before. This was a different James Baldwin, almost a James Baldwin at ease. For once, for an entire month, I managed not to be angry. Can you believe that?"

I sighed, staring up at the stars. "But then," I continued, feeling my voice going down, "I was dragged right back to reality. And the cruelty of it all is that this racism follows me wherever I go. I'm here, and it is here with me. I go home, and it is there. The entire world is my prison. My racial prison."

"And then?" Dela asked, taking the last bite.

"What do you mean?" I dug my hands deeper into my trouser pockets.

"What are you going to do about it?" He rubbed his hands together, shaking off the dust of the naan bread. "You are a scholar. What are you going to do about it?"

I sighed, searching the stars. "I don't know. It's been with me all my life." I watched the shuffling of my feet. "I really have no idea what to do with it."

"Corruption has been with me all my life. The state eating itself, and the state eating its own citizens, has been with me all my life," said Dela, looking away. "Ever since I became conscious of who I am, it has been with me, my state slowly eating me away."

We walked on up St Giles. I watched two young men, one chubby and short, who had been stealing kisses from each other in an alley across the street. They turned back into the dark alley, the skinnier one collapsing on the other's shoulder. A black cab wheezed by, with its light on top lit up for service.

"And since I became conscious of who I am, I have fought corruption," Dela continued.

"You fought it?" I felt nervous at the weight of his fight.

"But you fight because you don't want to die," Dela went on. "If you don't fight, you die. That is how you frame your fight. In specifics, not general, abiding emotionalisms. When you can't drink clean water from the tap without risking a sickness that would require you to go to a hospital that is not there, you fight. You fight because when you've fallen sick you're going to be taken by a private car, on a seriously potholed road because there has never really been an ambulance. Then you fight. And, anyway, you cannot call an ambulance when there's no public telephone and no telephone book where the number that has never been there is supposed to be listed. And so you fight. You fight because you don't want to die. When your grandfather's small farm, where he's lived all his life, is taken by the big government man with a big stomach, then you fight. The big government man has a big stomach because he eats a big salary, dead people's pensions, tax, bribes, revenues from diamonds and bauxite, his wife's *toto*, other people's wives' *toto*, then you fight."

I followed Dela's fingers plucking words out from the air, one after another, and hurling them into his mouth – this *toto*, that *toto*, bribes, dead people's pensions, big salary, tax, diamonds, bauxite.

"You fight because the sight of seeing your grandfather die of heartbreak never leaves you. Ever. You've seen him pray a thousand times, and he still dies of heartbreak. Then you fight. That's what I do, because I don't want to die. That's why I'm here, in exile, stateless. Because I don't want to die."

I stopped, turning to stare at him, my mouth slightly open. "I cannot imagine living in such a country."

"In a heartbeat, I can take your spot." Dela snapped his fingers.

"You don't mean that."

"I do." He smiled, leaking out a small laugh. "Oh, I so do – with all my mind, with all my heart, and with the entirety of my breath. Racism in a democracy can never really drastically alter the quality of your life so adversely."

I stopped again, turning to look at him. "I still cannot, by any stretch of imagination, conceive what it would be like living in such a corrupt country, where the state eats itself, and eats its own citizens."

"Pray that it doesn't come to South Africa. Pray hard that it does not reach South Africa. There was also, once upon a time in Togo, a brief time, when we thought it would never come to us. Pray hard."

I could see St Antony's far ahead of us – the limestone building and the wooden gate. The Late Bar was late because it remained open after two in the morning. Of course, there wasn't any 'Late Bar' sign anywhere inside the college. But we all called it the Late Bar.

"I'm truly lost, Dela." I drew my hands from pockets, wringing them together. "I just can't get anything right. My thesis work is not going as smooth as I thought it would. I'm struggling to write my fiction. My father is no more, and I didn't even get a chance to bury him. My girlfriend dumped me. I just can't get anything right. I can't write right. And I don't even know why I'm here."

Dela watched the shuffling of his feet as we got closer to the college gate.

"Perhaps I should focus on just one thing, my thesis," I went on. "And forget about fiction. I mean, a lot of people focus on writing only one medium at a time. Who writes all over, anyway?"

"A writer's a writer's a writer," Dela said, his eyes still distracted by his own shuffle.

"Mmh?"

"A writer is a writer is a writer." He cleared his throat. "You write to communicate to the people, to the reader. In any medium, in any form that suits your message best, you write. Sartre did it. He wrote academic papers, philosophy tracts, biographies, plays, novels. Iris Murdoch did that expertly for the longest time, writing philosophical books and penetrating, serious literary fiction. Your James Baldwin wrote fiction and essays. It's the same with Graham Greene and VS Naipaul. Nawal El Saadawi. Ngũgĩ wa Thiong'o. Chinua Achebe. Lewis Nkosi writes fiction and literary essays. You won't be the first, nor the last. I do it. I'm not saying it's gonna be easy. But it's better than not doing it, if you can do it."

"But my fiction is not getting anywhere."

"Because you're missing some fundamentals, some techniques."

"Mmh?"

"You know why Wole Soyinka's novel, *The Interpreters*, was a flop? You know why it was a flop, and yet it came out of such an illustrious playwright?"

"No."

"Because he didn't tell a story. What kind of an opening sentence did he use? What are you trying to prove? That you think far more deeply than many people? That you can write complicated sentences? Soyinka imposed themes over storytelling. He might as well have written political pamphlets, like the ones Lenin used to write. And that is the problem with your fiction, Luzuko. Fiction is important, Luzuko. When a person visits a country, the first thing he or she does to see into the soul of that nation is to seek that country's leading novelists, that country's leading fiction writers."

A short silence fell between us.

"And your short fiction is finite," Dela continued. "It's far too finished. There's nothing lingering and loose at the end for the reader. I saw it in 'Run, Afrika, Run!', that short story you published in *Icarus* last year. You write to yourself, for yourself, and you're far too expository. You want to explain everything. That's why your entry didn't make it to the finals of the Commonwealth Short Story Prize.

I breathed out the stab.

"See ... see, for instance, Alex La Guma's *A Walk in the Night*. It remains long in your head after you've put it down, because it's not finished."

Another short silence wafted between us.

Dela cleared his throat again. "And cut out the adjectives, adverbs, similes. A lot. Cut them out. As far as possible, use them only to describe shape, form and colour. Every other description, take it to its basest, its simplest nakedness."

We walked on, crossing St Giles, past the Seven-to-Ten

pharmacy with its green-and-white illuminated cross. We passed the white-stoned St Anne's College for women, where Iris Murdoch had taught.

"What's your take on Jesus Christ?" I asked, feeling an empty passage of air coming between us.

"Wha-wha-what are you talking about?"

The stutter was back. I'd barely noticed it had dissipated. Now it was back, albeit only briefly.

"I mean …" I hesitated. "What do you think of this whole business of Jesus Christ as our … as a kind of Saviour and stuff?"

Dela suddenly grabbed my shoulder. "Don't you ever, ever, ever, go there!" His voice spiked. "Don't you ever make that terrible, disastrous mistake!"

"But I am tired of all this. This anger, this misery, this hurt. I'm tired of it all. I want peace."

"You are a writer!" Dela yelled. "Don't you know that? You are a writer, and any pains and desperation you feel, you are supposed to take them onto your pages. That is the fire of it all. Imagine if Byron had accepted Jesus Christ as his Saviour? Imagine if Okigbo, if Beckett, if Marechera, if James Joyce, if Bukowski had accepted Jesus Christ as their Saviour? Would we have had their works? Imagine if Neruda was a born-again Christian? Imagine if Can Themba and Nat Nakasa had accepted Jesus Christ as their Saviour. Would we be reading their fires?"

We walked on quietly. "Luzuko, do you know that guy, the one who is a potter in college? That guy from Nigeria?"

"Yes. The quiet chap. Jonathan, right?"

"Yes," Dela went on. "You know, that guy, about ten years ago, was Nigeria's finest young poet."

"Really?"

"He was the best. He wrote such gripping and insightful poetry about the state of the nation. And then he started seeing this girl who was a born-again Christian. And now, boom! He's born again. Does he write poetry? No. No!

Now, I warn you, don't go that route. You are a fine young writer, we need you, and I do not want to see you wasting away your talent. Some of us, writers and artists, were not meant to water down the fire in us. We are meant to throw the fire back at humanity. We were born to be consumed by the fire, not to extinguish it. If the fire is not there, if all this confusion and anger and hurt are not there, then our roles cease to exist. We cease to exist."

Fire. And not a hint of the stutter.

THIRTEEN

"I'M LOST." BONGANI caught a whisper straying out of him. "What's happening to me?" The low echo of his voice surprised even him. And then he saw himself on top of a ball of the planet, a lonely image, walking alone in some random spot. In all that blueness and greenness and brown, he did not know where he had come from or where he was going. But he kept walking, just as he had been all along.

An icy brush of wind stiffened his shoulders. Rubbing his eyes, his breathing faltered. The wheezing and the panting slithered out of him. A whirl of icy vapour sliced through his breath. His head spun, the pace swerving and gathering in the vastness of the night and the dotted streetlights. Then he gasped. Collapsing on his knees, both hands plastered on the pavement, the ice cold of the concrete seeped through the tips of his fingers.

Do not run in the presence of the law, he reminded himself again, his eyes firmly on the St Aldates Police Station up ahead. The Job Centre, with its walls of orange, blue and yellow, stood on the corner opposite the police station. A steady bright light flared out from a pole with police insignia emblazoned on the glass. Never run in the presence of the law. The mantra had always helped. It had come to his aid once at Heathrow. And again in Manchester.

The candy colours outside the Alice in Wonderland curio shop reminded Bongani that he needed sleep. Blinking, he stared down St Aldates. A right past Ben & Jerry's would be the shortest route to Commonwealth House, but the presence of Thames Valley broke all the sleepiness inspired by Alice and the Christ Church Meadows and the grand churchy Corpus Christi College. Tilting his head sideways, Bongani lifted his left hand and checked the time: 03h32.

For the first time, it hit him: he was on the run. Was it worth it? Bongani wondered, shunting his hand into his jacket pocket. He walked towards Pembroke Street, crossing the street, past Thames Valley. It wasn't, no. It wasn't worth it, he made up his mind, scratching through the barbs of short dreadlocks. Walking that short distance only to be snapped up by Thames Valley.

Was any of this worth it? Remaining here? Chasing after what? That big, beautiful money? Black numbers flashed on the screen in front of him. That was all he had the last time he had checked his account's balance at the ATM: five thousand, seven hundred and seventy-seven pounds and twenty-one pence. After four years of chasing after the pound, only five thousand, seven hundred and seventy-seven pounds and twenty-one pence.

"You can't chase after the pound, *baba*," Mkhize's voice hovered over him. "You found the pound here, you leave it here." Mkhize had said, downing the dregs of his Stella Artois as a blast of a wet cough came out in the other direction. Tasting his lips, Mkhize had finished off: "It vanishes, to appear again far ahead of you, around the corner. And you have to chase after it again. Then you catch it and eat it here again. You eat it here. And it leaves you again. You found it here, *baba*, and you leave it here where you found it."

Had it been worth it? He listened to his feet pounding the pavement. Had it? The police? The ducking? The running? Was it worth it? But then, going home, was that even an option? To begin again in Shaka's Kraal township outside Ballito in KwaZulu-Natal with five thousand, seven hundred and seventy-seven pounds and twenty-one pence? Was it worth it? Was it worth going back? With everyone there waiting around me with their mouths wide open? Two brothers who dropped out of high school, always out of work. And a sister with two kids from different dads, all crammed in one small house with my mother. Was it worth it? They would ask. Was it worth it? Working in motor-assembly lines, washing dishes, sweeping the streets and emptying dustbins overseas? Was it all worth it? They would ask. For five thousand, seven hundred and seventy-seven pounds and twenty-one pence after three years? Had it been worth it?

Rankitseng had saved almost double what Bongani had managed by the time he was deported. Within eight months of his return to Rustenburg, Rankitseng had gone back to square one. Back to waiting tables at his local Spur, his old job, his old haunt. The last time Bongani had talked to Rankitseng on the phone, he had barely heard him over the loud and catchy, fast-tuned 'Happy birthday' sing-along delivered to some kid at his Spur. A grown man jumping and singing his heart out for some strange youngster, clapping hands in his tight blue jeans uniform, dishcloth over his shoulder. Frowning, Bongani shook his head. No, it wasn't worth it.

He kicked at a stone in front of him. It rolled and tumbled off the pavement and onto the street, as he turned to face Commonwealth House. On his left appeared a small light, a yellow-painted church. What he had once encountered there on the steps of that church continued to spook him:

the humping he and his friend Patrick once saw on the steps. The woman had sat on him, facing the church, panting and huffing over the man as he and Patrick came back from a nightclub. Passing the church, he thought of Chino. His friend once worked at the small computer and electronic gadgets shop around the corner from Ben & Jerry's.

And last summer, on that same one-way road, he, Chino and Patrick had shared sweltering long-drawn afternoons of ice creams and cold beers and pizzas and sticky chicken wings and hitting on Zimbabwean and Ugandan girls. They had sat on the pavement of Commonwealth House, lazing around Patrick's pork barbecues. They were long, balmy summer nights, the night curtain falling long after eight, and they had gone on long walks.

Crossing the street, Bongani walked straight into one of the many apartment blocks of Commonwealth House. Standing in front of an old wooden door with its flaking sky-blue paint, he knocked. He knew that the bell in front of him would not crinkle out any sound. At the sixth knock, he heard footsteps pounding down the stairs beyond. The door opened to a middle-aged Chinese man crackling as he chewed. He held, close to his chest, a bowl of cornflakes with milk and sugar. A hard-boiled egg with teeth imprints sat dunked in the centre of the cornflakes and milk in the bowl.

"Mmh?" The Chinese man chewed on, loud, with an open mouth.

"Is Patrick available?"

"Patrick?" He continued chewing loudly, tonguing a morsel of a soggy cornflake from his lower front teeth.

"Patrick from Uganda." Shivering, Bongani swallowed hard, trying to soothe his parched throat. He felt a heaviness settling on his eyes. Another rush of icy wind sent his shoulders jittery.

"Oh, Patrick." The Chinese man swallowed. "Come in." He opened the door wider. His other hand fished the egg out from its nest in the cornflakes and milk and quickly bit into it. Returning the boiled egg to the bowl, he chewed on louder with his mouth open. Drips of milk slid down his lower lip and chin.

Bongani shut the door behind him. In the hallway, the rustic yellow of the wallpaper drew the narrowness of the passage much closer, while somehow lifting the sogginess from the beige and maroon carpet. Bongani followed the man. The small TV in the corner was the only light in the living room. The Chinese man dropped the bowl on the table and took up the remote control from the small table in the centre.

The trailer on the screen had come to an end, so he quickly rewound to the beginning. The Chinese man's crackling chews ground to a pause as he watched the piercing cliffhanger, yet again. The trailer rewound itself and began yet again, another sneak preview of *What Women Really Want*, a soft-porn spoof of Mel Gibson's *What Women Want*. Then the man opened his mouth, hanging on to yet another repeat that cut him inside his crotch. Commonwealth House had not paid the channel's subscription fee. And another rewind of *What Women Really Want* began.

Bongani followed him out of the living room and into the kitchen. At the far end stood a tall, slim man in a black suit, white shirt and black tie. Loud music streamed out from a passage that led off the back. The Chinese man led Bongani past the black gentleman in the black suit, and pointed down the passage to Patrick's room, where the music came from.

At the door of his bedroom, the stocky, bald Patrick held a blonde by her waist. Pinning her legs between his, Patrick swayed fast, grinding against her thigh. Stifling a giggle, he took a gulp from a glass of Guinness. The woman's naked breasts, bulging and heavy, bobbed up and down. Just inside the room, a small, lithe and bespectacled man sat on the bed in front of a giant CD player on a table next to the wall. He, too, was drinking from a long can of Guinness.

At the sound of thudding footsteps fast approaching on creaking wooden floors, Bongani turned to look over his shoulder. An old, bald man wearing a powder-blue shirt and the white collar of a church minister squeezed past Bongani. Elbowing the topless woman out of the way, the minister stormed straight into the bedroom, killing the music. Patrick spun around, his hand still firmly around the woman's waist.

"Patrick!" The minister yelled, his thin lips trembling. "This is an Anglican home. This is church property," Reverend Markham bellowed, flailing his arms about.

"Reverend," Patrick burped, "you can touch my woman. You can touch my alcohol. But don't touch my *kwasa kwasa*." Patrick's deep bass was followed by another burp.

"It's four in the morning, and you're—"

"You can touch my woman. You can touch my alcohol. But don't touch my *kwasa kwasa*." Patrick wagged a finger at the reverend.

"You're disturbing Osman's sensibilities with your naked lady friend." Reverend Markham's voice was strained. "Osman is complaining. This ... this woman, she's practically half naked. And your music can be heard two doors away."

"Reverend," Patrick went on, flapping a finger at him, "I said, you don't touch another man's *kwasa kwasa*. No matter what happens, you never touch another man's *kwasa kwasa*."

"You're drunk, Patrick. See me promptly in my office at eleven this morning."

"And now you come here with your headmaster mentality. Am I a schoolboy?" Patrick retaliated. "*See me promptly at eleven. See me promptly at eleven.*" Patrick twisted his face, repeating in the voice of a little boy. "What would you do, Reverend, if you caught your woman under another man? Red-handed, mmh? What would you do, Reverend? A woman you were planning to take back to your village for your mother to see. What would you do?"

"But he warned you, Patrick." The little bespectacled

friend, his legs crossed on his knee, almost shouted. "He warned you not to come to her house unannounced."

"Shut up," Patrick growled.

Patrick turned to face Reverend Markham. "What would you do, Reverend?" he burped. "What would you do if you found your woman under another man? If you caught your woman red-handed under another man?"

"And he wasn't on top of her – she wasn't *under* another man," the little man went on. "I was there."

"I said, shut up." Patrick sent out another howl, turning to look at his friend.

Reverend Markham stomped off.

"And you, Osman?" Patrick pointed at the black man in the black suit who had now emerged from the kitchen. "What is wrong with you? What kind of a man are you? Sensibilities? Sensibilities? Another man would have joined us. What are you, anyway? And who dresses in a suit and tie at four on a Saturday morning? You don't even have a job, you. You are on dole."

Osman stared at Patrick with a blank face.

"Patrick ... Patrick." Bongani stepped closer.

Patrick smiled, patting him on the shoulder. "Bongani, you and I knock them back any time of the day, any time of the night." Another belch came out of him. "Come join us." Patrick turned to look at his friend in the bedroom. "And you," Patrick pointed at the little man on his bed, "you put back on my *kwasa kwasa*."

"Patrick, wait." Bongani blurted out. "I need your help. I need a place to crash."

"What happened to your place, mate?" Another burp.

"Thames Valley. Thames Valley happened," Bongani sighed, looking down.

"Again?"

"Just a place to crash, mate, until I figure something out."

"My man, my man, my man." Patrick patted him on the shoulder. "That's fine. You sleep here. But your time's up, mate. I'm sorry. Your time's up. Accept it and go home. When they close in on you again, like this, it's only a matter of time before they catch you. What do the Nigerians say? 'Thames Valley-man go catch you.'" He burped again. "Me, I have papers." Patrick let out a hiccup and stumbled back into the bedroom with a little jive, heading for the CD player.

FOURTEEN

"Luzuko." My name leaked out of his mouth. His thin lips held tightly onto a wobble. It was just a "Luzuko", no need to bother following it with a surname. Or perhaps a "mister". I breathed out between my heart's skipping beats. It had been a long walk up the stairs, up to that college room – a small lecture hall, or a spacious tutorial room. The flight of stairs was short, but it had been a long, hard climb.

"You know why we are here." Dr Eric Davidson, the Bursar, cleared his throat. Shuffling papers under hooded eyes, a strand of black hair struggled loose. The bottom jaw of his angular face tightened. Smoothing his college tie, he bowed his head, lending an ear to Dr Camilla Jenkins, the Dean of Students.

"Yes, Luzuko." Dr Davidson dangled the starkness of my name. I rubbed the dankness of the palm of my hands against my trousers, leaning my elbows closer on the table. "For the sake of formality and procedure, I shall read the charge sheet." Charge sheet? I was at a police station. When I walked out of my room in Summertown House that morning, I knew that there was no going back. There was no walking back from the slaughterhouse I was headed to. Even if the abattoir hadn't been in that college room, I would have been cut up elsewhere in Oxford.

I had no idea how I had managed to lug myself up to that college room that morning. I knew I was going to be killed, slaughtered. I knew I was going to die. Even taking a bath had seemed an impossible feat. As I dressed, my head spun. And then I had stood at the bus station farther down, across from the Dancing Dragon, the Chinese restaurant and bar Bafana and I often patronised. I took the S4 Banbury Road bus to the city centre, disembarking outside Sainsbury's on Banbury Road. And in all the madness of George Street, an eerie silence hugged me. On my way to the abattoir, I breathed in, trying to shake off the silence that comes before death. But I couldn't.

"Barney McIntosh," Dr Davidson's voice stood out, martial, "he says you endangered his life."

"I'm sorry." I looked down.

"You threatened to kick the ladder out from under him."

"I know," I said. "I'm terribly sorry."

"You threatened to kick the ladder out while he was perched on the church roof!"

"I know. I'm sor—"

"He was on top of the ladder," Dr Jenkins interjected.

"You could have killed him."

"Or you could have hospitalised him."

"But I didn't."

"There were witnesses ..."

"How is there a possibility of hospitalising him when I didn't even touch the ladder?"

"Should I read the statements of the two witnesses?"

"But they'll tell you that I didn't even touch the ladder. I merely threatened him with words."

"Mr Goba, a threat is as serious as an attempt," Dr Davidson butted in.

"That's just nonsense."

"You're insouciant." Dr Jenkins slapped her open palm hard down on the table.

"You're talking nonsense. A threat is not as serious as an attempt. Did Barney McIntosh tell you what he said to me? Did he tell you how he insulted me?"

"That doesn't matter!"

"It matters! For fuck's sake, it matters!"

"Sit down!"

"It matters, or I wouldn't have threatened him."

"Stop shouting!"

"F—"

"Sit down!"

"We shall not tolerate your outbursts or any of your theatrics here."

"Why don't you tell your bloody Barney McIntosh to stop throwing around his racist comments before he has his head smashed?"

"There we go again."

"Just like you smashed Mr Cornrow with a bicycle chain last year outside the nightclub Mood, mmh?"

"He called me a monkey."

"He said he had been joking."

"So, you joke around calling a black man a monkey?"

"In England, Mr Goba, a monkey refers to a silly person."

"Racism is racism everywhere."

"That is not an excuse …"

"Anyway, I told the chaplain I had just lost my father who—"

"Still, that is not an excuse!"

"You do not dishonour my father's—"

"Sit down …"

"Keep quiet!"

"Fuck!"

"Sit down!"

"Or what, hey? What?"

"Camilla, let's wrap this up."

"Mr Luzuko Goba, you are herewith, with immediate effect, banned from entering college premises for a full year. This means that you are not to enter college premises for any activity or event, except to consult with your academic supervisor for your thesis work. We will send you communication by e-mail to that effect. Is there any question of clarity, Mr Goba?"

I heard her last words only faintly behind the door I had already slammed shut behind me.

FIFTEEN

"*Paperless.*" Deputy Ambassador Dr Lufuno Mudau let out a polite cough. Over that podium in one past Hilary term, Trevor Manuel, South Africa's Minister of Finance, had unflinchingly charmed the entire hall. In a beige suit, Manuel had virtually downed a full glass of white wine right there on the podium. Smiling and taking a liberal sip, he had opened his address on the restructuring of South African macro-economic strategies. Gangly and sinewy in wafting trousers, our deputy ambassador to Russia peered to the far back of the Examination Hall. A taut potbelly slanted slightly sideways lurked behind his jacket. He piled the weight of one leg onto another. Shuffling a sheaf of papers, he shifted the old weight back to the other leg. Moving with a creak, I winced in anticipation of a tumble or fall at any time.

"Are we hurtling towards paperlessness?" he began. "And what about those who have already literally slid into paperlessness? Who are they? And where are they?"

I don't know how I found myself at the Examination Hall that late afternoon. Since my showdown at the slaughterhouse four days earlier, I carried my carcass on my shoulder. Winds moved me. Only the sheer forces of gusting air. Motions and legs carried me from one point to another. Nothing else. That was how I found myself in places I ought to be, taking care of things that had to be taken care of. No heart in it at all. And so, on that cold, icy late afternoon, I moved to a seat in the Examination Hall, listening to *Paperless*.

I'm not sure I was really interested. Intellectually, the notion appealed to me, of course, but I had nothing to do with paperlessness. It really didn't concern me. And so I didn't know what to do with it. Even with its intellectual appeal, I just didn't have the appetite to bounce with it. My mind had been muddied, minimalised by the college ban. I had to learn to live with it. I had an entire year to live, carrying my new burden of humiliation heavily.

"Keep your eyes on the ball," Josh had whispered loudly into my ear just a few minutes previously at the bicycle racks outside the Examination Hall. It had been 'Mighty Atom', Jack the porter, who had leaked it. Josh had heard of my college ban from the college porter. "The college is not the university, yeah? It's just a building. And a year runs fast, yeah? And forget about that tosser, Barney, or whatever his name is. We're black here in a sea of white, yeah? A sea of white. So keep your eyes on the ball."

Across from me, in the middle of the row opposite, sat Josh. I watched as he waved his hands about in conversation with his Sudanese friend from Merton College, a doctoral candidate in Astrophysics. I guessed that they were talking about the political developments in South Sudan. A little farther in front sat Osman and Wilson. In a black suit, white shirt, a tie and a cream scarf, Osman sat cross-legged, listening to Wilson.

Dela didn't turn up for the address. I hadn't seen him

for over a week. He was busy with his thesis write-up and his Togolese newspaper column. The last time we chatted, he had said something about a "concerted democratisation campaign" he was co-launching in Togo, partly through his column. And, in that chat, he had recruited me to be part of it – to write pamphlets and leaflets. To distribute them. To respond to enquiries. I had agreed. I supported pro-democracy campaigns in Africa. But I suspected I also wanted something to hang my self-worth on. I had begun to dissipate.

I looked into our deputy ambassador's eyes. His address was slowly turning into a ramble. It was not that he was faltering, though. It was my mind. My mind was numb. He prattled on about globalisation, and how borders and state sovereignty were becoming increasingly meaningless. Borders were mere lines on the map, hollow delineations in shaping political and social challenges, he said. And, as we hold on so dearly to our closely guarded borders against outside forces, real and perceived, we birth aberrant nationalisms. These carry the potential of quickly metamorphosing into neo-fascism and xenophobia, because we then begin to breed siege mentalities. Mentalities under siege, in turn, generate fundamentalisms and right-wing politics. And these were fast becoming institutionalised. They garner popularity and gain centre-hold in the political fulcrum.

"We promote static nationalist lifestyles," Dr Mudau went on. "We then believe that outside ways of life sully these constructed, fixed nationalist lifestyles. We generate national fears, perceived and over-inflated realities. These, in turn, become more and more 'legitimate fantasies'. We then elevate these fantasies to political threats militating against the integrity of our 'national' communities.

"But people move and then plant themselves all the time, leaving imprints wherever they go. And so it becomes more and more of a numbing hair-splitting exercise to determine who belongs where. We become all mixed up, everywhere, all over. Why? Because identities are always flux historical processes. They move and mutate all the time. And historical processes of the formation of identities – cultural, national identities – are always on the move." There was a brief, almost imperceptible pause.

"I was once paperless," he said. It was then that I sat up.

"At the port of entry at Heathrow in that autumn of 1985, the first two British immigration officials didn't understand any of the things I told them about myself. And for the life of me, I couldn't figure out what was not understandable about what I had said. And so they took me to a secluded room somewhere in the airport. Then the British immigration official began:

"'What is your name?'

"'Lufuno Mudau.'

"'Lufuno Mudau?'

"'Yes.'

"'But you also called yourself by some other name earlier on?'

"'My *nom de guerre*? Sorry. I've grown so used to that name.'

"'*Nom de guerre*?'

"'My alias.'

"'Why do you need an alias?'

"'It's a war name, to protect myself and my family from the terrorist South African state and their friends.'

"'Why is that so?'

"'Because I am a freedom fighter.'

"'And what is your profession?'

"'A freedom fighter and a student.'

"And my interrogator stood up, excused himself, and left the room. Soon after that I felt the temperature in the room drop significantly. It started off as a sting. Then a sudden, terrible chill came over me. About twenty minutes later, my interrogator returned.

"'Say again, what is your profession?'

"'A freedom fighter and a student.'

"'From?'

"'South Africa.'

"'And where is your South African passport?'

"'I don't have one.'

"'You don't have one?'

"'Yes.'

"'Why is that so?'

"'I've never had one.'

"'And you also don't have any documents proving your South African citizenship, right?'

"'I'm in exile.'

"'And in your so-called current passport, which is in the form of an A4 one-pager, it indicates that your point of departure is Lusaka, Zambia.'

"'Yes.'

"'But you don't have any Zambian residency papers.'

"'My passport was issued and authorised by the United Nations High Commission for Refugees, and guaranteed by the African National Congress, the ANC.'

"'The ANC? The outlawed, terrorist organisation?'

"'Yes, but—'

"'Let's move on, Mr Mudau. You pointed out earlier on that you lived in Lesotho before?'

"'Yes, for a few months. I skipped the country to go to Lesotho.'

"'Skipped the country?'

"'Illegally left the country for exile.'

"'Aah, okay.'

"'Then, after that, I moved to Zambia, then to Nigeria. I lived in Lusaka, Zambia, for a year. Then, from there, I moved to Nigeria.'

"'So then you lived in Nigeria?'

"'Yes. Then I moved to Nigeria, and lived there for two years, to complete my high-school education.'

"'You travelled on this … this A4 one-page passport?'

"'Yes.'

"'Then, from Nigeria, you moved to Moscow?'

"'First I moved to Dodoma, in Tanzania ... I attended the Solomon Mahlangu Freedom College for a year, and then on to Moscow.'

"'For a year?'

"'Yes.'

"'Still travelling on this one-page passport of yours?'

"'Yes.'

"'And then you moved to Moscow?'

"'Yes, to Russia, to enrol at the Patrice Lumumba university.'

"'And you travelled on this A4 passport?'

"'Yes.'

"'And since you've lived in Russia for just over eight years, you didn't acquire any Russian residency?'

"'No.'

"'And what do you call yourself, Mr Mudau?'

"'A freedom fighter ...'

"'Yes, yes, yes, I get that. I mean, what nationality are you? What do you call yourself in all your paperless travels on this ... this A4 one-page passport?'

"'A South African.'

"'A South African with no documented proof of South African citizenship?'

"'Well ...'

"'And what do you want here in Britain?'

"'To consult with my doctoral co-thesis supervisor at the London School of Economics.'

"The interrogator had sighed, reclining on his chair. Then he reared his head. I saw a mound of his eyebrows coming together, thickened.

"'You want me to believe that you move around with this decrepit, floppy, crumpled, lousy A4 page you call a passport, living in all these countries, working for an outlawed, terrorist organisation, calling yourself a freedom fighter and a student? Any bloke can come off the streets right now and call himself a freedom fighter of all manner of causes. And you want us to release you to wander around on British soil, a paperless so-called African freedom fighter from Russia?'

"Shaking his head, he then excused himself again. And I hugged myself once more. It had become a tighter hug to stave off a colder shiver. I couldn't understand what had irritated him. It was just a passport. My passport. And no one had ever called me *paperless* before, anywhere. I didn't even know what paperless meant. And I couldn't figure out anything amiss with who I was and who I had been all along.

"From the exchanges between myself and the British immigration official at Heathrow back in 1985, many of you may interpret my responses as the jitteriness of a refugee. Perhaps you see in all this how I had rattled neat categories – of citizenship, non-citizenship, of documented and undocumented status. It was all about how I should have existed on paper. It was all about how the sum of my movements, of my entire breath, should have been summoned onto a paper.

"But I did not see myself as a refugee. I was a freedom fighter. I had been displaced from my own country. For me then, freedom could come the next day, or the following week. It had been coming 'tomorrow' ever since I was displaced from my home country in 1976. And it continued to come 'the following day' throughout my exile. Until that 'tomorrow' eventually became 1990. And so, until my freedom came, I lived in other lands – lands that considered me foreign.

"The challenge of my paperlessness is how foreign lands – Britain and the rest of Europe, in this context – consider otherness. Their perceptions of the other are fixed. They feel that they ... others ... need to be put in their place. The 'other' must be there, because he is not us, not 'we'. And so, when the other is separated, set apart, when he is put in that space there, he becomes unproblematic. He becomes acceptable only when he is placed separately, there. For Europe, for Britain, the identity of the other ought to be embedded in not being European, not being British. Being in a foreign land means being alien. Full stop. So when the British and Europeans realise that the identity of the other is rather shifty, fluid, flexible, that becomes a problem. It is quite normal for European and British identities to change all the time, even in lands not their own. But it is not acceptable for the identity of the other to change shape over time, particularly on European and British soil."

There was another pause as the deputy ambassador caught his breath.

"But identities have never been resolved. They are not meant to be resolved. They are not meant to be fixed, static. They move, travel, rather like pilgrims.

"What was paperlessness then? What is paperlessness now? What forces drove paperlessness then in Europe, in Britain? And what drives paperlessness now in Europe, in Britain? I befuddled the British immigration official at Heathrow in 1985 because my 'otherness' was an ideologically constructed alien form. At the height of the Cold War, in his eyes, I was a Third World freedom fighter acting in proxy for the communist Soviet Union. I was a myth they had constructed. I had to be that. That had to be my identity. I could construct my own identity willy-nilly, in any way I wanted, but in their eyes my identity – the way I had constructed it – was disruptive.

"And what is paperlessness now? What drives paperlessness now? Again, it is to preserve the idea of a clean Britain, Europe, cleansed from outsider infestation. The other is a plague in their historically well-constructed social order. And so the other remains a threat.

"Europe and Britain are not willing to allow any free-handed play when it comes to the identity formation of the other in their societies. Identities have to be predetermined in their rigidly defined European and British constructs. And yet Europe and Britain had no problem in allowing the determination of their identities in foreign lands they regarded as their own.

Britain must become open to social and cultural interruptions. The other comes from Africa, Asia, Latin America, the former colonies. They are considered disruptions ... disrupting the normal British social and cultural order by flooding British soil. It is as if this flood has no history. It is as if it has not emerged out of a historical continuum of the colonial and imperial core-periphery dynamism of relations.

"And so Britain and Europe have to demystify the myths of the social and cultural constructs, those identities of the other. They have to empty themselves, deconstruct, and learn who we are as we are, and as we change, in our own terms. History has made us part of them, of their lands, as much as it has made them part of us, our soils. These are relations of an endless dance, a dance demanding that our identities never be fixed at any time. If we do not take heed of these fluidities, the myths will spiral into conflicts and counter-conflicts of right-wing and left-wing and the centre, destroying the elemental core of what Britain, what Europe is."

SIXTEEN

I SEARCHED FOR MY FATHER in the eyes of the deputy ambassador. Had they ever met in exile? Did the ambassador know him at some point in Zimbabwe, Madagascar, Lesotho, Zambia, Tanzania? Did they ever meet? Perhaps in a military camp in Angola? Or at a conference in Lusaka? At a bar in Harare? A house party in Swaziland? What kind of a man was he, my father? How did he laugh? How did he walk? Did he swagger about? How did he look when he was serious? When he was being silly? How did he shove his hands into his trouser pockets when in a pensive mood? What were his idiosyncrasies? How did he treat women? What was his favourite drink? And his favourite colour? What was his favourite food? Who did he read? Who was his favourite writer? What kind of music moved him? Was he a gentle man? Was he a violent man? Deceptive, perhaps?

Loud applause stormed around me. I stood up, watching Josh and his Sudanese friend tiptoeing, filing out the door.

Osman and Wilson were still chatting above the din. I lifted my backpack from the floor and joined the queue to the exit. Osman and Wilson headed to the podium to chat with the deputy ambassador. I had heard that the Oxford Africa Society had organised a dinner for him at the Lebanese restaurant on George Street, and a drink after at the Late Bar. I was not in the mood for all that, and yet I didn't know what to do with myself. I missed my father. And I didn't know what to do with that either.

I unlocked my bicycle and walked it up High Street towards the city centre. At a pedestrian crossing, I crossed over. Out of my depth, I stopped and leaned against a wall. I took off my backpack and unzipped it. Lifting out the first letter in a white envelope, I ran it past my nose. I searched for his smell in that letter, the odour of a man I had only seen once in my life. Running my hand over the decoy Durban stamp of 1986, I noticed little smudges – old smudges – of my fingers on the typed pages. Since I had shown up at the slaughterhouse, I had kept the letters he had written me from exile in my backpack. Taking one letter out of the envelope, I saw that the paper had lost its crispness. The four-way fold had gorged deeper, with some finality. I brought the page closer to my eyes. The writing of his first letter stood firm in typed form:

Dear Luzuko,
I thought it would be difficult to write you a letter, my son, but nevertheless I have managed. The main thing I wanted to do is to send you that card so that at least you know what I look like.
Do not worry so much, your father is not lost, I am in the struggle for liberation and even if I die it will not be in vain. Next time I will try and send you a big photo which you may even manage to frame in your room. I have not forgotten that last time I promised to send you some things but the problem I am facing is

the person who will take those things to you, so please be patient.

I have also been quiet for some time because I was in another area which made it rather difficult for me to call and say how you are, for instance. Please do not forget to greet your mother and your grandmother.

Where do you study now and how do you do with your studies, Luzuko? You know what? I miss you so much because basically when I last saw you, you were so young and now you are a very big man with all the skills and expertise of judo and karate. Please do not worry about answering this letter otherwise I will try to keep in touch with you, sonny.

Your loving father

I closed my eyes, gasping in the air and the smell of the first time I had read that letter back in 1986. And what I had asked for back then, when I was crazy about being a botanist, rushed back to me. I had wanted a microscope so bad, to study leaves and stems of plants, just as I had seen them in my biology textbooks.

Looking up, I realised for the first time that, here on the High Street, Cecil John Rhodes had been hovering over me and my father all along. I had given Rhodes my back, leaning against the wall. For a minute, I studied his face above me. He looked more purposeful, a stark contrast to his portrait hanging in the hall of Rhodes House. In that painting, in his brown jacket and beige trousers, he sat, resting his elbows on his knees against an orange-yellow-brown sunlit backdrop of the bush. He seemed at ease and thoughtful, but he also looked drained, emerging out of a long day of hunting, perhaps? I took out the letter I had written to my father in 1990:

Dear father,

It had to be "Dear father". Not "Dear dad – Dear *tata*". *Tata* was reserved for my grandfather, who had raised me from day one. The first time my father and I had talked over the phone, in 1987, when he had asked me to call him *tata*, I had failed. I had tried. I tried my best. But my tongue got stuck. It just did not leap out of me as I wanted. I tried to swerve and pummel and shift my tongue to call him *tata*. But it had refused. Even after his death, I could not call him *tata*, only "father", or "my father".

There were rumours that you have arrived in South Africa. It is said that your name was announced through the radio. I was so glad! I couldn't wait to see you live before my face. But it was said that you were in Johannesburg, brought by an assignment. Someone then said you had never even been here. There was confusion.

I wish to know more about your private and personal life. I wish to know about why you became an exile. How you became an exile. When and where you were first exiled. What are your political views? What kind of assignments are you engaged in? What kind of people do you associate with? Who do you live with? What are your routines on a daily basis? Your experience there. The situation in Zimbabwe and other African states on aspects of social, economic, educational, political matters. Great important men you have encountered in your political life.

When I was young I hated politics. Then it was the time I call "The Dark Period". People were burnt by petrol and tyres if their political views were not similar to the majority. If a person had no political information and has received nothing about the African struggle, he would be called "impimpi" and "khwel' ecingweni"

– (politically neutral). Those who had received no information would be referred to as "akarhabulanga" (politically unconscientised).

Then I was young. I had no information about the African struggle, and what made me more negative and ignorant about the situation was the reaction to people like me by the so-called "enlightened ones", that means "abo barhabulileyo"...

Halfway through the reading of it, I folded the letter. This was the rambling of a kid. I lifted out of my backpack another letter my father had written me in 1988 from Antananarivo, Madagascar:

Dear son – Luzuko,
I was very happy after having received your letter, son. I received it here from one comrade who came from Zimbabwe.
I am still in Harare but I came to Tananarivo on an assignment. By the end of March, I'll be in Zimbabwe again, though I'll start in Lusaka.
Sometime last year, I got another letter in Harare with a card inside. When I compare yourself in the photo with the last one, there's a big difference, son, really. In this one you really look old and big ...

I folded the letters, shoving them into my backpack, and cycled down the High Street to the Oxford University Parks. Walkers and cyclists filed over the pebbled walkway that ran as far as the benches at the far end of the park. The grass here remained green even in winter. Clusters of students gathered on the lawn. At the centre sat a group of five students sharing a picnic basket. Three students in tight black pants were stretching in unison, exercising in the middle of the patch of green.

Far off, sitting on a bench, reading something that looked

like a pamphlet, I spotted my friend, Dr Vincent Jama. He had come to England two years back, to practise medicine, rotating around hospitals in England. He had come to visit me overnight from Manchester, before travelling back the following morning. Tall and somewhat hefty, his complexion seemed to have become much lighter in the coldness of the English winter. Now his reddened nose was poked deep into the pamphlet, all he had with him to while his time waiting for me. He had come to see me so we could come to peace over our dear friend's death.

We had all been at high school together, and had just learnt that Xhanti – or X-Man, as we called him – had succumbed to some complication arising from his bipolar disorder the previous week. The disorder had first crept up on him in the middle of his undergraduate studies. And then all petered out just after he graduated. Even at the height of day, he saw vile creatures. And more of them hung on blood-dripping crosses in the vastness of the night. He was found early in the evening, hanging from the rafters in his aunt's garage. The thick rope plugging his neck to the beams of the garage had long stopped swaying by the time his aunt discovered him.

It was not the riot of the disorder that had sent him to his death. The medication had him in balance. It was what it had reduced him to that killed him. The daily countenance of the dourness of his hollow self. This new, frantic grasping for acceptance, for companionship. The loneliness, a loneliness so eerie. It was the brokenness – from constant mockery, from redundancy, from us leaving him – that had killed him. As he was wilting away, we were here in England. And so, as in the old way of cows gathering in a kraal at the exact slaughter point where their fellow cow had come across its blade, we had come together to mourn the fall of X-Man. "Make it snappy" – that was all I could hear from him, his favourite saying when he had grown silently irritated. And I saw him, his eyes closed, snapping his fingers, lip-syncing our favourite song, Bell Biv DeVoe's 'Something in Your Eyes'. That was all I saw of him when he was happy.

We walked back, Vincent and I, all the way up Banbury Road to my place in Summertown. A sweaty jogger in yellow shorts and a long, white T-shirt passed us outside University Parks. A lover and his woman in a checked jacket and black sweater coiled around her neck pushed a bicycle. Two more cyclists with backpacks, two brown leaves floating around, followed them.

"Things are changing," Vincent said, kicking a pebble. "I don't think I'll be in England for much longer." I looked at him, my mind slightly distracted, switched off.

"Mmh? Why?"

"It's the Poles. The Czechs and the Slovakians." He sighed, shoving a hand into his trouser pocket. "They're taking half the jobs we came here for."

"Really?"

"It's an influx, Luzuko. It has really become an influx now," he continued, eyes downcast. "Since they've been accepted into the European Union, Eastern Europeans are flooding this country. There's so many of them. And now there's some kind of an announcement, a half-official rumour flying around that we're going to earn half of what we're earning now because of this new wave of Eastern European intakes."

"Is it that bad?"

"Did you not hear what I said? Soon we are going to earn half of what we are earning now. I came here to make money, Luzuko. I'm here to make money quickly ... to set myself up before I go back to South Africa. And there's no point in remaining here if I'm going to earn half of what I'm earning now."

We stopped at a pedestrian crossing. I watched the cars and traffic lights, sniffing a gathering of rain in that piercingly cold afternoon. We stopped at the crossing to gather our hearts – on change, on leaving, on what we had left back home, on exile, on mourning over the wreckage of ropes and blades, on death and the sadness of living in the here and now.

SEVENTEEN

PURPLE TURTLE HAD NO FUSS. Unlike Mood or The Bridge, queues were much shorter. Often, there were none. So there were no irritations about "one in, one out", or couples' night only, or even paying at the door. This was a haunt preferred by Oxford University students, almost exclusively. Even Oxford Brookes University students rarely patronised the club, if ever. Owned by the Oxford Union, it did not attract the garish townie crowd either. And so, that night, Bafana and I walked into Purple Turtle.

I had purposely sought out ventilation. Over the past month or so, I had thrown myself into my thesis work and reworking my novel. I had wanted to prove to myself that I could live beyond The Barney McIntosh Affair. The logic in it was simple: bury myself in my work to push away the pain, the humiliation of my ban, of not belonging, of missing my father, and the numbness left by X-Man's death.

And so I immersed myself in my doctoral work, and

rewriting, rewriting, rewriting my novel. I realised I had been skirting around the revisions, scared of ripping apart the monster and putting it back together again. Pacing had flatlined. And so the narrative had emerged as a rather long, straight road. The prose was often unnecessarily expository. Chunks of dialogue digressed, long winded. And the parts of it that actually worked were quite stilted. Themes shouted over loudhailers, hanging over storylines, the drama and the movement of conflict.

So I reworked my novel alongside writing and editing thesis chapters, and filling gaps in my literature review. What was important was that I was working really hard, staving off everything threatening to gnaw at my insides. And so I worked. I rode two horses hard and fast, as best as I could.

During the day, I worked away from Summertown House. It was all about staying away as much as possible from a place that had my bed. I worked myself to exhaustion during the day, and left the evenings for literature review and novel revision in Summertown. I worked in the postgraduate computer room not far from Oxford University Parks. And on some late Friday afternoons, Josh would rock up in his small, old, beaten blue Ford Fiesta. And then we would "head out for a jar", as he would have it. And a jar of lager would often take us to The Cock & Camel, his chic haunt on George Street, across from Mood and a block from Manhattan nightclub. It was a fairly small and modern bar with the ambience of a coffee bar. And later, sometimes, we would finish off the evening with a jive either at Mood or The Bridge.

Often, I worked at the library of the modern, glassy and posh Politics and International Relations Department. It stood at the far end of a winding road not far from University College, moved there from its old site, behind St Peter's College and across from the Gloucester Green bus station. And sometimes I worked at Queen Elizabeth House, pausing for lunch breaks to grab a bacon-and-olive baguette with a bottle of cranberry Snapple on George Street. Occasionally, I had Chinese from a small place on St Giles. For a fiver, it sold filling lunches with soup. I also worked at the busy School of Geography library, and then sometimes at the Rhodes House library. Slowly, I realised that I could live outside the college premises. I could live beyond The Barney McIntosh Affair.

But there was also the matter of belonging. That was something that work could not possibly cure. Where was I? Was I meant to belong here for the time that I was here? Was it a desire I was actually meant to have? For Oxford, for white Oxford? And belonging to the small, though visible and strong core of African and black students rather soothed me. But it was a temporary, irritatingly illusive sooth. They looked West, enthralled by the West, the glimmer and the glitter of whiteness.

So many African students did not want to return to Africa. That repulsed me. I truly wanted to vomit up the disgust when I met elated African students on the streets of Oxford excited at the prospect of landing a job in England or Europe or in the US or Canada, or when they went on and on about careers in the oil industry, at multinational firms in some western country. I could smell the greed and selfishness coming out of their mouths – the West Africans, the East Africans, the few Central Africans, the Zimbabweans, the Zambians. With the exception of South Africans, Batswana, Namibians and a handful of other southern Africans, the whole African student lot were determined to turn their backs on Africa after Oxford. They did not want to go back to Africa, back home.

I thought about belonging as I stood in front of the Afro-Caribbean man handling the door at Purple Turtle. There was a sense of contentment I wanted so bad from belonging. But everything I wanted had been a hand-catch of the wind. And so I stood at the door, hauling in the steaminess of the lager and the ale, the sharp sweetness of the spirits and the schnapps, the hazy cigarette smoke, and the musky sweetness of the hubbly-bubbly circling the air. The doorman let us through.

Bafana cut ahead of me, swiftly descending the stairs. I watched him heading for the bar, ordering two pints of Stella Artois. Then I recalled a snatch of a moment that night last year in Hilary term, at that same spot. I had stood with Dela and another English literature student from Keble College, discussing the stream of consciousness in Iris Murdoch's *The Sea, the Sea*. Dela had abrasively cut me out. Struggling to shout above the din of the retro seventies' music, he had laid out the abomination I had committed: You don't critique a writer over his or her work unless you have read the writer's entire oeuvre. "Have you read all of Iris Murdoch's books? If you haven't, then keep quiet."

I rushed to my spot, a couch in the back corner looking up at a poster of Bruce Lee in *Enter the Dragon*. The retro seventies' music and the steaming hubbly-bubbly pipes yanked me to a high. There were other movie posters of seventies' cinema on the walls, of Steve McQueen in *Inferno*, of Blaxploitation movies with high Afros. I took in the smoky purple and yellow and orange, the wounded, topless, sweaty Bruce Lee. As a kid, I had always imagined that the four-striped bloody scratches on his pecs came from a baboon's maul. It was an imaginative fancy that took over me. I had never seen a baboon in real life. And I loved staring at that poster with beer whirling in my head. Inside that fermented zing, I dreamt and listened to some of the exciting snatches of my novel's prose, the written and the still to be penned.

I was taken back to Kole Omotoso's *The Edifice*. There was a bit of pubbing and clubbing in England in that novel. There was also a certain unease, perhaps a sadness in the main character grappling with the notion of belonging. I would then drift into Dambudzo Marechera's short stories, 'Oxford, Black Oxford' and 'Black Skin, What Masks?' And there, I would cackle to myself, imagining Marechera awkwardly socialising at college bops. Then there was that conversation he had with his African college mate at New College dormitories who had scratched the blackness off his skin again and again and again. So eager to score a girl but constantly failing, Marechera, rolling tobacco, had advised him to rather masturbate, or try men.

Bafana moved carefully, but still the two pints spilled a little over his hands. As I cleared the foam off the top of my glass, I shuddered. Sitting down, Bafana lunged for my twenty pack of Marlboro Reds on the table. When he was sober, he did not smoke at all. But when he was drinking, he ate my cigarettes and never bought replacements. I took a gulp, sighing at the smooth coldness of the lager.

"Where's your friend, Dela?" Haltingly, Bafana heaved in the half-inhaled cigarette smoke, looking up at the ceiling. Watching his twitching cheek, his round, light-complexioned face came out much lighter against the abundance of orange.

"He's writing."

"Writing what? His thesis?"

"Yeah. That, and his column. He's launching a Togolese pro-democracy campaign through his column. And he's asked me to help with the campaign."

"Doing what?"

"Writing pamphlets, leaflets, and distributing them."

"So, there's no democracy in Togo?" He tapped the ash of the cigarette on the ashtray.

"It's a façade."

"And you know that for sure?"

"Yes."

"Because Dela said so?"

"No. Because I know so."

"You talk about this as if you've been to Togo, as if you know Togo."

"I don't have to have been there to know that democracy in Togo is highly flawed. I know that …"

"Who cares, man?" Bafana killed the cigarette butt and took a long gulp of his lager.

"What do you mean, 'Who cares'?"

"Why do you care?" He fished another cigarette from the pack.

"I care about democracy in Africa."

"For democracy in Togo, Luzuko?" And I knew that when he enunciated my name, he was about to say something I was not going to like. "Who cares about Togo?" he continued.

"I care. You should care. Togo is an African country," I said, listening to his throat croaking at the last dregs of his pint.

"It's just a drumstick on the map." Bafana licked the wet beer from his matted moustache.

"No, Bafana. Benin – next to Togo – looks like a drumstick on the map."

"Yeah. Togo is smaller. I remember now." Bafana laughed. "It looks like a drumette, then. Yeah, you're right. I remember now. It's a drumette." He looked straight into my eyes. "Just get us another round, man. What's in it for you, anyway?"

"Nkrumah said that …"

"Just go and get us another round, man!"

I stood up and headed for the bar, shaken by how he had managed to strip me down. I returned with the second round and a packet of pork scratchings. He had already eaten another cigarette and taken out another. Puffing on half-inhaled smokes, he ogled the girls flowing to and back from the dance floor. I tried to mince in sensible conversation as much as I could between the second and the coming third round. The tilt always came halfway through the third pint. It always came. Every time.

And so I packed in as much sensible conversation as I could ahead of the tilt. I adored the man so much. It was the casual seriousness of his conversations that fascinated me. Off the cuff, he could come up with the most brilliant statement in just one sentence, all still while silently taking in the sight of girls passing by. He started off by brushing aside my college ban. It happened to the best of us, he said, snacking on another cigarette. He took a sip, eyeing another girl. He was once banned from Worcester College for a year, he said. For sexual harassment, they said, sniffing and peeking at a girl on the dance floor.

Sometimes, he would come up with profound things. Once, almost casually, he told me of how his mother used to run after cars in the streets of his township, trying to pry open the doors. She had been mentally unstable, in an on-and-off sway. His father had passed on before he was born. He told these stories with a smirk that straddled a frown and a smile, all in a pensive mood.

He told me of how he had accidentally landed at university, when all he had ever wanted for his life was to drive a mini-bus taxi for the sole purpose of getting laid often, just like his cousin the taxi driver. But, somehow, he had ended up at university. At first, he resisted. His cousin had seen five stars next to his name in the newspaper carrying the matric results at the end of that year. Bafana, then a fifteen-year-old, had no idea that a star meant a distinction. His cousin had convinced him to enrol at a university. In exchange, he had promised to take him for joy rides in his taxi in search of girls over weekends.

Then there was the story of how, for almost a year, he had embraced Islam and changed his name to Rafiq. In his politically radical undergraduate years in the late eighties, Rafiq sold the ANC's banned *Umrabulo* newsletter on the streets of Johannesburg. Often looking furtively over his shoulder, he never walked the same route twice, he said. He then returned to sipping on his pint of Stella Artois, letting out another puff of cigarette smoke while swivelling his head to take a fuller look at one passing girl.

As Bafana drank down the last silt of his second pint, I reminded him of the origins of his alias, Slimy.

"Come on, man. Come on." He frowned, looking away.

"Remember the Oxford Africa Society party at Lincoln

College that night in Hilary term last year?"

"Stop it, man."

"She gave you your alias then. What's her name again? That Jamaican Jehovah's Witness chick from my college? Julia or Julienne or Julianna? I forget."

"She also called you a glutton, Luzuko." He huffed out a laugh.

"I know." I laughed it off.

"But how do you eat two full, long baguettes one after the other?"

"I was hungry, man."

"You're always hungry. And you eat a lot and too fast. You are a glutton." We laughed, taking sips of our pints.

"You remember that night you arrived drunk at another party at Lincoln College?" I reminded him. "The minute that Nigerian woman saw you coming up the stairs, her mood changed. Completely. She was so ticked off when she saw you coming up, because you always hit on her. Every time you were drunk, you hit on her. All the time. And then you came up to her that night. Straight into her face, you said, 'You remind me of the Queen of Sheba.' And I know she reminded you of the Queen of Sheba because she's quite dark skinned, as if you've ever seen a picture of the Queen of Sheba."

Rolling with laughter, we tossed ourselves back on the chairs. I saw tears rolling off Bafana. He tried to take out a cigarette, but then launched into a fresh, new hail of laughter. Then he stood up, heading to the bar for the third round. I flinched at how he looked at the girls on the dance floor. His stares had become lingering. His sniffling had become heavier, his eyes redder, wetter, rolling loosely around their sockets.

"I'll be back now-now." He staggered off again. And I knew it. The tilt was upon us. Exactly halfway through his third pint, the tilt had come. After that, there was no returning to sensibility. It came at Mood, at The Bridge, at Purple Turtle, and there was never any reeling him back from the tilt. And so I sat back, watching Bruce Lee and Steve McQueen, nursing my pint, and waiting for the inevitable, yet again.

Five minutes into it, as the zinging had begun to brew in my head, Bafana passed our table with two Afro-Caribbean bouncers flanking him. One held his hands tightly behind his back, all three heading for the exit. Again, he had snuck up behind girls on the dance floor, grinding against their behinds. Just as he had done at the other clubs, he pounced on them from behind, touching and grinding against them. Slimy. And one night when we went out as a group of friends to The Bridge, we had to pass by the entrance and slyly check who was working the door, lest it be the same bouncer who had chucked him out the previous weekend.

"Luzuko, let's go," Bafana yelled, sniffing. Returning his eyes to the bouncers, he said, "You know who I am?" The bouncers stared at him. "I'm a doctor – three times over. Triple doctor." He sniffed again. "One, two, three …"

"Let's go, Triple Doctor." One of the bouncers shoved him towards the door.

Bafana immediately launched into a list of his major degrees, tallying them up to make him a triple doctor: medical degree from the University of Cape Town, DPhil from Imperial College in London, and a second DPhil from Oxford.

"Let's go to Sodom," he shouted as the bouncer released him at the door.

"Is that a new nightclub?" I asked. "Is that the name of a new nightclub? I've never heard of it."

"No, it's a house. Let's go, man." He staggered out in front of me, into the light drizzle, still sniffling. "Tata Linda invited me to a party. In Sodom."

"A party in Sodom?" I huffed out another laugh.

"It's a South African party," he said, turning right onto Cornmarket Street. "We have to catch a cab to Blackbird Leys."

"A South African party? What South Africans?"

"Black South Africans."

"Darkies?" My heart leapt. "Our darkies? In Oxford?"

"Yeah, black South Africans working and living in Oxford."

"What?" I smiled, my heart taking another leap. "You must be joking. I thought there were only students in Oxford."

"They're numerous here, man."

"I had no idea," I said as I tried to catch up with him.

"I want to score a girl there." Bafana stopped. "That's the only reason I'm going – to score a girl. There's this girl called Nomusa – fit, fit, fit, fit, fit! You hear me? Fit! Give me a cigarette."

"Really?"

"I want to sleep with her tonight. Don't you want to score, Luzuko?"

"Maybe."

"Come, let's go then. And when you get there, stop with your nonsense intellectual talk with girls, okay? No intellectual political and literary talk tonight. It's a party. These are working-class people. We hit on girls and take them to Summertown, finish. There're lots of girls there tonight. Our girls. And don't be slow, going round and round and round the point. I know you're scared of approaching girls. Just hit. Hit to the point. Let's go and score some girls and drink and party. Forget about Purple Turtle. It's too white anyway. I want Nomusa tonight. That girl is so fit, yho! Give me a cigarette."

He's right, I thought to myself: I was slow with girls. How did I miss that gene from my father and his father? My father had been a scheming playboy. And his father had been an unrepentant philanderer. But somehow the gene had skipped me. How on earth was such a misfortune possible? I always thought five times before talking to a girl, mulling it over in my head again and again and again. Turning phrases inside out, shifting words from the end to the middle and out and back again, it was chilling sometimes. The very idea left me heated through all the pores of my skin. And just when I thought I was getting the hang of it, the fright would all flood back in again.

Breathing hard and sniffing, Bafana hailed a cab. Then he looked at me. "But Nomusa is mine. Don't you dare go near her, okay? Cigarette, Luzuko."

EIGHTEEN

Run. Run to where? Run from who? From what? Nomusa listened to the rattling in the plastic bag Nomzamo carried. She tried to recall her train of thoughts. But the swish-swash of the jacket and the clinks and thuds in the bag and the wind and its chilled air had taken over. Looking up at the half-moon, the cold wind had dried her eyes.

Run. Another brush of cold snapped at the tip of her nose, freezing her thoughts. Perhaps Nottingham. I know people in Nottingham. Some South Africans. KZN guys. My mother will take care of herself. She's made up her mind. There's nothing I can do about it. If I stick with her any longer, we're bound to be sent home. Nomusa paused, listening to her shoes padding on the pavement. But I can't run away again. No. Not again.

She turned to look at Nomzamo, who tried to hide it. But she could see through Nomzamo. Things were changing. Nomusa saw it in the shiftlessness of her friend's eyes. Then there was the rapt lone laugh that came out of a long face, the sudden interest in red wine, the tousled hair. There were also the telephone calls she had made to the fathers of her two children. The first had been a shouting match – "When are you going to pay maintenance?" – and he had dropped the call. The second call to a second father had been almost whispered. Nomzamo had blown long tired sighs down the phone to a fairly sozzled man at some loud party.

"Bongani's really making me mad." It came out of Nomzamo like a random leaf snapped from a random tree. "He's going to unstitch everything I've knitted together." Nomusa turned to watch Nomzamo. Big Mavis could go back to teaching if she was sent home, Nomusa pondered. But Nomzamo? What about Nomzamo? She had been a caretaker at a crèche back in Durban. What would she be if she got sent home? With her job in Oxford, Nomzamo was already paying a mortgage for a three-bedroomed house in the more middle-class section of Umlazi Township, and she had been making double monthly payments since she bought the house last year. Her mother and her two children lived in that house, moving from a shack, because of Nomzamo's job in England. They all depended on her. What would happen to all of that if Nomzamo were deported? Nomusa's forehead wrinkled.

The bitch-nun is back, Nomusa thought. They were going to say that. They were itching to say that. No ways. I can't go back home. Not now. I've lost too much, and I haven't gained enough to make up for anything I've lost. Not yet. This, this running away? Making money in England? Does it help? Will it help? Covering up for what I've lost? For what I could have been? For what I should have been?

How the hell did I end up here in the first place? How did it get to this – to this point, this place, here, with a baby? With a master's degree in Social Work? Back in South Africa, teaching at a university? Is this where I should be? A nun, perhaps? A nun and a social worker? A nun-social worker?

That was the original plan. So how did it get to this – me, illegal, walking in the middle of a freezing night to Sodom?

"Maybe I should get myself a British man," Nomzamo announced into the cold.

"And then he rams you hard and leaves you dry," Nomusa lifted her voice, "with nothing and still no papers. He rides you hard, again and again and again, and then he disappears into his England. His England. Not yours. And where will you search for him? How will you search for him? Search for him as who? Who are you going to say you are? What are you going to say? That he rammed me hard and disappeared with the papers he promised me? Haven't you learnt anything from Sis' Zuki? They rammed her hard, even at her age, and left her as paperless as she had been before."

They walked on in silence, Nomusa's thoughts running away with her: her mother, Baby Angelina. She had thought of calling her father, Jacob, to try to help change Grace's mind. But that would have made things worse. Grace would have dug in her heels. I never picked that up, Nomusa thought, sniffing the icy air. It never occurred to me that my mother was unhappy. I didn't sense it at all. But then again, what do I know about marriage and raising a family for thirty years? This is going to tear our family apart. Nomusa hugged herself tighter. But who's going to break? We're all adults now, living on our own. Is it going to break Dad? How? But this is foolish. An old woman breaking up with an old man she's lived with for the past thirty years and has children and grandchildren with? And then, just like that, you break up with him? Boom. No wife. Gone. Empty. Boom. Just like that?

"But this new group is annoying, you know…" Nomzamo broke the silence.

"Everyone annoys you." Nomusa's teeth almost rattled against the icy wind.

"I mean Tshidi and her Jo'burg group."

"How are they annoying you?"

"They do things on their own, separately. They cut themselves off from everyone. They don't even join us at JD Wetherspoon's. If they do go, they go alone."

"But Tshidi's nice," Nomusa said.

"When she's alone, yes, she's nice," Nomzamo went on. "But when she teams up with her Gauteng friends, she changes. They cut us out."

"So you think they think they're better than us?" Nomusa asked.

"Yes, Nomusa. It's a language thing — Sothos and Tswanas from Gauteng. They think they're different from the rest of us."

"Like that woman, Irene." Nomusa raised her voice, her cheeks tightening.

"Really?"

"Have you seen her, Nomzamo? Just because she's a registered nurse, and has papers, owns a brand-new car, and lives alone in a posh two-bedroom townhouse, she thinks she's all that, better than us."

"Yeah?"

"Have you seen her, Nomzamo? I mean, have you watched her? Listened to the way she talks? She tries so hard to sound British, to sound white."

"She can be British or close to British because she came through the front door, unlike us. She's legal. She has papers. And we are not."

"Do you want to be British, Nomzamo? I mean, really?"

Nomzamo stared heavenwards, snorting out a full steam of icy vapour.

"As long as being British gives me a decent life, that's all. Being British for me is all on paper. It's all about a decent life I'll never have back home. Shame, being British beats being South African."

"We can't have decent lives back home because we don't have degrees or diplomas, Nomzamo. You can sweep the streets here and still have all the decency and dignity of a teacher or a nurse, better than back home. You can empty municipal bins and have all the decency of that nurse. You don't need a university degree or a diploma to live a decent life here, to earn good money, to buy a decent apartment, or own a nice, comfortable running car. Back home, cleaning the streets or emptying municipal bins will only give you a three-roomed shack in an informal settlement."

Turning into a dark alley, Nomusa listened to the tapping of her shoes on the pavement. Soon, the darkness of the alleyway gave way to a cul-de-sac. On the left, a fire swelled up from a braai stand, a group of men huddled around it. Even from a distance, Nomusa could make out the face of Major General with his shiny, sagging cheeks. He hung on to a long can of Carling lager. Sir Khaps leaned with one hand against the wall, a small glass of vodka and orange juice dangling in the other.

Nomzamo shifted her plastic bag to her other hand.

"Has that idiot, Bongani, not arrived yet?" Nomzamo shouted at the huddle around the fire.

"I see you haven't been taken to Campsfield House Removal Centre," Major General bellowed at Nomusa and Nomzamo. Laughing, he wiggled his can of Carling from side to side.

Nomusa and Nomzamo crossed over.

"Is Bongani here?" Nomzamo asked.

"He hasn't turned up yet." Major General opened a fresh can of Carling. "To be honest with you, my sister," Major General belched, "we haven't heard from Bongani for four days now. I have no idea if he's coming."

"Maybe he's hiding somewhere," Sir Khaps coughed.

"News is already out, Nomzamo, my sister," Major General went on, "of your daring escape through the window."

"Our lives in this country ..." Nomusa mumbled, rubbing her hands together over the fire. "How long are we going to live like this, dancing with Thames Valley, my brothers?"

NINETEEN

Making his way down the two steps of Odd Bins, Bongani released a long, thin sigh. With a box of Foster's Lager cans snuggled in his armpit, flakes of percussion and scratchy saxophone notes lingered behind him, along with a stream of clanky piano chords. Facing the top of Little Clarendon Street, Bongani watched the icy vapour cloud out of his mouth and vanish. To the right, towards Wellington Square, the regular weekend buzz had been cut short by the cold.

His hands in leather gloves swished around inside his jacket pocket. A warm, moist, sour smell seeped out of his beige turtleneck jumper. It was the third day and night the turtleneck was stuck on his skin, in and out of bed and on the streets with him. Oils, sweat, cold and cotton had become one, leaving a wet and scratchy stickiness on his chest and arms. His blue jeans felt cold and wet.

A young man with long, pushed-back hair and carrying a backpack rushed past him. A scarfed middle-aged woman from behind Odd Bins tapped on his shoulder in order to pass. He stepped aside, the piano chords settling into a steady stride behind him as he turned north, shifting the weight of the lager to his other arm. At the meeting of Little Clarendon Street with St Giles, two Oxford Tube buses whizzed past him in a flash of red and green. He gripped his load tightly against the jostling swarm passing through and, walking slowly towards the bus stop, passed Ponana. An icy wind brushed his face.

Sniffling as he went, his eyes caught a poster pasted on the bus stop ahead of him. Beneath the large blue *Sunday Tribune* caption, the headline became clearer as he neared: 'David Blunkett: Deportations on the Rise.' Moving the weight of the cans back to the grip of the other armpit, he stopped to read it again, finally offloading the lager in front of his feet.

"Illegals," Bongani whispered, blowing warm air into his gloves. 'We're illegals, dog,' Chino had said once as they marched out of Ponana, heading for the nearest kebab van. 'They want us to bounce, my nigger. They want us to bounce, dog. We're bloody illegals.'

Bongani wondered how a blind Secretary of Homeland Security could be so spot on and so fast when it came to nabbing "illegals". He blew more warm air into his hands.

And they are so quick, it's scary, Bongani mused, wriggling his shoulders about in a warm-up. He thought back to the last time he'd talked to Sis' Nomfundo over the phone.

"I've been back in Umtata for a week now," she yelled on the other end of the line, above the background noise of a crying and screaming crèche.

"A week?" Bongani had shifted his phone to the other ear.

"It happened so fast, Bongani. So quickly," Sis' Nomfundo had gone on. She had panted, stopping to shush a screeching toddler. "Be careful out there, BB." Bouncing the little girl on her hip, her voice was tossed about.

"Okay."

"But I'm coming back, Bongani." Her voice had returned but was quickly swallowed by the hip bounce again. "There's no way I'm staying here for long. I'm coming back. I'm coming back to France or Ireland next time. Not England. Yhoo! Not there again. Maybe Dublin. Not Belfast though. It's easier there, I gather. But, for now, I lay low for a while. So I can just breathe, cool down and plan. Just breathe, BB. Yhoo! My head is still hot right now. This whole thing of deportation is painful. It's humiliating." And then another baby let out a frothy yelp. A woman's booming voice and the loud slip-slaps of sandals descended on the phone. And then a rushed goodbye had cut them off.

The last time Bongani had seen Sis' Nomfundo was at Sodom. She had rushed in, her eyes rolling, lugging three massive black plastic bags. And she had sworn to avenge herself, to seek out Big Mavis for snitching on her to Thames Valley. Between sniffs and tears, she had sworn again and again that she was going to take Big Mavis down. And then she had run off to see someone in Jericho.

Bongani carefully picked up his weight again, and waited for the traffic light to clear. Shoppers filed out of Debenhams department store onto the busy corner, others from Waterstones bookshop across the street. The traffic lights changed, and he crossed over to Cornmarket, caught up in the stream of people.

Where am I going to sleep tonight? Bongani wondered. Where am I going to live? I don't think Major General will put me up. And there's no way Mkhize will take me in. And where am I going to find another job now? Bongani pondered as he passed KFC, the warm, comforting steam and aroma of fried chicken gorging his insides out. Sodom, he huffed. Sodom will surely provide a way out. Little by little, things will work out, starting at Sodom. He sighed, stopping to shift the weight of his lager to the other arm.

At the narrow alley leading to Purple Turtle, the peaceful

musical man with the Lenin-style hat strummed his guitar. Bongani slid his hand into the back pocket of his jeans and fished out a quid. Pitching it into the basket, the music man gave him a silent nod.

Bongani thought back to the previous day.

That morning, Patrick had woken up a bit woozy, his memory wiped clean of the previous night's scuffle with Reverend Markham. Bongani had sat him down, slowly drilling into his head that the Reverend Markham wanted to see him sober that morning. Trembling, Patrick had taken a cold Guinness from his bar fridge, Bongani recounting blow by blow what had happened the previous night. By the end of Bongani's story, Patrick was sucking the last dregs of his third Guinness.

Between pauses and rewinds and cringes and many nods and more pauses, Patrick had downed four more long cans. At twenty to eleven, Patrick had burped, slurred a few words, straightened himself up, and staggered off to see the reverend. Almost crying, he had said, between burps, that he wanted to share his pain with Reverend Markham. "Reverend, how would you feel?" he had rehearsed with Bongani standing at the door. "How would you feel seeing your woman underneath another man, Reverend, mmh?" Then he had slammed the door behind him, leaving Bongani to return to bed.

When the Blackbird Leys bus stopped, Bongani quickly hopped on, unloading his cans on the front seat. He punched his monthly ticket into the machine near the driver and, shifting the weighty cans to the floor, rested his feet on top of the box. Resting his head against the window, he shut his eyes, listening to the steady rolling of the bus.

He awoke just as the bus was turning away from the small pub near Sodom. When it came to a stop, he picked up his cargo and, carrying it like a tray, stepped carefully off. Where am I going to sleep tonight? At Sodom? he asked himself as he headed straight for the yellow house with its fire and house lights glowing in the yard.

Major General, Sir Khaps and some other fellows he didn't know were hovering over the fire. He would ask them anyway. He knew what they were going to say, but he was going to ask anyway. Asking wouldn't kill him. They would say he was going to get them sent home. No one wanted to be deported. Not then. Only when they were ready to go back. Not then.

"Mister Havoc," Major General shouted as Bongani offloaded his burden.

"Where the hell have you been?" Sir Khaps asked, resting his chin on a folded arm.

"I'm tired," Bongani said, taking off his gloves. "Let me catch a breath and warm myself first." He shoved the gloves into his jacket pockets, and rested his fingers over the flickering fire.

"Where have you been, Bongani?" Sir Khaps lifted his glass of vodka and orange juice.

"Everyone's been worried," said Major General.

"Worried because Thames Valley will also come for them?" Bongani said without taking his eyes off the flames.

"Yes, Bongani," Major General yelled. "And also because we care about you."

"The question is, who snitched on me?" Bongani asked, still looking into the fire.

"Eish! Names are expensive," Sir Khaps said.

"Was it Big Mavis?" Bongani asked.

"I said, names are expensive," Sir Khaps went on.

"Even if names were not expensive, Sir Khaps wouldn't know," Major General continued. "And, besides, this theory of people snitching on others to the police is just talk. Loud talk. People should stop saying such things. We should stop believing stupid things." Major General cracked open another can.

"I need to take these to the fridge." Bongani lifted the weight to his shoulder and headed to the house.

"Let me warn you, Bongani," Major General said, watching Bongani retreating back. "They're inside."

"Who?"

"Both of them, they're inside."

"Nomzamo and Nomusa," Sir Khaps answered.

A kwaito song by Trompies jumped at him as he opened the door. At the centre of the dance floor, Tata Linda had sagged onto his knees, shuffling his shoulders to the jerking beats. A woman Bongani recognised smiled and waved at him. He smiled back, swirling his index finger around, indicating that he was coming back. Then he turned into the kitchen and dumped the box of beers on the counter.

"You!" Nomzamo, glass of wine in hand, yelled from across the kitchen. "I'm on the run because of you."

"I'm sorry, Nomzamo. I'm sorry."

"You're sorry?" Nomzamo edged closer, but Nomusa cut in front of her just as Nomzamo was about to tip her wine over him.

"How's your sorry going to help, mmh?" Nomzamo screamed.

"Nomzamo! Nomzamo!" Bongani flailed his hands. "I have no idea how this came on to me. I think someone must have snitched on me."

"Someone snitched on you?" Nomusa snorted. "You've been on the run from the law for two years, ever since you escaped from Heathrow," Nomusa shouted. "Now you have no idea how this came on to you? Come on, man."

"Don't you think Heathrow haunts me?" Bongani yelled.

"Who escapes from a Heathrow holding cell, anyway?" Nomusa shouted, flailing her hands.

"It was not a holding cell, Nomusa."

"Whatever, man. Whatever. You were captured in a room at Heathrow, about to be sent back home. You ran away from a Heathrow deportation centre. That's the point. That's what matters. That's what I'm saying. And now you've put all South Africans in Oxford in jeopardy."

"I mean ..."

"Only you, Bongani," Nomusa went on. "Only you have the guts and the foolishness to escape from Heathrow."

"We're all illegal here," Bongani shouted. "Sooner or later, we'll all be sent home. Who was kept at Heathrow and who was not doesn't matter anymore. What matters is that none of us is supposed to be here, and we're all going to be sent home. And, you know, people like Big Mavis ..."

"Don't you dare!" Nomusa screeched, shoving a finger into Bongani's forehead. "You leave her name out of this."

"But she—"

"I said ..." Nomusa cut herself short. "You're putting all of us here at risk." With her arms akimbo, she turned her back on Bongani.

"Just leave the kitchen, please, Bongani," Nomzamo said, staring down at the floor.

Bongani ripped the beer box open, and took out two cans. Shoving one into his jacket pocket, he retreated to the living room. Cracking open a can, he leaned against the wall, looking for a chair. His feet were slightly swollen, and he could feel a rush of blood up and down his legs. All the plastic chairs and sofas had been taken, so he headed towards the door and right into Sir Khaps and Major General.

"So, Bongani, after you escaped from the police, where did you go?" Major General asked, as he swirled around a fresh can.

Cab lights flooded the yard, and Bongani watched the figure step out.

"It's Bafana." Major General's voice dropped. "I bet he wants to get laid." He huffed out a long laugh. "He's a goat on heat. Goats go on heat in seasons. But Bafana is on heat off and on – doesn't matter the season."

Bongani watched Bafana and another guy he'd never seen before as they approached.

"So, Bongani," Major General continued, "where did you stash yourself after Thames Valley pounced on you?"

He tossed the empty can onto the grass.

"I slept at Patrick's."

"Patrick? From Uganda?" Major General snapped. "The one and only? Patrick, the Prince of Chaos? Why, Bongani? All the time, Bongani, all the time chaos follows you."

Bongani said nothing but kept his eye on Bafana and the young man.

TWENTY

I PROPPED MYSELF UP IN the back seat of the black cab and watched as it whistled past St Aldates. Squinting down the street, I caught a glimpse of the Alice in Wonderland shop. I imagined Lewis Carroll strolling across Church Christ Meadows, caught up in the wondrous world of literary nonsense. I often imagined him there, the mathematics fellow of Christ Church College hand in hand with a colleague's daughter, the little girl who inspired him to conjure up Alice.

Last summer, I kissed and caressed Amanda under a tree in the meadows. A squirrel had paused and stared at us, watching me kiss her supple lips. Perhaps I took my love life for granted. Maybe I didn't really care much for it? Were there other Amandas to unfurl in the future? I had asked myself, tending to my heartbreak – that short, deep stab. When I grieved, Bafana had quickly snapped at me – that I fell in love too easily and hurt too fast. And he had taken one last swig of his lager, ogling girls passing through the beer garden of some pub whose name I couldn't remember. Perhaps I hadn't been that different at all to Chet Baker in his 'I Fall in Love Too Easily'. I may be lost in the same languid, hazy tones.

The cab munched its way slowly down the High Street, heading for Cowley Road, then took a slow turn into Between Towns Road. On my right, the shiny leaves of the ivy creeping up over the offices of Macmillan Publishers gave the mansion a stately form. In my mind's eye I saw young Harold Macmillan, his mind not particularly there, briskly making his way across the grey-pebbled driveway. Perhaps he had been at the Macmillan Publishers' offices in London. But I fancied seeing him there at Between Towns Road, soon after the end of the First World War, before the 1921 general election in which he stood, for the first time, for a parliamentary seat. I recalled a hardback volume of his Downing Street memoirs, *At the End of the Day*, sitting on my grandfather's bookshelf at home.

Next to me, I listened to Bafana sniffling, his knees friskily knocking against each other. He was high on expectation. Nomusa might or might not come to pass. What was it again? What was his theory again, that drunken algorithm? Yes. Out of a hundred girls, with ninety-nine passing through his fingers, he was surely going to net one. And so I listened to the swishing brush of his jeans, the knees snatching against each other.

I reclined against the headrest as the Oxford I knew changed into the Oxford I had only heard of. Blackbird Leys seemed a neater working-class suburb than the colourful, often rowdy Cowley Road. The houses were bigger, not as terraced, more suburban in a modern way. And I tried to size up my heart, at what I expected to encounter at Sodom, a party of black South Africans. For the first time in Oxford, I was not going to put on airs. I was going to be myself.

But was I? What was going to be expected of me? I wondered again. I didn't know how I was meant to carry myself in the presence of black ordinariness. In my entire two years in Oxford, I had lived most of my life behind the Cowley Road roundabout at the Plain, on the other side of the river. On my arrival, many British and European postgraduate students had warned me against lingering beyond the roundabout. Their nightclubs and bars, even the townie ones in the city centre – Manhattan, Old Fire Station, Que Pasa – were "cheesy, mate," they said. "Cheesy" was another way of saying hoi polloi without appearing snobbish and judgmental.

And so I rarely ventured so far in this direction. If it were not for grocery shopping at Tesco, or to buy bulk meat at bargain prices from that Pakistani butchery or getting a haircut, I wouldn't go at all. And on those rare occasions that I went with Dela, Wilson, Josh, and sometimes Bafana, we were on a hunt for colour. For a loose jive. For outlandish creativity.

There had been occasional dips into the lively 'isms' of Cowley: intense discussions on working-class consciousness, Left Labour, New Labour, encounters with a band of Trotskyists. Often, we'd hopped to jazz joints. And a few Afro-Caribbean poetry sessions in cloistered and poorly lit bars. Then it was back to the dreaming spires again, to be closed up in libraries and theses and books and writing and even more theory.

I stared out the cab window, watching flickering streetlights pass me by. How did it come so suddenly? How did the belonging I had so yearned for come so unexpectedly? I smiled, my eyes still fixed on the passing landscape beyond the window. And was I going to get a girl? Perhaps? I shrugged it off. The thought didn't excite me as much as it thrilled Bafana. But then, he had a way of brutally cutting himself off from debauchery as soon as his own Cinderella cut-off time tick-tocked him back to his senses. He would swiftly switch back to his post-doctoral work as if he'd never ventured to that world. With the same gusto, he'd throw himself into his work for weeks and weeks on end. And then he would reappear, a sudden gust of wind coming from nowhere, to indulge in another bout of depravity and brushes with meaty bouncers and my cigarettes.

Bafana had drilled in me that it had taken rigorous practice for him to clinically separate random, technical sex from intimate lovemaking with a woman he truly loved. "It takes time," he once said. "Time and practice, practice, practice." I could never do that – the draining labour of the entire affair of compartmentalisation. It seemed impossibly inhuman.

The cab slowed down at the unfenced yard of a modest yellow-painted house. What seemed like a freshly started fire glowed from the front porch, lighting up a slightly unkempt lawn. There was something dry and forlorn about the yard: the overgrown grass, weeds jutting out of what seemed like a hastily cemented porch. The headlights of the cab threw out the other three houses hugging the yellow one in the centre of the circle cul-de-sac. This was Sodom. A fading Mafikizolo song yielded to the throbbing beats of Glen Lewis. Soon, a hail of Zulu and Xhosa voices erupted. I smiled. I knew that I was home. At last.

I shoved my hand through the window opening separating the back seat from the driver. The driver snatched the fiver and seventy-seven pence with a huff. When I spotted Bafana staggering towards the five men hovering over the curling fire on the wide net of steel of a braai stand, I slid out of the passenger seat to catch up with him. Purple Turtle's lager had fermented well in my head, so I had to steady my gait. But still I felt a new thirst for beer brewing. Bafana stood in front of a rotund fellow with a round and rough face. Sucking from a long can of Carling lager, his eyes heavenwards, he stuck out his hand to Bafana.

A young man dressed in hip-hop style, with short dreadlocks, faded baggy jeans and a fashionably oversized white-and-navy striped Calvin Klein sweater, stood facing the round fellow with the round face. He sucked on a cigarette. The wetness of his inner lips had already dampened the filter. Dragging on the last of the cigarette, he tossed the soggy brown filter into the flames.

"All the time," The rotund fellow shouted above the swirl of house music from Glen Lewis, his hand remaining stretched out to Bafana's, while still talking to the younger dreadlocked man: "With you, Bongani, chaos follows you all the time." I thought of Seth, the Egyptian god of chaos, disorder, confusion, wars, thunder, deserts and storms. But, like many of us, Seth had changed. He had not always been chaos. He had not always been like that. In the beginning, Seth had been a good god. He saved the sun god, Ra, from the serpent Apophis, who had tried to stop Ra's journey through the night sky on his way to dawn. Apophis had tried to keep the world in perpetual darkness, but Seth had ensured that the sun would rise again the next morning. And yet no one really knew when, why and how Seth had changed from a hero god to an enemy of order.

"I try," Bongani replied. "I try to avoid chaos, Major General."

I couldn't believe that they called him Major General.

"What do you mean you try, Bongani?" Major General took his hand back from Bafana. "How do you try to avoid chaos when you hang out with Patrick from Uganda, the Prince of Chaos?"

"But, Major General …"

"And what happened to your other friend, the Duke of Chaos, that Chino from Zimbabwe?" Everyone around the fire laughed. Sir Khaps, a tall man whose head nearly reached the outline of the roof, clutching a glass of vodka and orange, laughed the loudest.

"Don't laugh, Sir Khaps," Bongani admonished the tall man.

"Major General," Sir Khaps began, "did they tell you how Thames Valley grabbed Chino from Ponana?"

"Come on, Sir Khaps, you're making fun of my friend now."

"Who cares?" Sir Khaps waved a hand. "He's been deported to Zimbabwe anyway." Sir Khaps talked inside the glass, draining the last of the vodka.

"Major General," Bongani came in, "you know I had no choice. I had to go to Patrick, because I didn't want to go to any of you guys. You know how it is, *mos*? They catch one of us, they catch many of us."

"No, Bongani," Major General tilted the can of Carling slightly and peered with one eye into it, "it's because you know that you've set Nomzamo on the run."

"And maybe Nomusa also." Sir Khaps jumped in. "Who knows?"

"*Ja*, guys," Bafana quickly chirped. "And where's Nomusa, anyway?"

"It's because you want to mount my sister, Bafana. That's why you're asking." Major General took another swig. "And you haven't even introduced us to your friend because you're in a rush to climb my sister."

"This is Luzuko," Bafana sniffled. "Luzuko Goba from Grahamstown. He's a doctorate student in Politics and International Relations."

I greeted everyone. Major General gave me a hug, his smile blowing out his flabby cheeks. His eyes moved around me. He stood back to study me. Sir Khaps stooped lower, bringing me closer to him with another hug, my head barely reaching above his belly. "I'm not far away from you, my brother. I'm from Port Elizabeth," Sir Khaps said with a broad smile.

"And me? I'm from King William's Town," Major General offered throwing the empty can onto the lawn.

"And where's Nomusa?" Bafana fidgeted inside the pockets of his jacket.

"Nomusa," Major General said, "she's where she's not in a mood to be mounted by anyone." He set his eyes on

Bafana. "Gents, we need more alcohol. Let's go inside." Major General was already walking towards the door.

I felt Bongani's hand creep up my shoulder. His smile reached his ears. When Major General threw open the door, the first thing I saw inside Sodom was an old man wearing a Lenin hat stumbling around in front of a vigorously jiving young woman.

"Welcome to Sodom!" Bongani yelled. "And what do you drink, my brother?" He tightened his grip on my shoulder, and then let it loose with a massage.

"A beer," I shouted above the noise.

He dashed off without another word, snaking his way through the throng on the dance floor before disappearing beyond the crowd. From the door where Bongani had left me, I sized up everything. I dribbled mental notes of every step, every smell, colour, the hazy warmth, every buzz. I was heeding Graham Greene's advice on writing when interviewed about his novel set in colonial Sierra Leone: You have to have walked the streets and smelled the air of the place in order to write about it.

My body tingled, my heart opening up to a new light and a new song. I had found belonging in Oxford. Sweat broke out on my forehead. Tata Linda, the old man, was still swaying, down and down in front of his woman to the thumping beats of Glen Lewis.

Bafana got chatting to Tata Linda, as three young women in their late twenties danced around the old man. In a flash, Bongani appeared again right in the centre of the throng on the dance floor. He pulled one of the three women closer to him, grabbing her by her slim waist. I listened to the swishing of her black leather skirt frolicking against the firm grasp of Bongani. And then he pulled her shaved head to his, sliding his tongue between her lips. She let it in, and let out hers, the pair wiggling and wobbling around each other. His effortlessness in getting these women to do what he wanted sent a rush of blood through my body. Then

Bongani disappeared, laughing, into the swarm again.

A tall, light-complexioned woman, a tight brown dress hugging her well-proportioned body, stepped through the dance circle. Her slightly bowed legs stood out in the black cotton leggings and long brown leather boots. I had rarely seen such sensuousness and confidence in her own beauty in a middle-aged woman and she captivated me. Holding, with both hands, a silver tray of raw meat – chicken, pork and boerewors – she stood next to Tata Linda, Bafana and the three young women.

Calling for Major General and Bongani above the din of Mdu's kwaito hit, the group made their way over to me, standing at the door.

"Hi." The meat-carrying beauty greeted me, sticking out her hand.

"Welcome to Sodom, Luzuko," Tata Linda laughed, holding a long glass of gin and tonic, his bright white teeth gleaming. "I'm Linda. And this here is Original Fitness – Pam, the lady of the house Sodom."

"Guys," Bafana coughed. "I'm off to the kitchen. Where's Nomusa?" And once again slithered through the horde.

"Here." Bongani handed me a long can of Foster's. "A beer is a beer," he said, and I grabbed it. I did not particularly like Foster's, with its steely taste and rather weak bite, but a beer is a beer. And I was parched. Soon, Major General and Sir Khaps retreated to the porch, following Original Fitness with the silver tray of raw meat.

"Come," Bongani said, and I followed him. A rather good-looking, cornrowed young man wiggled through the throng, his eyes moving with me.

"Maybe he likes you." Bongani twisted his smile. "You're not a bad-looking chap, after all." Then, with his hand on my shoulder, he whispered: "Bisexual, but more into the homo side." Bongani winked. "But he thinks we don't know." The hand on my shoulder quickly switched to a rather bony massage. "He a bit of everything, let me say. Straight. Gay.

Black. Jewish. Student. Worker." I listened to his laugh over the hissing foam of my lager.

Three women in their mid-thirties sat hunched in a corner. One, a rather large woman in tight blue jeans, wagged a finger as we passed by.

"That's Nomzamo," Bongani went on. "Don't mind her. She's a gossipmonger, like her two friends. All they talk about is who has done what to who, where and how."

Slouched on a chair next to the loudspeaker was a squat, middle-aged man sporting a huge, potbelly. Fast asleep, he clung to a can of beer nestled on top of his tight paunch.

"We even have Zulu taxi drivers in Oxford, imagine?" Bongani went on. "That's Khumalo, from Ulundi. He was a taxi driver back home. But he doesn't drive taxis here. He's working, like all of us. And he's always drunk, or almost all the time." He cracked out another laugh.

TKZee slipped into the mix with the hit 'Dlala Mapantsula', and the whole house jumped up. Back in the kitchen, I saw a young woman shoving Bafana away with one hand that sent him crashing against the cutlery tray, his head smashing hard against the cupboard. I wondered at this beautiful woman, her face all smooth and natural – the kind of beauty you did not have to search for even when she'd just woken up.

"Nomusa," Bongani shouted, hoisting Bafana to his feet from behind, "be careful."

Nomusa returned her hands to a fold under her breasts. Bafana stood up, panting and fixing his shirt.

"I told you, Bafana," Nomusa's voice came out in halted breaths, "and I'm not going to warn you again." Nomusa pointed a finger at Bafana across the kitchen.

"That's Nomusa," Bongani whispered. "And that's her best friend, Big Mavis, next to her. But don't call her Big Mavis. Just Mavis will do."

I watched Nomusa as she turned to Big Mavis at the kitchen table. Big Mavis drank slowly from a glass of red wine, swaying her generous hips to TKZee.

There was something sad in Nomusa's angry outburst. I guessed Major General was right when he said she was not in the mood to be climbed by anyone that night.

"This is Luzuko from Grahamstown," Bongani shouted out my name.

"Hello." I stuck out my hand to Nomusa.

"Hi. Nomusa, from KZN."

"He came with Bafana. Also a student at Oxford."

"I hope you're not like your horny friend," said Big Mavis, her face wrinkled, glaring at Bafana.

"Your friend's horny all the time," Nomusa almost whispered, watching Bafana as he walked out of the kitchen. "Why is he touchy-touchy and fiddling all the time? Can he not just dance and drink and have fun like everyone else?" Nomusa lifted the glass of orange juice to her lips.

My eyes still on Nomusa, I wondered whether Bafana's drunken ninety-nine per cent algorithm had crashed that night.

"My man," Bongani drew me closer, "I need to ask you a favour."

"What?" I slurped my Forster's.

"Can I put up with you?"

"What?"

"Just for a while?"

"What do you mean?"

"Can I stay with you?"

"No, no, no, Bongani. Sorry."

"Just for a while?"

"I can't. And what's a while? I don't know you. I've just met you."

TWENTY-ONE

O<small>NCE UPON A TIME</small>, there was a young prince who lived in a northern kingdom of China who was spellbound by dragons. With all his heart, with all his mind, and with the entirety of his breath, he wanted to see a live dragon. He thought about dragons day and night. He dreamt about them. He drew them on paper, on scrolls, on walls. He composed poems and songs and stories about them. And yet, despite all his riches, and all the fantasies he could bring to reality with just a snap of his royal fingers, he could not will to life his one true wish.

The prince travelled the length and breadth of China seeking stories and legends of dragons – red dragons, green dragons, blue dragons, brown dragons that spit two-split fires. He knew everything about them – the long ones, the wavy-necked ones, the flappy-eared, the wise ones. And still he could not conjure one true, living dragon.

And then one day, a wiry old man with a long white beard

and bony, trembling hands arrived at the palace to seek an audience with the prince. Having announced himself as a wizard of the southern kingdom, he was welcomed into the palace by the young prince. The wizard told the prince that he had heard of his one truest wish, and that he was able to bring it to pass. The wizard enthralled the young man with the most spectacular stories of dragons and magic he had ever heard.

The wizard had been drawn by the prince's sincere faith that his wish would be realised – determination the wizard had never encountered in any other man or woman before. And so he promised to bring one live, fire-spitting dragon for the prince to see with his very own eyes. The wizard was unwavering in his vow. The prince could barely believe it. And so the wizard left the palace, beseeching the young prince to awaken at the midnight hour.

And exactly at midnight, just as sleep was beginning to steal him, the prince heard a strange, heavy thud. Then there was a cloppity-clop-clop at the giant doors of the palace. The prince ran to the door in his flowing white silk sleeping gown, and when he threw open the door, a giant red dragon stood looming over him. The young prince froze. He had no idea what to do with the one true, living dragon standing right in front of him. He simply did not know what to do when his one true wish came to pass right in front of his eyes.

•••

Bongani sat next to me at the back of the black cab. My one true wish – to belong – was right there, next to me. My dragon, my red dragon, next to me in that black cab. And I had no idea what to do with him. I had no idea what to do with it. Who would have known that one random night of revelry that started with Bafana at the Purple Turtle would bring my one true wish to life? Who would have known?

At four on a Friday morning, my head spinning with

lager, I tried to hold myself together. We bundled out of the cab outside Summertown House. My knees wobbled, and an air of stale beer breath surrounded me. When the cab drove off, I turned and, taking four long strides, led Bongani into the grounds of Summertown. As we made our way through the grand entrance to the property, I blabbered on about Summertown House – how the rooms had been designed differently for singles, married couples and married postgraduate students with children. Gibberish that passed right over Bongani's head. I began to see that what I had to say had nothing to do with the price of the bread in his market.

At the main steel gate, I took my key tab from my jacket pocket and placed it on the reader on the wall next to the gate. With its usual electronic creak-crack, the gate opened, and we staggered together towards the lift. I had agreed to put Bongani up for a week. He had disarmed me with that come-what-may, we'll-see attitude of his. I had never shared my living quarters with anyone before. But, somehow, I had agreed to this.

Downing our fourth Foster's back in Sodom, that woman whose lips he had licked came to join us. And then, rolling her index finger, had beckoned her friend over. Her fingers, slim, brittle, seemed capable of unleashing unspeakable depravity from even hard-boiled men. She had leaned into me, and I had given her my ear. And she had breathed into it, giggling. And I smelled a faint whispering laugh. When she pulled away from me, I stared at her eating her lower lip. She hung on to the bite of her lower lip, smiling.

Her friend had joined us in our corner, leaning into the wall, Ringo's 'Sondela' wafting loud above us, calling on his lover to come closer. Bongani's head softly butted hers, whispering, kissing her forehead. I felt his rough hand reaching for mine to connect my hand to that of the first woman. She had grasped it, slowly toying her fingers around mine. She then plugged her lips onto my neck, wanting to nibble on my ear.

Bongani moved my hand from the first woman's and planted it on the belly of the second woman whose lips he was eating. I watched him, as our joined hands caressed the woman's flat stomach. Together, our hands reached her front mound. Lunging forward, the second woman had moaned inside Bongani's mouth.

I floated. It was in how Bongani had made them lick each other's lips. I kissed both women, my tongue snaking through the sticky warmth of their tongues. The moistness, their musky breaths made everything in me stand up. Bongani's woman allowed me to grasp at her titties, brush them. And I had felt the rising bumps of her hips grinding against the might of my sex. I slid my hands and tongue to all the crevices I could find in those two women in Sodom. And they did the same to me. Ringo's 'Sondela' beckoned us closer to each other. Bongani had stood back, watching us, sipping on a Foster's that was fast losing its chill.

And then Aretha Franklin's 'I'm in Love' set everything loose into a floating slow. In that moment, I forgot about white Oxford. And I forgot about the black Oxford of Dela, of Josh, Bafana, Wilson, Maud, Francois, Nneka. I had found another, illegal Oxford.

The lift opened. I pressed the fourth-floor button. I stared at my dragon, my red dragon, leaning against the wall. The lift whooshed us up to the fourth floor. Slowing down the pace on landing on the fourth floor, Bongani blinked his droopy eyes. My red dragon wanted to sleep.

·•·

I woke up at quarter to twelve, still smelling that ball of rotting, stale beer breath swirling around my face. I heard Bongani rustling about in the kitchen. Finally, he emerged, already showered and in fresh clothes, and stood over me, smiling, clapping his hands. That was his order for me to get up and take a shower. He said something about taking me out for lunch, and then seeing a friend somewhere in Summertown.

I threw off the sheet and rushed to the bathroom. Bongani had taken to phone texting, his cheekbones firmed and taut. By the time I had leapt out of the shower, Bongani had switched the TV to Channel 4. I watched him sitting there on my little sofa, quietly sipping on coffee. Suddenly he stood up and walked over to my bookshelf next to the window. He lifted out Max Weber's *The City*, nippily flipping through it. He then put it back and took out Sidney Tarrow's second edition of *Power in Movement: Social Movements and Contentious Politics*.

"You read all these books?" He turned his eyes on me, as I pulled the brown turtleneck over my head.

"Yes. I have ..." I coughed, smelling the toothpaste and the mouthwash jostling with the beer breath. "Well, not all cover to cover. I didn't need to."

"So, you're a full-time student?"

"*Ja.*"

"Aren't you too old to be a full-time student?"

"Late twenties?" I stroked my chest.

"Yes."

"No."

"Man," Bongani rested his hands on his matted dreadlocks, "for how long have you been a full-time student?"

"Well," I searched the ceiling, "it's been an unbroken eight years now since matric, and the count continues."

"Eight years? No, man. Everyone I know goes to school for two years max after matric, and then gets a job."

I pouted my lips.

"Damn!" Bongani let out an almost whispered exclamation. "Eight years? How many degrees is that?"

"This is my fourth."

"I guess you're the first graduate in your family."

"Not by a long shot, man." I sat down to pull on my

sneakers. "My grandfather and three of his cousins were university graduates. Then there were grandmothers, four of them, who had college diplomas. I even have a great-grandmother who graduated from college and was a school principal. Then there was also a great-grandfather who graduated from college and became a church minister. So, both my maternal and paternal families ... they graduated from colleges and universities. And then there's my mother and father and aunties and uncles from both sides who graduated with degrees. So, no, I'm not the first graduate in my family by a long, long, very long shot. Even if I publish a book, I won't be the first to do so. One of my grandfathers published five or six books – I've lost count. They were plays and short stories and other books, grammar. No novels, though." I stood, feeling the snugness of my feet inside the sneakers.

"So, brains run in your family then?"

"No." I stomped one sneaker on the floor, then the other. "It has very little to do with brains, but more to do with particular historical and sociological explanations."

"You talk like you're reading from a book sometimes. I've already noticed that with you."

"If I accomplish any first in my family, it'll be graduating with a DPhil."

"A D what?"

I stared at the ceiling again, and let out a full steam of breath. "Let's go eat, man." I straightened myself. "I'm famished."

"But first we need to go see Hugo. It's urgent," Bongani said, leading the way to the door.

The urgency of this Hugo came to me in Bongani's hurried footsteps as we headed towards the lift and plummeted to the ground floor. Our quickened pace turned to a run as the steel gate creaked open.

Bongani tossed out snatches of Hugo's story as he ran, and I struggled to string together the pieces of his account of Hugo: Congo – Umtata – parents here – Umtata again – isiXhosa speaking. A series of fast, jagged pants. Summertown – council estate. Three more panted breaths. At the corner of Summertown House, he sprinted. And I followed as fast as I could.

I raced after him up to Banbury Road, chasing his pacy breath, running behind him north of Summertown House. By that point, he had stopped talking. And I had given up trying to piece together the Hugo story. I was feeling more and more stupid, chasing after him, catching up to something I knew nothing about.

Just before the roundabout that would take us towards Manchester, Bongani crossed the road. Dots of sweat broke out on my forehead. Up ahead I saw a multistorey red-faced brick building overlooking a large weed-infested lawn. By the time we reached it, a tall, skinny fellow was tumbling down the steps towards us. Two big black-and-red suitcases flew fast and hard over his head and past him. Quickly picking himself up, he grabbed hold of the suitcases and lugged them behind him as he stumbled down the rest of the steps. I stopped to catch my breath just as Bongani held out his arms to catch the first suitcase.

TWENTY-TWO

BONGANI STARED AT THE pint in front of him, licking his lips and swivelling the bottom of the glass. The brewed swirl spun in his head. He stilled himself. It had been his first fresh and cold Foster's pint that Friday afternoon. Then four shots of tequila gold with slices of lemon and salt. And then two shots of Jägermeister, followed by more pints of Foster's to wash them down.

Rustling voices at JD Wetherspoon's levelled up to a brashness. Lady Marmalade's 'Voulez vous coucher avec moi' swung high. One young woman in tight black jeans swayed and bounced her hips at the Zimbabwean table behind them, waving a white scarf above her head. Bongani had another try at calming his head.

Massaging the back of his neck, he watched Luzuko across the table. His eyes droopy, Luzuko had resigned himself to a certain numbness. Perched over him, one hand resting on Luzuko's chair, an old Kenyan prattled on and on about Machiavelli's *The Prince*. Crossed at the ankles under the table, Luzuko's feet twiddled fast. He turned to look up at Bongani, and then quickly turned away.

Bongani stretched his neck, surveying the Kenyan table in the East African corner. He thought of ways in which he could swat the old man back to his table, right next to the Burundian table. Bongani blamed himself for bringing the old Kenyan over. He had told everyone in the East African corner and at the Zimbabwean table that he was in the company of an Oxford student, a doctoral student in Politics and International Relations. And the old man had followed them over to their table.

The old Kenyan man with a head of uncombed hair and ragged white beard, wearing a thick brown tweed jacket and grey cotton trousers, lingered over Luzuko. Tasting his lips, he began, "How do you think former President Daniel arap Moi survived the politics of Kenya? How do you think Moi's presidency survived the late seventies, the entire eighties and nineties, up to 2002?" He took a swig from his pint. "How do you think he withstood the rowdy politics of the Odingas and coup attempts and backstabbing? Mmh? Machiavelli. It was Machiavelli!"

Sliding the empty pint glass away from him, Bongani blew out a plump sigh. 'Dancing in the Moonlight' slid into the mix from the speakers around them. Luzuko bobbed his head to the rhythm. Bongani felt at ease that Luzuko was drunk. Chairs flew as one man after another from the Burundian table shunted themselves to the dance floor. On the other side, a Sierra Leonean couple and two Nigerian men remained seated, feasting on mounds of rice and some oily, yellow-and-red delicacy. The young woman from the Zimbabwean table ran to the dance floor, joining the Burundian men. And two burly middle-aged Tanzanians in black leather jackets also shuffled their way over, talking above the din of 'Dancing in the Moonlight'.

Rallying his tongue around his lips, the old Kenyan

continued, "You know, my friend, President Kenyatta's cabinet ministers used to mock Moi all the time. They never thought that a Kalenjin would ever ascend to the highest office in Kenya. And not only did Moi survive, but he became the longest-serving president of Kenya, from 1978 to 2002. And I'm sure Moi read Machiavelli back to front. He knew that being feared is more useful than being loved. As Machiavelli put it, 'It is much safer to be feared than loved because … love is preserved by the link of obligation which, owing to the baseness of men, is broken at every opportunity for their advantage; but fear preserves you by a dread of punishment which never fails.'" Clearing his throat, his quote verbatim and virtually faultless, he took up his pint again.

Luzuko turned to look the other way. 'Dancing in the Moonlight' reached a fever pitch before the old man took it up again, "And, my South African brother, Moi understood quite well the art of deception, confusing the enemy. That is why he outsmarted his enemies all those decades. As Machiavelli said, 'Never attempt to win by force what can be won by deception.' Also, my friend, Moi was politically astute. As Machiavelli wrote, 'How laudable it is for a prince to keep good faith and live with integrity, and not with astuteness, everyone knows. Still the experience of our times shows those princes to have done great things who have had little regard for good faith, and have been able by astuteness to confuse men's brains, and who have ultimately overcome those who have made loyalty their foundation.'" Again, verbatim.

The old man droned on. Suddenly, Khumalo appeared behind Bongani, standing short and nervous and clasping a pint of lager. Rubbing Bongani's shoulder, his potbelly brushed the back of his chair. Blinking and breathing heavily, Khumalo downed another giant gulp.

"I told you, Bongani," he said, "I'm not leaving this country until I eat a white woman."

"When did you come in?" Bongani turned his head up at

Khumalo.

"Just now."

"And you're already drunk?"

"Come on, man."

"But, Khumalo, you remember what Tata Linda told you that night at Sodom?" Bongani sighed, returning to his glass.

"Come on, man. No one is going to deport me." Khumalo took another gulp. "Thames Valley is not going to catch me," he laughed. "As I said, I'm not going anywhere until I eat a white woman." He walked away, laughing loud all the way to the dance floor.

"I did not sign up for this, Bongani! I did not sign up for this at all!" Luzuko had stung Bongani in the bus, all the way from the city centre to Blackbird Leys. Everything had been a mad rush. Hugo had toppled down the steps outside the Summertown council estate, two bulky suitcases in tow. Then, just as they had crossed the road to Summertown House, he had spotted the Oxford municipal supervisor's car driving into the parking lot of the council estate.

Outside Summertown House, Luzuko had yelled at Bongani and Hugo, demanding an explanation. Hugo, smiling, skinny and tall with bowed legs in baggy black jeans, had dropped the two suitcases at his feet. Then he had quickly explained, rattling off a list of bullet points: He, Hugo, was from Bandundu in Congo, but had lived in Umtata for some time. When his parents left Bandundu for England, he had immigrated to South Africa, settling in Umtata back in the nineties. He had just joined his parents, along with his sister and cousin. His parents had been granted refugee asylum, but he and his sister were here illegally, their visas having expired. He then joined his sister and cousin – also in the country illegally – to live with his parents in the Summertown council estate. And, as per the Oxford municipal regulations, a supervisor checked on his parents and their needs and progress regularly. Regularly turned out to be once a month. Sometimes regularly was twice a month.

As per his parents' registration for the council estate flat, they had to live alone. Hugo and his sister and cousin thus had to vacate the two-bedroom flat every time the supervisor paid them a visit. For that hour or two, they had to pack everything they had and leave. Then later, when the coast was clear, they returned to the flat. That was what they had just done, Hugo explained. He needed a place – Luzuko's flat in Summertown House – to store his suitcase for a few hours.

"I did not sign up for this, Bongani!" Luzuko had said, his voice coming out high and thin. "I did not sign up for this at all!" Bongani had stared out the bus window, straining his neck farther out. All of that had brought back to Bongani the nagging of his ex-girlfriend, Thandi. Luzuko sounded just like her, Bongani thought, the way his voice reached full crescendo pitch in a matter of seconds.

"Bongani, Prince of Chaos." Major General's laughter came through his head from the previous night in Sodom. "You hear me, Bongani? I did not sign up for this." Luzuko had gone on.

Why can't I get what I want? Bongani had asked himself, batting away two drops of tears. I'm a decent man. He sighed, resting his chin on the palm of his hand. I've tried. I've tried my best to do things the right way. I've tried to be normal. To be decent. I've tried to do things the legal way. But now I'm this homeless, paperless thing.

Turning the empty pint glass in his hand, Bongani scanned Luzuko across the table, slumbering on the chair. He looked away as the old man launched into yet another chunk of Machiavelli. Hugo stretched his long legs out underneath the table, chewing on the skin of a lemon slice. The old man had cut Hugo off from his story rides of Umtata police's Operation Qhaqha Zonke – 'Tear apart everything'.

And there, in Hugo's stories, Luzuko had come alive. Hugo had slammed down one anecdote after another of Operation Qhaqha Zonke in perfect isiXhosa. The stories sat somewhere in the middle of fact and fiction. They were too bent to be real, yet laced with too many thick layers of logic and reality to be made up. And Hugo delivered them with a serious poker face.

Bongani stood at the bar waiting for some lout to take his order. And then, from the Burundian table, a chair flew out and a tray crashed to the floor. The Burundian table shook and trembled in Kiswahili and French and English. A hefty oaf with a large spread of shoulders stood up, his eyes bloodshot and peeled out. A half-filled pint glass smashed on the floor. Across the table, a tall, slim young man stood up and reached out to the tall Burundian.

"*Rafiki yangu*" – "My friend." The old man shouted to his friend at the Kenyan table.

"*Rafiki yangu Mrundi, anaona vizuka tena.*" – "My Burundian friend is seeing ghosts again."

"*Kachini, rafiki yangu.*" – "Sit down, my friend." The old man yelled at the Burundian.

The large-shouldered Burundian began to tremble. The old man rose and sped across the floor to the Kenyan table, mumbling fast in Kiswahili. Luzuko let out a long sigh and turned to face Hugo.

TWENTY-THREE

THREE MORE WEEKS OF these jobs, then I'll move on to my Summertown nursing-home dream job. Nomusa assured herself, sliding the machine forward. Her arms took on the shakes from all the tumbles and the trembles. I hope the bloody Poles have not snatched up my Summertown nursing job. They're all over the show, she mused, shifting the machine to another dirty spot.

She wondered how she was going to pay back Mavis for all the fuss she had put up with in securing her the nursing job. Perhaps a perfume, she thought. No, a perfume and a dress. No, it would need to be much bigger than that. More meaningful. The machine steamed out a loud steady wheeze. Wagner's 'The Valkyrie' buzzed out of her mobile phone in the depths of the front pocket of her navy work uniform. Sniffing, she straightened herself up, her slim and nimble fingers reaching for the phone.

Reading the screen, she saw it was a number she did

not recognise. 'The Valkyrie' purred on. She glanced at her watch. It was 11:47. Just thirteen minutes before her knock-off time. And she had another cleaning job from two to five that afternoon at Wolfson College. In between, she had planned to take a quick trip home, for lunch and to check on Baby Angelina and her mother.

Staring at the screen, she prayed it was a call from the Summertown nursing home, that they wanted her to start sooner.

"Hello." She let out a small cough.

"Hello." The voice on the other side of the phone came out flat. "Is that Miss Linda Liso?"

"Yes."

"My name is Brenda. Mrs Brenda Briggs, from Social Services."

"Yes? Yes ... ma'am."

"My colleague and I are outside your house as we speak. It appears that your baby may be in the house all by herself."

"What?"

"She's crying her lungs out, Miss Liso."

"I'm ... I'm ... I'm coming over right now."

"Your annoyed neighbours have been barraging us with calls for the past two to three hours."

"Yes, ma'am. I'm coming over right now."

"If you're not here in twenty minutes, I'm calling the police. Do you understand me?"

"Yes, ma'am." Nomusa breathed fast and hard, stripping off her work uniform as she spoke, and heading for the main door. She tossed the clothes to the floor just outside the exit and ran.

It was 11:58. The next bus to Blackbird Leys was at five minutes after twelve. I have to make it, she thought. And now I'm going to lose my job at Wolfson. She swiped at the sweat on her forehead. What if I end up at the police station? Deported? I have absconded from work. She folded her arms under her breasts, tapping her feet. I cannot have my child taken from me, she thought. Tears welled in the corners of her eyes and trickled silently down her cheeks. How could my mother do this to me? A tear landed on her arms. I have four minutes left. Maybe I should take a cab? Perhaps I could dash back to the college and leave a message with the porter. I can't lose this job. Turning around, she saw her bus approaching.

At three minutes after twelve, she hopped onto the bus. Standing in front of the driver, she fingered through the insides of her handbag, and pulled out a bus pass. Slipping it onto the bottom of the card machine, the instrument gave the congested, hurried chime. She wiped her forehead, looking for an empty seat. There was one at the back of the bus, and she scurried down the aisle. Out of breath, she plonked herself down and stared out the window, drawing in the hustle and bustle outside, beyond the glass. Everything seemed to have gone in slow motion. I can still take a cab, she thought as the bus moved off gingerly towards High Street.

Dabbing her forehead, she watched the hastiness of Cornmarket Street, and raising her left hand again, checked the time. Then, just as the bus was settling into a steady pace, it stopped again for a passenger at the next bus stop.

"Nomusa!" a man's voice boomed.

"Mkhize." Nomusa looked up and wrung out a smile.

"Yho! My sister!" Mkhize almost yelled, his fist plastered to his lips. "Have you heard about Big Mavis?" he coughed out a loud, wet blast. Nomusa shook her head.

"Word is going around that Big Mavis sent that Limpopo boyfriend of hers back home."

"Mmh?"

"What's his name again?" Mkhize squinted. "Phineas." He laughed. "This Phineas fellow was supposed to pick her up from her new job at the Odeon cinema in Blackbird Leys. The new Odeon there, you know, *mos*? Now that Phineas has a car, he picks her up from work every day. But he did not turn up this time. And I'm talking about the beginning of last week here. And she had knocked off at one in the morning, and there are no buses to her place at that ungodly hour. And so Big Mavis took a cab and headed *straight* for his place." *Straight* came out pressed. Nomusa turned her gaze back to the window, tapping her feet.

"And when she walked into his place, what did she see?" Mkhize whispered. "Remember that she has her own keys ... And there he was," Mkhize almost yelled. "There he was with an old, fat British woman in his bed. And so the arguments and scuffles began." His hands flailed around. "Phineas gave Big Mavis a few slaps. And Big Mavis? She walked away. The following day, the police picked Phineas up at his work. He was deported three days later. And Big Mavis, she is not denying this one. Not this one."

"That's terrible," Nomusa said, still gazing out the window, tapping her feet.

"Are you all right, my sister?"

"I'm fine. I'm fine."

"And," Mkhize leaned forward in a whisper, "Luke was caught red-handed, just last week, kissing and fondling a college boy."

"Oh."

The bus stopped at the top of the hill on Barns Road, a few feet outside her house.

"Nomusa," Mkhize hushed his tone, "that's Thames Valley outside your house. What's going on?"

"Nothing. It's nothing, Mkhize." She straightened herself up. "Probably came for the Arabs next door." Nomusa quickly made her way to the bus door.

"But I haven't seen any Arabs in your neighbourhood. Didn't you say your neighbours are an elderly English couple?"

"The elderly couple moved out. We have Arabs now." Nomusa headed down the steps and out onto the pavement. There was a burst of steam, the door shut behind her, and the bus glided away. Mkhize stared out the window behind her, his eyes following the two uniformed officers and two plainclothes women. Baby Angelina's cries climbed higher and higher, reaching out to Nomusa across the street.

Panting, she ran through the gate. A big woman with bouncy, curly hair, in an overflowing red dress, fetching her mid-fifties, looked at Nomusa with a firm, straight face. The two officers watched her flailing through the gate, their hands resting on their armoured belts. Nomusa guessed that the big woman in the red dress was Mrs Brenda Briggs. To her left stood a lanky brunette, smiling at her.

"Good afternoon," Nomusa panted.

"Miss Linda Liso, right?" Mrs Briggs's voice came out loud.

"Yes."

"I'm the one who called. Can we come in, please?"

"Yes. Yes, of course."

Nomusa stuck her key in the latch, her hands quivering, and opened the door. Baby Angelina's cry descended on them from upstairs.

"Where's your baby, Miss Liso?"

"Upstairs, ma'am. In my room."

"Well, it's obvious from the rank smell that she needs attending to, if that's not an understatement. And when you're done with her, bring her downstairs."

"Okay." Nomusa galloped up the stairs.

Baby Angelina's chest and neck were soaked. Nomusa reached over and picked her up, bringing the baby to her chest. Baby Angelina's cries had turned into a screech. Quickly, she returned her to the bed, cooing and massaging the child's belly. She reached over for the wardrobe, and pulled out a black gym bag. Placing it next to Angelina on the bed, she picked through it for the baby wipes. The child screamed and kicked, her fists punching the air.

She unbuttoned the babygro, parted Angelina's legs, and gently pulled the soiled nappy from under her buttocks. A heap of a mushy turd. Lifting the baby's legs, Nomusa quickly wiped her buttocks and put her back on the bed. Rushing to the bin in the corner of the bedroom, she deposited the soiled nappy – only to return to find a load of fresh, squishy waste drenched in urine on the clean nappy she had just slid under her buttocks. Touching the child's forehead, she sensed it was hot. Nomusa pulled the nappy from under the baby and took out a fresh wipe. Her tears silently dropped onto the duvet cover.

Stripping the baby, she wiped her neck and chest, and pulled on fresh clothes. Finally clean and smelling of baby powder, she brought Baby Angelina to her chest, bouncing and cooing her. The child's cry grew faint. Looking around, Nomusa noticed a full bottle nestled inside a jug of water on the bedside drawers. Baby Angelina took the teat immediately and, as she suckled, silence fell upon the house.

Scrambling back down the stairs, the clickety-click and kash-kash sounds of walkie-talkies stuck out loud. Mrs Briggs sat on the sofa. The two police officers moved around the living room, picking up and putting down objects and papers and books. Carrying the baby, Nomusa settled herself on the sofa across from Mrs Briggs. Baby Angelina sucked on heavily from the bottle, stopping only for a breath in between.

"Miss Liso," Mrs Briggs started, exasperated, "this … This is beyond negligence. It's criminal."

"Ma'am, let me explain …"

"Do you know that Social Welfare can take away your baby for this? That you can be arrested for this?"

"Please, ma'am, let me explain …"

"This is beyond any explanation."

"I left my mother to look after my baby. She was supposed to remain in the house and look after her until I return from work."

Mrs Briggs sighed. "This is a baby we are talking about, not a car or a piece of furniture or household appliance.

You're clearly not fit to be a mother."

"No, ma'am, it's not like that at all."

"It's like what, then?"

"My mother was ..."

"You've said that already."

Silence.

"And now," Mrs Briggs wagged a finger at Nomusa, "Social Welfare is compelled to take away your baby until we have ascertained that the circumstances under which your baby is being raised are conducive to a happy and healthy infant."

Nomusa rushed towards Mrs Briggs, falling to her knees.

"Please, ma'am," Nomusa gasped, her hands up.

"We have no choice."

"Please, ma'am." The tears threatened to spill again. "I promise you, ma'am ... I promise it won't happen again."

"And may I add something here, Mrs Briggs?" The policewoman coughed faintly, walking over to Nomusa. "The father of your baby, Mr Joe Hart, a Liberian national, is currently being held in prison in Manchester on a number of fraud charges. And he uses this address for his fraudulent activities."

"Please, ma'am ..."

"And," the policewoman continued, once again resting her hands on her belt, "we are also investigating your papers. Apparently, you hold a student visa, and are registered for a diploma in Information Technology with Oxford Brookes University. And yet you've never attended a single lecture, nor submitted a single paper or any assignment for two years now."

"But ... but ..."

"And there are no records of your student visa application in this country or in South Africa."

"Miss Liso ..." Mrs Briggs came in.

"If that is truly your name, anyway," the policewoman interrupted.

"Miss Liso," Mrs Briggs gave the policewoman a sharp look, "we'll give you a few days' reprieve. If the circumstances here are found wanting, Social Welfare will have no choice but to remove the infant from your custody. Yes, Miss Liso, they will take your baby away. Almost certainly."

"Thank you, ma'am." Nomusa was still on her knees.

Mrs Briggs stood up.

"And we will call again soon," the policewoman barked, heading for the door.

All Nomusa heard was the door slamming behind her.

⁂

"Nomusa!" Grace yelled from downstairs. Nomusa listened to her mother's heavy footsteps on the stairs.

"Nomusa." Grace stood at the door of the bedroom wearing a soft smile.

"Where have you been?"

"Guess what?"

"Where have you been?"

"I have a job. I have a job at a supermarket. Seven pounds and fifty pence an hour, eight-hour shifts, four days a week …"

"You left Angelina all by herself."

Silence.

"Social Welfare people and the police were here. They nearly took Angelina away. All because of you."

Silence.

"I'm sorry, Nomusa."

"You're sorry? I nearly lost my baby!"

"Don't you ever talk to me like that."

"Leave now. Leave!"

TWENTY-FOUR

Do FIFTY-FIVE-YEAR-OLD married women fall in love with men they are not married to? Grace listened to the rhythm of the question. She listened to his snore, a drizzle coming up and slowing down. Then it quickly rose to a summit and lay flat again. "A Scottish purr," Eddie had whispered, smiling, one upper rabbit tooth slightly slabbed in front of the other. "I'm working on it, my love," he had sniffed, rubbing his forefinger back and forth beneath his nose.

Again, that night before he had gone to sleep, Eddie had tried. His hand had crept up her silky beige nightdress. It had been an unhurried trip up her thigh. Sharp electricity had sent spasms through her, collecting and sliding far into the depths of her inner thighs. And she had wanted to open her clamped knees. "Not yet, my love." Do fifty-five-year-old married women fall in love with men they are not married to, men on whose beds they spend nights? She had asked herself, slowly closing his fingers together, gently turning them back to him. "Too soon, my love." And she had run her fingers round his cheeks: "Please wait, my love. Please." And then her fingers had moved up to his face, ruffling his tousled sandy hair.

Everything had felt good. He touched her as if he was begging. It was in the way he folded her hands into his. The feeling of her brittle bones warmed up in his. The vastness and the hardness of his skin. It was the bones of his hands curtaining hers. Do fifty-five-year-old married women fall in love with men they are not married to?

She smiled. It was in the way he asked her permission to do things to her – to run his fingers over the gorge beneath her throat, and then plant a soft kiss on her neck. It was in the way he made coffee for them both. And then fried eggs and bacon and hash brown, with tomatoes and fried onions. It was in how he brought over her plate of dinner, and how they ate together in silence sometimes. And how he poured her a drink and listened to her every word. Do fifty-five-year-old married women fall in love with men they are not married to?

She wondered if she could already have fallen in love in just three weeks. Eddie pulled up the pants of his blue pyjamas, sliding into his grey-check slippers. Taking up his dressing gown hanging on the back door of the wardrobe, Grace picked up a whiff of his body odour – a mix of mildly stale armpit and a spicy, woody fragrance. And then he had hurried down the stairs to the kitchen.

That morning, she felt a smile widening on her. Heaving in the crisp wintry air, she wondered how long it was going to take to get used to the cold. The brittleness in her fingers, the joints growing creakier. Beads of sweat all over her had become bolder. Sharp jolts of pain and hot flushes lingered longer. She was running out of her medication for high blood pressure and arthritis. Opening the low wooden gate, she felt the creaks in her fingers crawling out.

She walked out the gate and up towards the bus stop.

The tightness of the maroon, purple and white flowery dress Eddie had bought for her at Debenhams embraced her in a hug. Watching the bus heading steadily down the road, she walked faster. The bus released a burst of steam as it drew closer to the stop. Grace filed behind a burly middle-aged man with a lunch bag tossed across the shoulder. Piling herself up the bus steps, she punched in her weekly bus ticket.

Taking the third seat from the front, she let out a slow breath, watching the houses glide slowly past. One week to pay day, she snorted out a quick soft laugh. One week to my first pay day ever. She smiled, loosening her fingers and clawing through her handbag. She ran her fingers over the envelope. Slowly unfurling it, she wondered whether she was finally ready to post it to Durban during her lunch-hour break from her supermarket cashier job. Grace straightened out the letter on her lap:

Dear Jacob,
  I hope and I trust that you are keeping well and safe at home. I'm sure that this letter comes as a surprise to you. No one writes letters these days. I guess I want you sitting down when you learn of what I'm going to say. Maybe I don't have the guts to tell you over the phone. Maybe I don't have the appetite to listen to your voice barking on the other end of the line. So it is better that I say this here, on these pages. Perhaps I am a coward. Am I a coward? I don't know. All I know is that I don't want to listen to your voice. I've heard enough of it over the last thirty years. Perhaps I respect you. I respect what we have, what we had, so much to say what I want to say now in these quiet pages rather than through a loud rush of barks and insults and cries and sobbing.
  You don't listen to me when I sit you down to tell you what I feel, anyway. You've never listened to me, ever. You haven't listened to me over the past thirty

years of our marriage. And so I think, in this letter, you will listen to me. It is the best way to sit you down and make you listen. Letters are serious matters. And so I guess you can tell that what I'm about to say here now is serious.

Jacob, I am not coming back home. I'm not coming back home, ever. I lied to you. I even lied to Nomusa when I promised to return home in three months with our granddaughter, Angelina. I have chosen to remain here in Oxford for good. I know that this decision that I've taken will make you angry. It has made Nomusa very angry. As a result, we no longer live together, and we are no longer on talking terms.

If you had listened to me over the past thirty years, I would not have done what I've just done. If you had listened to me, things would have been altogether different. I would now be talking about how good a time I'm having in Oxford, spending valuable time with Nomusa and our granddaughter. If only you had listened to me, if you had made me feel human, this would not be happening now. If you had listened to how badly I wanted to be a nurse just after we married, I would not be writing this letter now. If you had allowed me to complete high school and enrolled at nursing school thereafter, we would not be here now.

Jacob, now I'm here working illegally. I am paperless. I don't know when they'll catch me and deport me, send me back to you. I don't know how things will turn out. Perhaps they won't catch me, just as they haven't caught Nomusa yet. I have never in my life had my own money. If your money comes to my hands, it leaves as soon as it lands, because it is not mine. You have no idea how I've always wanted to have money of my own, in my own hands, and to do with it as I want. That is freedom. That is my own freedom. For many years, every day, many nights, I dreamt of having money of my own. And now I am a week away to my first pay day ever. And you are not here to tell me what to do with it.

I don't know if I'll ever see you again, Jacob. Even if I do, I'm not sure if our marriage will ever be the same. There are many things that break a marriage. There are many things that break love. Do fifty-five-year-old married women fall in love again? Do they ever fall in love with men they are not married to? I don't know. But I know that question, if it were ever turned around to men, wouldn't mean anything to them. You've done as you wished from the time we got married. And all I did was watch. But what I know for sure is that I am no longer in love with you. And I don't have a care in the world how you take that.

Have I run away from you? Yes, with all my mind, with all my heart, and with all my breath. And now I am completely free. I am now on my own. I am now myself.

Bye-bye,
Grace Gama

Folding it slowly to its creases, Grace made up her mind that she was going to post it during her lunch hour. The bus chugged steadily past a row of terraced houses in Blackbird Leys. Slipping the pages back into the envelope, she made up her mind that she was going to open her legs that night.

TWENTY-FIVE

BENDING DOWN TO THE oven, Dela gathered the hem of his navy gown. Pulling open the oven door, the stiff wavy air of charred wheat wafted over the kitchen, its warmth hazing over the calypso flakes and the scampering trumpet notes of Dizzy Gillespie's 'Con Alma'. I stared out the window, to the frail sunlight beyond. The notes mashed together, leisurely fading out. Fishing toasted bread from the oven, Dela's slight fingers dusted off crumbs and slapped the slices on a red plate next to the stove.

Boasting a glorious brown colour, four sizzling pork sausages with mushrooms and fried onions lay in wait on another plate on the counter. Rejigging his gown and tightening its belt, Dela shut his eyes and breathed out slowly. I felt like sliding and curling into a restful sleep on the sofa with my bedtime read, Janet G Vaillant's *Black, French and African: A Life of Léopold Sédar Senghor*. But, with my red dragon next to me in the weeks that were fast becoming many, I hadn't had any bedtime read. It was Sunday morning, and it had been long since I had woken from a restful sleep.

Coffee dripped gently from the plunger into my mug as Dela poured, the steam sending out a tight, slightly nutty aroma.

"Co-Colo-lombian stuff, mmh?" Dela moved the plunger over to his mug, the *t* in his 'stuff' bounding out naked and wet. "Not in-ins-tant coffee, mmh?" Sitting at the table in the centre of Dela's kitchen, I watched his face, his round John Lennon spectacles threatening to slide down the ridge of his nose. I marvelled at how everything here was custom made. The bottle of honey on the table next to the coffee plunger came from Togo, its label in French. And on the far left of the kitchen counter sat a plastic bag of Togolese rice, also labelled in French.

Alongside the kitchen window, looking four storeys down to the open park on the far side of Warneford Hospital, Gilchrist Olympio stood at an angle in a big, brightly coloured picture frame. Smiling, he waved a yellow scarf to a crowd of followers in what looked like a stadium. Standing on the back of a van, a sticker on the side read: *'Forces Unies pour le Changement'* – the United Forces for Change, the UFC. Olympio's opposition party in Togo, the UFC of Dela, the party he had moved to exile with.

A similar image hung in the hall leading from the front door, this time of Gilchrist Olympio's father, Sylvanus Olympio. With a somewhat tighter, slimmer and fresher face, he beamed health and life in contrast to his son's oily, sweaty and podgy face. Gilchrist's eyes, drooping slightly, looked tired. The small parting in Sylvanus's short, natural hair showed that his black-and-white portrait was taken some time in the 1950s. His hands were cropped off in the picture, but he had been waving to a crowd, much like his son had been. Dela always wondered how Sylvanus would have turned out had he not been the first head of state in

Africa to be assassinated in the continent's first military *coup d'état* in January 1963.

Hung next to Sylvanus on the corridor's wall was his arch-nemesis, Ghana's Kwame Nkrumah, the reason he had hesitantly kept an army of two hundred and fifty officers. To Sylvanus, that number of soldiers in his country's army was enough. But his stubbornness at keeping such a small national army had been the very trigger for his death. He was gunned down by Étienne Gnassingbé Eyadéma, an officer who had wanted a bigger army for himself and his colleagues who had just returned from overseas military campaigns. Eyadéma soon made himself president and installed his soldier friends in the government of Togo.

Gilchrist Olympio completed his doctorate in Economics at Nuffield College in the city centre, just up the street and across from the Oxford municipality offices.

Dela's short hallway ended abruptly with his bedroom on the right, a rather spacious room with his desk against the far wall. Above the desk hung the black-and-white portraits of the writers he admired the most, mostly African. This was his shrine, where he dipped his head before and after writing.

A shuffle of papers beneath the chair bore a scruff of handwritten notes. There too, on the floor, lay a library copy of Mahmood Mamdani's *Citizen and Subject: Contemporary Africa and the Legacy of Late Colonialism* alongside some rather old editions on African nationalism. William Faulkner's *Absalom, Absalom!* lay prostrated, opened midway beneath the unbound first four chapters of Dela's thesis. Strewn around these was a mishmash of papers written in French with footnotes and a single page of a select bibliography.

Dela slid towards me the red plate now with tomatoes, two sunny-side-up eggs and two slices of brown toast on it. Mary Stallings' voice dangled 'Yesterday' in the air. 'Dreaming of yesterdays,' she sang before her voice slowly slipped away, stretching the last 'yesterdays' in a slothful, want-to-be falsetto soprano pitch.

I pushed aside the printed copies of his past newspaper column to make space for the red plate.

"Su-sus-tenance for in-inte-intellectuals, my good sir, mmh? And Co-Colo-lombian brew, mmh?" He slid the spectacles back up his nose, laughing as he did so. And everything came up to my face – the heady aroma of the brew; the greasy, taut air of the fry-up; the warmth of the toasted bread.

"I-I'm ... soon p-pu-blishing a book on those co-co-lumn pieces." Slowly, he dragged the chair out from the table, scooping a blob of butter and spreading it on a slice of toast. "The ... pur ... kind of ... p-pur-pose is to have this book available in the rural areas of Togo, mmh? North, south, central provinces."

I bit into the toast. The smoothness of the butter skated down my throat. Then I marshalled into my mouth a chunk of sausage and a piece of the sunny-side-up egg. Washing it down with a sip of the Colombian brew, the combined greasy delicacy, the buttery smooth toast and the brew dug deep into me. A rumble of satisfaction came from my belly, taking hold of the warmth of the fry-up. Art Farmer's 'Wonder Why' drifted above us. The two trumpets blew – one solid and brave, and the other hesitant and coy.

"It's important that people read." Dela looked down on his plate, forking playfully at his mushrooms and fried onions. Searching his plate, he chewed on, gently slicing his toast. "Not just about the Togolese pro-d-de-mocracy struggles against Eyadéma's t-ty-ranny." He lifted a forkful of mushrooms and fried onions to his mouth. "But to read. Mmh? To read. Kind of ... yes!" He chewed slowly. "Just to read. To have b-boo-books available, to ... to have them around to read." He scooped in another forklift of mushrooms and onions, and thrust in another bite of toast. I listened to his gentle crunching.

"When I was a teenager," Dela went on, "living in my village in the south of Togo, living among the Mina people, I lost my mind." He slurped in his coffee.

"What do you mean, lost your mind? I don't get it."

"Wh-what ... what's there n-no-not to get, mmh?"

"Lost your mind? Because you had no books? What do you mean by that?"

"It's ... it's ... a terrible thing, mmh? It's ... kind of terrible. I fear it."

"You fear it?"

"A lot. Losing my mind again. The thought of it stu-stu ..."

I waited. Dela looked away, chewing on, taking off his spectacles. His eyes looked small, bloodshot.

"I didn't say I had no ... no ... books." He returned his eyes to me, putting back his spectacles. "I didn't say there were no books. I kind of ... went mad, crazy, because there were no *more* books for me to read. I had read everything there was to read, and there were no more books left to read. Then I kind of ... lost my mind. Just like that. I snapped. Kind of, yes!" Flailing his hands, those two gorged, round, deep scars on his wrists showed.

"That's not possible. There's always something to read lying around. Even if it's an old, unimportant newspaper or magazine. There's always something to read."

"I said I had read everything there was to read in my village."

An honest laughter welled up out of me. Dropping my fork and knife on the plate, I threw myself back on the chair and laughed. Dela looked away, his fingers clasped together under his chin. But my laughter braved the air alone. Dela stared away, into the hallway beyond.

Art Farmer's two trumpets had both grown full of themselves.

"It is ... that is ... my ... my ... kind of ... greatest fear, Luzuko." He stared straight into my eyes, his chewing chin bouncing on the clasped hands beneath.

He shunted out his chair, stood up and turned to the cupboard behind him. Opening it, he took out a can of baked beans in tomato sauce. He snapped open the cutlery drawer, and took out a can opener. Slowly winding the can, he hummed: "*Oga*, drive your motor *jeje*" – "Sir, drive your car slowly." The song brought back to me the ambience of Chinua Achebe's *No Longer At Ease* – the new *ogas*, the young good sirs in slender black Kennedy ties being turned out by their hundreds from universities in England and America; the heady, new independence era; the vintage cars of the sixties. The old Nigerian pidgin-English folk song stumbled out like a hooligan, the song of drunk men staggering home as the bar behind them shut down for the night. In between, Dela hummed a cautionary line of what would happen if the good sir did not drive his car *jeje*, slowly. And then he returned with speed and zest back to the line, "*Oga*, drive your motor *jeje*." The "motor" came out with a stark-naked *t*.

As he poured a mound of beans onto my plate, I wondered whether Dela knew that I had, of late, been moving around with illegal immigrants. Was I driving too fast? About to careen into something dragonish? And where was I driving to? In search of what? I watched Dela slide a dune of beans onto his own plate. Shaking the last dregs of tomato sauce from the can, he hummed the cautionary line. Where was I going with this car so fast, I wondered.

I toyed with the mound of beans on my plate, and wondered about the three Oxfords I had begun to mount. I slapped a second fried egg over the beans. Slicing a piece and forking it into my mouth, Blue Mitchell's 'March on Selma' trotted happily along after Art Farmer, all from Dela's CD playlist. His notes lay hidden behind a trombone, sitting uneasily with the mess in my mind. How had I mixed up three Oxfords? I munched on, staring up at Gilchrist Olympio. How did I end up mounting white Oxford, black Oxford and illegal Oxford? How?

Dela chewed on decisively. Hunting my eyes, I sensed that he was wrapping up. Unlike me, he had the stomach of a bird. And I sensed that we were about to begin with the serious discussions of that Sunday morning.

"Just last year, in 2003," Dela began, sliding the plate away from him, "Étienne Gnassingbé Eyadéma and his Rassemblement du Peuple Togolais, the Rally of the Togolese People, the RPT, won power again. He apparently – fraudulently, of course – won the election by 57.78 per cent of the vote, and was reinaugurated as Togo's president. Eyadéma has been in power since 1967, with or without his military junta, with or without his façade of multiparty democracy.

"The year before that, in December, he managed to wrangle an amendment to the constitution that removed the term limits of the office of the president of Togo. This is because he would have been forced to step down after the 2003 elections. The constitution was also fraudulently amended to reduce the minimum age of the president from forty-five years to thirty-five years. We suspect he is grooming one of his sons, Faure Gnassingbé Eyadéma, to take over the reins when he steps down."

Dela let out a slight cough, drawing in his chair.

"Now, Luzuko, where am I going with this? This is a multidimensional and long-term game strategy. We, as the opposition, the Union of Forces of Change, the UFC, led by Gilchrist Olympio, have embarked on a long-term strategy. On one front, we are continuously discrediting the Eyadéma regime in the hope that they'll call new elections. On the other end, we are preparing and galvanising all our opposition forces in Togo and outside, ahead of the 2008 elections.

"Again, where do you and I come into all of this? Well, I have been mandated with mounting an effective advocacy drive to inform our people and friends on all manner of Eyadéma's draconian rule. This ranges from killings and massacres to detentions, human-rights violations, corruption and a complete lack of service delivery. And much of this drive, the success of this drive, hinges on the support we get from our bases in the West."

He paused, but I said nothing.

"So, this is where you and I come in. You are to help me write pamphlets, information bulletins, on all these key areas of how Eyadéma's RPT regime violates our people. You are to write and distribute this literature in Oxford. We'll work together from time to time, but I will also spend a significant amount of time in Brixton." Dela shoved a fat mound of papers to my side of the table. "You start with these," he said. "This week, I would like you to write a ten-page pamphlet, and a three-page bulletin." He moved back to his chair, spreading his hands far apart on the kitchen table.

TWENTY-SIX

Bongani held on to the rail of the bus seat. The bus swayed as it took the corner, moving into Blackbird Leys. The case of Foster's Lager sat balanced between his feet. Luzuko had fallen asleep on the seat next to him. But he didn't mind seeing him gone. Lately, Luzuko had been quiet, but fidgety. Bongani wondered how long he would remain at Luzuko's apartment. Ever since the Hugo affair, he had been twitchy. It was in the way he searched his eyes, as if for an answer. But then Luzuko would look away.

Bongani watched Patrick and Hugo seated across the aisle. Leaning back against the headrest, he wondered whether the job Patrick had promised him would come through. Perhaps it'll be a good move, Bongani wondered. Moving to Banbury, far into Oxfordshire and away from the city itself. Patrick had promised him a bar job in Banbury. It was a good, well-paying job and they would work together because, in a few weeks, Patrick would also move in with his new German girlfriend who lived in Banbury but worked in Oxford.

How long would he survive on his savings? Three to four months, perhaps five? He watched Luzuko softly snoring. After the Hugo affair, he really couldn't annoy him any longer. If it were not for Luzuko, no one would have helped him.

The bus whooshed to a stop, and a stream of passengers climbed aboard, among them a limping Mkhize carrying a bulging plastic bag. Bongani smiled. Blabbering an isiXhosa song, Major General hopped on behind him. Luzuko raised his head, sniffing and coughing. Quickly, he sat up, wiping sleep from his face. Laughing and bouncing as the bus trundled off, Mkhize and Major General sat on the empty seats in front of Bongani. Major General sneaked a bottle of whisky from his bag, showing it off to Bongani. His smile fading, he nodded twice at Patrick and Hugo when he noticed them seated across the aisle. Then he turned and looked deep into Bongani's eyes, his stare lingering longer there. He shook his head.

"Anyway," Major General began, "I think it's going to be a slow and gentle night. So, I bought two bottles of our favourite."

He turned his stare towards Luzuko. "What are you still doing here?" Major General barked.

"What do you mean?" Luzuko fidgeted in his seat.

"He means exactly that." Mkhize let out a wet cough blast.

"Here, where?" Luzuko sat upright.

"And where's your friend, Bafana?" Mkhize's head inched closer to Luzuko's.

"I don't know."

"Aren't you supposed to be with him?" Major General barked again.

"Why should I be with him?"

"He means," Bongani gently came in, sliding his head closer to Luzuko, "because you two are Oxford students, doing the same thing, you know?"

"And so?"

"We mean," Mkhize raised his voice, "what are you doing here with us?"

"We are going to Sodom, aren't we?"

"We are not talking about going to Sodom," Major General went on. "We are asking: What are you doing here with us?"

"Look here, man," Mkhize butted in, "we just don't get it. We work here in Oxford. We came to work here in England. We work hard for our money. For every penny and every pound we get here – we've earned it. Every day, we wake up very early to go to work. Do you have any idea how bitterly cold it is at four in the morning?"

"And you, on the other hand," Major General chimed in, "you sit on your arse and receive money for reading books. Just for reading books. You earn money for doing nothing. You live a cushy life for nothing. And you don't even struggle for papers. They organise papers for you."

"It's a scholarship." Luzuko raised his voice. "And you can also get one if you want to."

"And study for all those years?" Bongani interrupted.

"Seems you've made up your mind then," Luzuko said, resting his head. "You don't want to study for so many years, and you want to work instead. So go for it." He threw his hands up.

"Besides, Luzuko, you come from a comfortable life," said Bongani. "Your grandfathers and grandmothers went to universities and colleges. Ours were domestic workers and gardeners and factory workers."

"And so?" Luzuko sat up straight. "What do you want me to do about it?" He raised his voice and, turning his head around, looked into their eyes, one by one. "What do you want me to do about that? Mmh? You want me to collapse at the weight of my knees and weep because I've been solidly bourgeoisie from day one? Mmh? Listen, you can summon all your many heavens to conspire against me and call me all manner of uppity names, but I will not collapse at the weight of my knees and weep for being solidly bourgeoisie from day one."

"There you go again." Bongani threw up his hands, rolling his eyes. "Talking as if you're reading from a book or poem or something."

"We know why Bafana comes to see us sometimes," said Major General, his chin resting on the rail of the bus seat. "He wants to get laid and party, and then he returns to his people. But you, it seems as if you've come to stay. You've lingered on. You want to be here with us for good. Where are your people? Why don't you go to your people?"

Luzuko again threw himself back against the headrest and stared out the window.

"Don't worry, man," Bongani leaned into Luzuko, whispering. "Maybe," he coughed into a fist, "perhaps you've got to go into yourself." Luzuko's eyes were bloodshot and droopy. "Listen, Luzuko," Bongani sighed, looking down and then levelling up with Luzuko, "you've got to go into yourself too if these guys are throwing you out. No one will chuck you out from yourself."

Bongani wondered if he had lost favour with Luzuko. He felt guilty. Luzuko hadn't been doing his work properly for over a month. He hadn't seen him writing or going to his libraries. At times, Bongani had wondered how Luzuko fitted among them. Often, Luzuko spoke above their heads. Even some of his jokes were lost on them. And Bongani could tell that Luzuko could not find his pace with their visa stories, running out of visas, fixing papers, hiding from the law, finding jobs.

The bus came to a stop, and the driver whooshed open the doors. A slim policewoman in her late twenties stepped onto the bus. Then a middle-aged policeman followed behind her, his arms resting on his black armoured belt.

"Right!" the policeman shouted, a mound of his ginger moustache shifting nimbly on his upper lip. His breathing was hard, his potbelly stretched out. The policewoman scanned the passengers.

"Look down, look down," Bongani whispered hoarsely to Luzuko. "Don't panic. Just look down." Bongani's words came out in sharp lisps. He fished his phone from his pocket and fiddled with the screen. Bongani watched Mkhize and Major General as they stared at their feet, Major General twiddling his fingers. Mkhize stared out the window.

The policewoman walked slowly up the aisle. Balancing against the edges of seats, she looked down at the faces of the passengers. And at each, she paused and looked into their eyes.

"You!" Ginger Moustache shouted from the driver's seat area. "The geezer in a black jacket and black beanie."

Bongani continued staring down at the floor. The policewoman took four steps further up the aisle.

"You, sir," the policewoman said, "please come with us." Her voice came out soft and calm, but stern. Bongani listened to a shuffle of footsteps across the aisle. He dug his eyes deeper and longer onto the floor, listening to the thud of shifting feet.

Three lanky yobs in white tracksuits with blue stripes down the sides jumped onto the bus. They moved jumpily around the area around the driver's seat.

"Wanking coppers looking for trouble yet again, if you ask me." The tall one in front yelled out to the policewoman, spitting on the floor at her feet.

"This is police business," Ginger Moustache boomed.

"Shut up, you fat fuck," the yobo in the middle retaliated.

"Oi," the policewoman warned, "we'll take you in to the police station if you're not careful, lad ..."

"What's stopping you then, love?" the yobo in front sneered, licking his lips.

"Bloody yobs," Ginger Moustache whispered to himself, shaking his head, staring at the floor.

"Who you calling yobos?" The yobo shoved the other

two out of his way. "Come here and stand in front of me and call me a yobo, mate."

"Shut up, you lot," Ginger Moustache yelled.

"What's it gonna be? Cowley or Aldates, love?" one yobo asked.

"Come, you," the policewoman said, slowly hoisting Hugo out of his seat. "Up we go, sir."

Bongani kept his eyes on the floor of the aisle, watching Hugo's feet shuffling slowly and hesitantly.

Ginger Moustache moved farther up the aisle to the policewoman.

"Oi," the yobo in front shouted again. "Why don't you leave that geezer alone, yeah, fat fuck?"

"Insult me again and I'll take you in," yelled the policeman, his moustache snarling too.

"Yeah! Yeah!" The yobo moved quickly towards the officer. "Fucking racist pricks. Racial profiling and harassing that geezer just because he's black."

..

Tata Linda crossed his ankles and shifted his glass to his thighs. Bongani watched him blink up at the ceiling. Lifting his glass up to his lips, he took a slow sip. Bongani cracked open a Foster's, handing another to Luzuko sitting next to Tata Linda. Pam came in from the kitchen, holding a bottle of vodka and a large glass of orange juice. She placed the orange juice on the table alongside Tata Linda. Balancing the bottle of vodka against her chest, she twisted the cap and, smiling, poured two tots of vodka into his glass.

A slow drag of piano chords emerged from the sound system. Bongani took a swig, moving his chair closer to Tata Linda, Major General and Patrick slouching on the sofa opposite. Major General sighed, slowly shaking his glass of whisky. Bending down to the floor, he grabbed three cubes of ice from the bowl and dropped them into his glass. Mkhize stared quietly into a light ahead, sipping occasionally from his glass.

Bongani rested his head closer to Tata Linda. "It's going to be all right, Tata Linda," he said.

"How, my boy?" Tata Linda continued searching the ceiling. "How?"

"She'll find help."

"From whom? She has no family in Cape Town. All her family is in Jo'burg and East London. And they don't have resources to help her anyway."

"So, what does that mean, Tata Linda?"

"It means I have to fly to Cape Town, soon, before she overdoses." Tata Linda took another sip. "I have to, my boy. My daughter's in a bad state, all twisted up. I have no idea how she came across these drugs. I should have enrolled her at a university in Gauteng."

"And what's Ma Aggie saying?" asked Bongani.

"She's flying down in three weeks. And she's talking a different language now."

"A different language?" Bongani came out sharp.

"Yeah, yeah, yeah ... I'm cheating with Original Fitness and spending so much of my time in Sodom that she's had enough and wants a divorce. It's bad."

"Yho!" Bongani exclaimed into his lager.

"She wants to go back to South Africa for good, take care of our daughter. We don't know how long her recovery will take, what with her pregnancy and all of that."

"Pregnant?" Bongani sat up straight.

"First trimester."

The piano chords changed to long, searing, dry saxophone notes. Tata Linda returned his eyes to the ceiling.

"They say she loses her mind sometimes." Tata Linda wiggled his feet to the tune. "Talks gibberish and sees things that are not there."

"Man!" Bongani sighed.

"It reminds me of exile," Tata Linda went on. "Takes me

back to Angola, to the military camps. There was a guy in our camp who lost his mind. Every morning, he would take his briefcase and disappear into the bush, mumbling about heading to Moscow for a meeting with Premier Leonid Brezhnev. And then, late in the afternoon, he would be back, carrying his briefcase. Every day. We didn't know what to do with him. It was enough that the movement had to take care of all of us young exiles in foreign countries. Now imagine taking care of a young man who loses his mind in exile, far away from home. And we couldn't take him back home."

"In exile?" Luzuko shifted the seat to the edge of the sofa. Tata Linda stared at him.

"*Ja*."

"My father, he was also in exile."

"With whom?"

"The movement."

"Where?"

"Zimbabwe and Madagascar, most of the time."

"Where's he now?"

"He passed on, not long ago."

"Sorry, man. Condolences."

"It's okay, Tata Linda."

"What did he do in exile?"

"Department of Information and Publicity. A radio and print journalist. A propagandist."

"The Radio Freedom and propaganda guys?"

"Yeah."

"And what was his *nom de guerre*?"

"Aaron, Aaron Teketa."

Tata Linda sat upright, putting his glass on the table. Sidling to the edge of the sofa, he leaned closer to Luzuko.

"Comrade Aaron Teketa? I knew him."

"Really?" Luzuko's voice sprung up.

"He passed on?"

"Yes. Not long ago. A few months."

"Comrade Aaron is no more?"

"I didn't get a chance to attend his funeral back home."

"I'm so sorry, man."

"It's fine."

"We met in a camp in Angola, he and I, when he had just arrived. We trained together."

"Wow," Luzuko smiled. "You have no idea how long I've been searching for information about him. I only met him once, at the end of 1995, a few years following his return from exile in Zimbabwe. I was a second-year university student then. I never saw him again."

"Why?"

"Shame. It was shame." Luzuko clasped his fingers together, staring into a blankness far ahead of him. "He was ashamed that he had done nothing for me, hadn't been around to help raise me. When he saw how grown up I was, the shock of it all just overwhelmed him. He skipped the country when I was about three years old. He finally returned from exile when I had just completed my second year at university. He felt so ashamed of himself. And he kept apologising that he hadn't been there to raise me. He kept saying, 'I'm sorry. I'm sorry. Please, forgive me, son.' He could barely look me in the eyes. I tried to reassure him that he had done nothing wrong, that he could not have done anything better. But I just could not reach him. And then he left again, promising to keep in contact with me. He simply turned away, got into his car, and drove off. He drove away, and I never saw him again. Just as he had driven away to exile when I was barely three years old ... " Luzuko heaved out a long sigh. "And then he died."

"I'm sorry, man," Tata Linda said. Bongani watched as Tata Linda patted Luzuko's clasped hands. "I can't even begin to express my sorrow for you. There are so many stories of heartaches that came with exile."

"You know, Tata Linda," Luzuko went on, "I sincerely thought freedom was the beginning of a brighter future."

"Exile." Tata Linda lifted up the glass to his eyes. "Exile

messes up your mind, messes up you and your spirit in so many ways."

"How so?" Luzuko shifted on the sofa. Bongani sat upright.

"Comrade Aaron, your father, suffered a nervous breakdown in exile. And then I heard he had a second one back home, soon after his return. Imagine waking up to a skirmish with UNITA soldiers and as you lift up your head from your bed in a camp in Angola you see a bullet fly past your ear, missing you by a hair's length. I'm not sure if you can ever recover from that."

"Mmh?" Luzuko almost whispered.

"I also see him," Tata Linda continued.

"Who?" Luzuko said softly. "Who do you see?"

"I see him now and then. It never really goes away. Comes and goes. But it never completely fades away. Maybe that's why I spend a lot of time in Sodom, to boogie-woogie the ghosts away." Tata Linda gave a short laugh and brought the glass to his lips. "I see him, Luzuko, that UNITA soldier I shot to death. Big, tall guy. I shot at him, running after him. I shot at him in the back, again and again, chasing after him. He ran so fast. He just kept on running, and I kept right on his tail. And then, all of a sudden, just like that, he fell. Just like that, he fell like a big log. After running for, like, two kilometres, he just dropped dead. But it's the look in his eyes that has stayed with me, even up to now. The shape his lips had taken. I can't wipe it from my memory. I can't. I just can't. Not even with all the boogie-woogie nights in Sodom, I can't."

"And how does a man suffering from a nervous breakdown behave?" Luzuko asked, gently resting his head against the back of the sofa. Bongani watched as Tata Linda moved his fingers around his short glass.

"The North is best forgotten," Tata Linda said.

"What?" Luzuko lifted his from the headrest again.

"Our travels to the North are best forgotten." Tata Linda

sighed. "We travel," he continued. "To the West is the House of Fortune. To the East the House of Fire. At times, we travel to the South. As for the North ... it is best forgotten."

"But how does—?"

"As for the North, Luzuko, it is best forgotten." Tata Linda looked away.

Bongani listened to the fading piano chords and muted notes of the sax. Wiggling his can nervously, he watched Luzuko's eyes, his feet tapping quietly to the music, and two tears escaping from Tata Linda's closed eyes.

TWENTY-SEVEN

WITH THE RAIN PATTERING down, Nomusa wondered whether to turn left or right. She fluffed open her wide beige umbrella, and flared the collar of her thick grey jacket. Earlier that Friday evening, in her mind, she had flipped between cooking her own supper or buying a takeaway. If she took the left turn, there was Pizza Hut on George Street. If she went right, she would head straight to the bus stop. So she turned her mind against serious cooking. She just didn't feel up to it. The cleaning machines had left a creaking stiffness in her fingers.

Taking a left off New Inn Hall Road, she quickened her pace. On the pavement outside the Methodist Church a scrawny man sat with his hood pulled up against the rain. A bowl containing a few coins squatted on his right, a trembling white-and-brown Jack Russell curled up between his legs.

Nomusa moved the umbrella over her head. A flash of a

poster of *Spider-Man 2* at the Odeon cinema appeared in the corner of her eye and soon vanished. She licked a petal of rain off her upper lip, tasting the smudge of rouge.

As she walked, she thought about her mother. A South African friend had rustled up a job for her at a supermarket in Blackbird Leys. That same day, Nomusa had thrown her mother out her house; on that day she had nearly lost Angelina to Child Welfare Services. Her mother, meanwhile, had been taken in by her new supermarket supervisor, a man called Eddie McKenzie. And now word had got around that the Scot and her mother had become lovers.

Mkhize had come up to her and asked if it was true that her mother was being poked by a divorced Scotsman. He had rallied his tongue around his lips, polishing off the last bit of a giggle. She had no courage to slap him across the face. And once Mkhize found out about her mother's new love life, the entire South African crowd in Oxford was let in on it. Everyone knew. The word had been spread around in gushes and received with mixed reactions. Some had been light hearted, egging her mother to do as she pleased. Others had been shocked, withdrawn. Many had been sneaky. And still others had met the news with sneers of disgust and shame.

At least she's out of my hair, Nomusa assured herself. She licked more rain from her lip. She had decided against calling her father. She could not bring herself to tell him about what her mother was up to in Oxford. Besides, they were nothing but rumours. And she had not yet shaken off the shiver of what she had done to her two weeks back. If she called her father, the conversation would inevitably reach there.

Nomusa shifted her thoughts, watching how her boots pounded the splatters of water on the pavement. Her own man, Joe Hart, had left her and his baby, Angelina, and had never come back. He went off to London and just never returned. Nomusa had met Joe in Manchester. Tall and slight, he was a man who walked as if he was on a cloud. Striding purposefully with his legs apart, he always looked excited, happy, and there was never a problem without a simple solution to him. That is what attracted Nomusa to him, even though she had warned herself to stay away from West African men. Joe Hart was special. He made her forget about all the stereotypes spread about West Africans.

But Joe Hart was also part of a crew of credit-card fraudsters in Manchester. So when his activities began to attract the attention of Manchester police, and Nomusa ran to Oxford, Joe Hart followed her. In Oxford, he had just begun to worm his way back into her heart with his charms when he vanished and left her big with himself. She had heard later that he had been nabbed, and was now serving time in prison. Nomusa did not visit Angelina's father in jail. She had not attended his trial. Joe Hart was gone. Just like that other man who had made her big with himself at university, he was gone. They came and left. Gone.

Nomusa blinked when she saw, just ahead of her, a man she had briefly encountered in Sodom a few weeks back. Dressed in a long grey jacket, beige turtleneck and a grey beanie sheltering under a black umbrella, he held on to what looked like a bundle of papers. Nomusa recalled that he had come to Sodom with Bafana, but he was a South African she had never seen before. But on that night, they had had an easy conversation. She had forgotten his name. All she remembered was that he was a student at the university. That was what Bongani said. And then she remembered that Bongani had also said something about him coming from Grahamstown.

He's sweet and handsome, unlike the bastard Bafana, Nomusa recalled thinking of him that night she had first seen him. She bit her lower lip, watching him as he stood under his umbrella on the pavement. He's a bit tense though, rather thoughtful, Nomusa pondered. A bit on the short side, but good looking in an innocent, wholesome way – not in a rough way like Joe. But what the hell is he doing out in the rain handing out papers? And the people, they are not even taking his papers. Oh, shame. Nomusa mused, walking straight up to him.

"Hi," Nomusa leapt out, shuffling in beside him.

"Oh, hello." He turned to look at her, folding in two a thick sheaf of pamphlets.

"Fancy seeing you here after Sodom," she smiled, gently swaying her body.

"Yeah, it's been some time," he shouted above the slush of a car speeding through a puddle. It shot a splash of water at them, and they both wheeled back off the pavement.

"Bafana's friend, right?"

"Yes. My name is Luzuko. And you're Nomusa, right?"

"Yes. Yes. You remember my name? I mean, we chatted only briefly, and you remember my name?"

"I do. Bafana had been going on and on about you that night on our way to Sodom."

"*Ja*, right. And I can guess what he had been saying about me, that horny bastard."

They both laughed, fluffing out their umbrellas.

"What the hell are you doing here in the rain? Aren't you supposed to be in a class?"

"No. We don't really have classes. You can choose to attend a class if you fancy. You're not obligated. I mean, I'm not supposed to be attending lectures. I'm way past that. Maybe I'm supposed to be in a room somewhere writing my thesis." Luzuko took out the bundle of pamphlets, showing them to Nomusa.

"Togo?" Nomusa almost whispered, running her eyes over the page and leaning closer into Luzuko.

"Yes."

"Is that your thesis?"

"No. It's a campaign."

"What campaign? Is it part of your thesis?"

Another car whizzed by. A huddle of four men suddenly appeared on the pavement in front of them. Bongani and his three friends.

"My man!" Bongani laughed, sliding in under Luzuko's umbrella with him. "What the hell you doing here?"

"Handing out pamphlets." Luzuko's voice crawled in on itself.

"We're still cool, right?" Bongani leaned into Luzuko's ear, whispering, sliding his hands into the pockets of his checked jacket.

"Yeah, yeah, yeah." Luzuko gently touched him on the chest, pushing him away.

"Busy with my sister, Nomusa, I see." Bongani winked at Nomusa. "You need a woman, my man. And Nomusa is just perfect for you."

"Yeah, yeah, yeah," Nomusa came in. "Bongani, guys …" Nomusa's eyes stayed on the huddled two. "Now please leave us, as you were going along your way, anyway."

"My sister," Patrick singled himself out and stood right in front of Nomusa, "let me take you out for something warm to eat and drink."

"And who's this, Bongani?" Nomusa wagged her finger at Patrick, looking Bongani straight in the eyes.

"Patrick," Bongani almost whispered, "please don't bother my sister, man." Bongani gently pulled Patrick away by the arm. "And how's your mother doing, by the way?"

"None of your business," said Nomusa in a huff. "Now please take your friend and leave us."

"I'm concerned, Nomusa." Bongani raised his voice slightly. "I'm worried. That's it. She's paperless. And we don't want Thames Valley chasing after her. She's too old for that."

"You should rather concern yourself with your own situation, and how it's already unleashed Thames Valley on us. You've roped us all into your shit."

"Now we're not sure about that," Bongani sighed, looking heavenwards. "Let's go, guys." He shoved his hands deeper into his jacket pockets. "Luzuko, I'll see you later." Bongani was smiling as he walked off with his huddle. "You'll catch us at the Bullingdon Arms if you so wish," he shouted back at them, raising his arm.

"Sharp!" Luzuko shouted back.

"This guy's got such a nerve." Nomusa's voice dragged low. "He walks about so freely as if Thames Valley is not after him." She turned to smile at Luzuko. "And now you ... you're coming home with me for a pizza, a bowl of soup and a chat. I'm sure you're done with Togo for the day. People are rushing home now anyway. They don't care to snatch up any of your pamphlets about what's happening in a place that many here have only vaguely heard of. They don't even know where Togo is in Africa. I don't even know where Togo is. And I couldn't care less. Now, come with me for a pizza and some soup."

...

Nomusa sat down on the sofa with a bowl of soup. Blowing softly, she took a slice of pizza from a plate resting on the table. She moved back, easing herself into the sofa.

"Do you think it's wise?" Nomusa chewed on.

"What?" Luzuko swallowed a spoonful of soup.

"Mixing with Bongani and his crew?"

"He needed a place to stay." Luzuko bit into a slice of pizza. His finger helped guide into his mouth a falling crumble of cheese and pepperoni. "So I helped him out. I'm just helping him out."

"He's chaos." Nomusa spooned around the soup. "He's going to blow up in your face."

"He's a bit playful." Luzuko scooped up more soup.

"You mean disorderly, Luzuko."

"Come on."

"You know how he ended up homeless? Did he tell you why?"

"No. Come to think of it, I never actually asked."

"Police. The police have been looking for him since he

escaped from detention in Heathrow."

"Mmh?" He hummed through bloated cheeks, a mouthful of pizza and soup.

"Two years back, they had him in detention, waiting to deport him back to South Africa. And he escaped. He just walked out of the airport building when an immigration official got a bit careless."

"What?" Luzuko shifted, seating himself on the edge of the sofa.

"So ... be careful around him."

Silence.

Nomusa bit into another slice.

"But I guess you're all sorted?" she said.

"What do you mean?" Luzuko fluffed the dust of pizza off his hands.

"Papers. You've got papers, right?"

"Yeah. I have a student visa. I had it renewed three months back."

"Wow. Just like that?"

"Yep."

"Then what do you want from Bongani and his crew?"

"I guess I want to belong. I just want to be part of something, part of a people, part of a community here in Oxford."

"I guess we all want something here, searching for something." She let out a quiet giggle.

"And what do you want here?"

Nomusa folded her chin into her hand, heaving out a long breath.

"I want to belong, Nomusa," Luzuko continued, shifting closer to the edge of the sofa. "Is that so hard to understand? Belonging brings so much peace and comfort and confidence to a person. White Oxford rejects me, unless I accept how it sees me, which is as just another anthropological curiosity, an Area Studies. And black Oxford leaves me with a deep sense of revulsion. It hankers so badly after whiteness and does not want to go back home. It makes me want to vomit."

"And so ... have you found a sense of belonging with us?"

Luzuko slid back on the sofa. "I'm not sure. I don't think so. I want to. I want to so bad. But I'm now beginning to think that I haven't found it with you guys either. You also reject me."

"Redemption," Nomusa almost whispered.

"Mmh?"

"That's the word I've been looking for. Redemption." Nomusa folded her arms across her breast. "'I have swept your offences like a cloud / your sins like the morning mist / Return to me / for I have redeemed you.' Isaiah 44, verse 22."

"Wow! The Bible ... You know your Bible quite well. I'm impressed."

"Well, I was meant to be a nun."

"Really?"

"I studied Theology and Social Work at university, before I made ..." Nomusa dropped her head, resting her elbows on her knees. A silence fell between them. "I'm sorry, Luzuko." She sniffed, swiping her nose with the back of her hand. "I guess I've never really told myself my own story. I've never confessed my story, even to myself. I've never said it out loud. I guess that's how scared I've been of my own past. Saying it sounds so strange and so foreign and so scary." Another silence fell between them.

Nomusa brought her plate closer, gesticulating with a slice of pizza in her hand.

"I was awarded a scholarship," Nomusa continued, "for university. From the Roman Catholic Church. We are Catholics in my family. I got a four-year university scholarship to study a Bachelor of Social Sciences in Theology and Social Work in Durban. It was a full scholarship, covering tuition, residence and meals. Well, the condition was that I become a nun. I was training to be a nun specialising in social work.

A nun-social worker, I suppose. I lived in residence, in the centre of campus, with two other students doing the same course, all of us trainee nuns. We went to lectures and tutorials, wrote exams, took Theology classes on campus and at the diocese on Umbilo Road."

She hesitated briefly before continuing.

"I was happy. I was fulfilled, Luzuko. I was the first person at home to go to university. I was going to be the first person in my family to graduate with a degree. And then, towards the end of my second year of studies, I let it all slip away in one act of recklessness. I really don't know what came over me. I guess it had been coming all along. 'Don't befriend that man. Don't befriend that man, Nomusa.' They warned me. The other two student nuns warned me, time and again. But I didn't see anything wrong chatting with, even befriending him – that security guard. He was twice my age. And he was married. He was like a father to me."

She cleared her throat.

"We had become close. Very close. And then, one evening, in an act of carelessness that overwhelmed me, I let him in, Luzuko. I had never known a man before that. I let him in. I let him inside me, Luzuko. And I swore that I'd never do it again. No one knew about what I'd done. It was our secret. But then, early the following year, I started becoming sick. Then, I realised that I'd fallen pregnant.

"And then, bam! Everything took a spin. I lost everything. I mean everything, Luzuko. Everything. I lost my scholarship. I was ex-communicated from the Church. I returned home with a bump. Then I had my baby, a girl. And two months later, my baby girl died. I became a source of humiliation to my family. I can't wipe away the memory of that disappointment, that humiliation, that look of shame from my mother. The way people in my neighbourhood looked at me. I can't wipe away that memory. I even tried to console myself that I hadn't done anything wrong. I came up with 1 Timothy 4, verse 3: 'They forbid people to marry and order them to abstain from certain foods, which God created to be received with thanksgiving by those who believe and who know the truth.' I went that far in trying to convince myself that I hadn't done anything wrong, anyway. But I was wrong. I had made a commitment, and I had broken that commitment. I had been insincere. Some began calling me a 'bitch-nun'. And then I ran away, from my past, from my shame. That's why I'm here, to seek redemption."

Luzuko stayed silent, looking away.

"And how do you want to redeem yourself?"

"Simple really, Luzuko." Nomusa sniffed, her head looking down between her knees. "My family is still poor. I couldn't remain in South Africa and face all that shame, the loss, the darkness and sadness. It was way too big. What was I going to do there to get us out of poverty with a matric certificate? Wait on restaurant tables? Work as a maid in the suburbs? A cashier in a supermarket? Answer telephones at a call centre? And earn what? For how long? I had to come here, to earn proper, decent wages so that when I return home, I can take the smug off of those people who called me a 'bitch-nun'. So that I can glorify myself in some kind of wealth in the presence of all those who mocked me. That's the promise of my redemption here in England, here in Oxford. Come rain or shine, I'm going to redeem myself, if it's the last thing I do, even if I hang with my last breath." Nomusa sniffed, lifting her head.

TWENTY-EIGHT

EDDIE SWEPT HIS HAND in a circle over Grace's behind. The hem of her silk nightdress rolled farther up to reach her waist. She turned to stare through the window, listening to the fray of electricity humping up her behind. Watching the yellow of the morning sun, the soft rays slivered through the parting in the curtain, leaving behind an outline of the window's small panes. Another volt of Eddie's static rushed through her.

His index finger moved slowly up along the edge of her white cotton panty. She pursed her lips and held on to a moan, her eyes fixed on a silhouette of a small bird chirping in a tree in the garden outside. On its third chirp, she felt his finger snooping through the side gate of her panty. The roughness of his palms worked her behind, up and around and down and sideways. She let out another whispering moan.

The roundness of the sun's yellowness became bolder.

The little bird flittered and flapped away. Eddie's finger suddenly slid down beneath and inside her panty, wedging itself along its edge. Two fingers slid fully beneath, teasing the hairs of the grove. Grace hauled her waist up, allowing the two fingers full reach of her. A wetness came out at all the scratchy moves of the two fingers. Hearing the rushes of her own breathing, she shut her eyes. The warmth of the sun descended on her face. And from afar, she caught the hiss of a bus door opening.

The electricity moved and swayed around her. She lifted her waist farther up, a hand roughly fondling the sheet. Three fast snaps, and the panty slid down her legs. Holding tight to everything, a rushed breeze slid under the duvet. Eddie's right hand slithered beneath her hips, gently flipping her over. The rays of the sun shone more brashly through the window now. The floral purple and orange and yellow of the thick curtain came out deeper. A thick sliver of yellow crept through the parting, settling on Grace's face.

"Yes." A lisp followed the sharpness of her whisper.

"Mmh?" Eddie groaned, his hand fondling one breast.

Grace nodded softly. "It's okay." She let out another whisper, her hand reaching for his cheek. "Come inside … Please. It's okay. Come inside." She drew him in, pulling his head to her neck. He heaved out a full steam of breath. And then he swallowed her lips. Breathing out full and slow, he circled her cheek with his finger.

"Come," she released his lips, grasping his waist with both arms and slowly parting her legs. And she felt his weight shoving inside her. She closed her eyes, biting her lips. She opened up, rolling and weaving and bobbing, rising and flattening. A well crashed inside her. And everything came flooding out.

Eddie scooped up her waist with one hand. Swaying her hips mid-air, she threw up her hand, drawing him closer by the back of his neck. Flipping out her tongue, she gasped. He slotted himself inside her with a soft heaviness. Two rapid breaths. Biting her lower lip, she swayed her hips around to a slow grind. He slipped inside her again, in and out, slowly working out a steamy moan.

Every pore in her body opened. Eddie threw himself back next to her. And then Jacob flew into her mind. When he had worked at the mine in Jo'burg, he had sent her back to the floor after sex. She hadn't come. And he didn't care, never asked if she was happy. When they lived in the rural areas of the Midlands in KwaZulu-Natal, the bed she had bought in Jo'burg was propped up against the wall. It waited there and was moved only when she swept the floor. It waited there, against the wall, for Jacob's return from the mines every four to six months. The bed only sat on all fours on the floor when he was home for a few weeks. And he slept on it alone – she took the floor. He only allowed her on when he wanted her for sex. And it had been his sex, and his sex only, for those few minutes.

Eddie lay his head on her breast. She listened to the bristling of his rushed breaths through the big hairs of his nostrils. Tousling and caressing his sweaty, sandy hair, Grace then came to know. It was possible. She finally came to know. It was possible for a fifty-five-year-old married woman to fall in love with a man she was not married to. She knew that she was happy. The kind of happiness she knew she would still find waiting for her the following day, and the day after tomorrow. It is such a pity that I have to find such love and happiness so late, and so far from home.

•••

Grace skipped up the staircase at Debenhams. Each step brought a breeze. Wind flapped past her face. Smiling, she held on to the rail as she climbed the stairs. The Saturday afternoon had a fresh, lazy feel to it. She had set her mind to buying herself a skirt and two blouses, a pair of stilettoes and a new pair of boots. She had to plunge herself deep into her first wage packet.

Standing in the women's clothing section not far from the coffee shop, she soaked up the polite clamour. A few mothers and their daughters swung skirts and blouses from the displays. In front of her, a lady flipped through a row of denim jeans. A matronly woman right ahead of her hovered over a tray of lipsticks. Grace strode briskly towards the cosmetics section. She was running out of rouge. And perhaps some face powder and mascara. With her back to the ageing matron, she picked up a rouge lipstick, wondering whether she should switch to purple.

A tap on her shoulder, and Grace turned around.

"Ma." In front of her stood Nomusa, clad in tight faded jeans.

"Nomusa." Grace smiled, instantly noticing the hesitation in her daughter's shy beam and the young man next to her.

"Hello, young man." Grace extended her hand to him.

"Sorry, Ma. This is my friend, Luzuko."

"Hello, Luzuko."

"Hello, Ma."

"So, Ma," Nomusa pointed at Luzuko, "Luzuko here is an Oxford student from Grahamstown."

"Wonderful." Grace shuffled out a whispered laugh. "New boyfriend?"

"No, Ma." Nomusa blushed. "He's just a friend. Really, just a friend."

"No shame, my girl." Grace turned to face Luzuko. "He looks like a nice, decent young man."

Nomusa pushed out a cough. "So, what a coincidence bumping into you here after such a long time."

"Come on," Grace said, "it's only been two months. It hasn't been that long."

"But you're at Debenhams, shopping," Nomusa went on. "You have money, I see."

"My first pay, my child. Imagine."

"Wow."

"Come, let's get some coffee." Grace waved at both of them. "I'm paying. And perhaps some muffins. Young man, Luzuko, are you joining us?"

"That's very kind of you, Ma," said Luzuko, "but I need to use the bathroom first, if you don't mind."

"Not at all," Nomusa cut in. "Go ahead. You'll find us at one of the tables over there – at the coffee shop."

"Good, good." Luzuko touched Nomusa's shoulder before heading off to the restrooms.

Grace and Nomusa made their way over to the coffee shop, sitting at the first open table they spotted.

"My child," Grace heaved out a slow, heavy huff, "you have no idea how happy I am to see you. And I hope – I sincerely hope – that we won't fight. Not now."

Nomusa twiddled her thumbs.

"I'm sorry, my child." Grace reached out her hands, resting them on Nomusa's nervous thumbs. Nomusa looked up, into her eyes.

"I know what I put you through, Nomusa. And there's no excuse for what I did. I ... I don't know what came over me. I really don't have an excuse for what I did to you and my granddaughter."

"They're still on my case, Ma." Nomusa sniffed, wiping away one big tear. "The police, Thames Valley, and the social workers, they're still on my case. And I just don't know what to do any more."

"I'm so sorry, my child." Grace tightened her grip on her daughter's hand. "I am so, so terribly sorry."

"I really don't know what I'm going to do, Ma." Nomusa wiped away another tear. "And now they've brought Angelina's father into it."

"Shh ... shh ..."

"It's just a mess, Ma. A mess."

A waitress, her blonde hair ponytailed and shirtsleeves rolled up, came over to their table to take orders. Nomusa asked for a strawberry smoothie. Grace turned the laminated menu over and ordered a bran muffin with a cappuccino.

"Nomusa." Grace let out a slow breath once the waitress had left with their orders. "Let's start over – please, my child."

Nomusa looked away.

"I know that it's going to take some time to close the wounds I have opened up. But let's start afresh here, in Oxford."

Nomusa rubbed her nose with one finger, her other hand taking Grace's hand in hers.

"But, Ma, how do we start living our lives on such shaky ground? Where we are now? We are now both illegal here."

"I don't know, my child. I really don't know." Grace looked up, her hand still enclosed by Nomusa's. "I started by breaking up with my present back in South Africa."

"What do you mean, Ma?"

"That I've left him ... more or less. It's over."

"How? In a letter? A married woman breaking up with a married man in a letter, Ma?"

"Yes. Breaking up with someone has to start somewhere. What matters is that I've started. I've begun my journey to freedom and happiness."

Nomusa sighed.

"And I have a new man now." Grace flashed a smile.

Nomusa stared at her. "So, it's true, Ma? Every South African in Oxford knows about it."

"It's my supervisor at work. He's Scottish. Eddie McKenzie. And we kind of live together now."

"I ... I don't know what to say. I don't want to judge. I ... I ..."

"Well, I was also startled by how fast it all went. But, Nomusa, in my whole life, I've never been so happy, so free, so womanly, so myself in my own skin."

TWENTY-NINE

EVERYTHING SAT AT THE split of the fork. I had grown not to trust anything Bongani said. And I didn't know how to feel when he assured me that he was going to spend the last night at my place at Summertown House. I could not yet leap for joy, nor collapse from the weight of anxiety. As I rolled my bike out of the lift on the ground floor of Summertown House, my heart sat at the split of the fork.

I listened to my bicycle chain. I had just laced it with oil, and there was a precise knack-knack sound. The main steel gate let out its usual creak, opening out onto the pavement across from the well-kept green lawn. I pedalled slowly to the main gate, passing Marcus, a Canadian History doctoral student at Mansfield College who was writing a thesis on the Second World War Battle of El Alamein. I waved and then took a swift right turn towards the city centre.

Three streets down, forking to the left, was Jackson Road where, a little bit farther down, Bafana and I had made a rather strange discovery. On one forlorn, dry and penniless Saturday afternoon, we had stumbled across an upmarket brothel operating from a modest, nondescript white-painted house with ivy running up the wall. And the exceptionally beautiful women we saw there had the smoothest and silkiest skin we'd ever seen.

I had left Bongani in my room, curled up under a duvet and heavy blanket. The night before, it had finally spilled out of me. I had to get tough with him. It had been close to three months since he had moved in and nothing had changed. Nothing had shifted in any manner whatsoever. And yet, everything about me, in me, had changed in ways that shamed me deeply. I had embraced a life other than my own. My red dragon had dragged me down with him, to a level I never thought I would see.

I had now grown to working scattered shifts. And those shifts were growing farther apart, more sprinkled. It had become a matter of touch and go. We would go on benders, often days at a time, and I would miss work for a week. The intermissions of recovery sapped my energy, leaving me hung over and dry. Once, I woke up with blood seeping from my nostrils. And I knew it was from the endless Foster's.

By the time I crawled back to work a week and a half down the line, I found myself grasping at straws. Touch and go, a flip and scratch and go – where I had left a chapter write-up; my notes on a literary review; where I had left off my data analysis and interpretation of the quantitative research findings I had collected from my fieldwork research; the marathon e-mail reads and responses. As recovery began to gain ground, and my strength slowly came back, another weekend with Bongani would start up. It was Sodom and JD Wetherspoon's and the non-stop drinking all over again.

"You need to go, Bongani." That was how I had started our conversation the night before, as I wiped dry the small pot I had used to cook the mushroom sauce for the chicken roast.

"Mmh?" Bongani had taken one foot from the small table in front of the TV.

I let out a staccato cough. "It's been nearly three months now, Bongani." I felt an opening in my chest pouring inner resentment. Until then, I had been shuffling and swerving around sentences and phrases and pauses and exclamation marks. They just couldn't come out. I knew that all they needed was a push, one slight nudge. And I had finally done that. I watched Bongani staring at his foot on the blue-carpeted floor.

"Three more weeks? Please, Luzuko?"

"No, no, no." They had all leapt out of me, each "no" filing fast after another, leaving a hard thud of a stomp. "You need to go. Tomorrow."

"You know I was supposed to move to Banbury with Hugo. And you know Hugo's been deported."

"Look, Bongani ..."

"He was arrested right in front of us. On that bus to Blackbird Leys. You were there, remember?"

"I don't care, Bongani."

"And now my plans have all been messed up. Everything. I can't make my next move out of Oxford. I need to think and reassess everything. Please ... just give me a little more time."

"I said I don't care, Bongani."

"Where am I supposed to go, Luzuko? Mmh?"

"I don't care. Just go. Leave ... tomorrow."

Now I pedalled past Marks & Spencer, leaving a pub with a beer garden and pavement café a block behind me. I thought of the tact, the stops and pauses, the hesitancy and swerving of my confrontation with Bongani the previous night. I didn't want to remind him of the near brushes with Thames Valley. I didn't go into any of that. At the Gloucester Green bus station in the city centre, on the way to the Oxford train station, Bongani had yanked me back to hide in the toilets at the sight of two oncoming police officers. When did I start hiding from the law? Bongani and his crew reminded me of hamsters on a treadmill ... endless running and running and running but getting nowhere. And I couldn't be on that wheel with them.

"Okay." Bongani wiped his forehead.

I didn't think it would be wise to offer my help in moving him out. Anyway, he had brought nothing with him but one large suitcase and a gym bag.

"But first," Bongani had continued, "we need to go out, the two of us." He stared at me.

"Didn't you hear what I said? I'm behind with my work."

"One last night, Luzuko. Let's drink one last night, and then we can part ways, please."

I heaved a sigh, flinging the dishcloth to the counter.

"Just ..." Bongani coughed, "just to thank you for your kindness, my friend, from the bottom of my heart."

I came to a stop sign. Summertown was behind me, St Giles just ahead, closer to the city centre. Admittedly, it had not all been bad though. Perhaps Bongani had pushed me towards finding myself – a self no one else had dared make me confront. And in Sodom, I might have begun to make peace with where my father had vanished to – the North. Memories of travels to the North are never told. They are not relayed. They are best forgotten.

"To the West is the House of Fortune. To the East the House of Fire. At times, we travel to the South. As for the North ... it is best forgotten." Since that evening in Sodom, I had rolled Tata Linda's poetry over my head, wondering over and over again. My father had suffered a nervous breakdown. Two, in fact. I could not for the life of me imagine a person carrying that kind of weight. I really wanted to understand what a person having had a nervous breakdown looked like. I had researched it. But still, I could not imagine it.

There was a sense of vacancy about losing one's mind, one's faculties. It was far too delicate for words to wield and mould into shape. I thought far back to a time when

I had seen a man grabbing at and letting go of his slippery faculties, like my father might have done, right when the struggle against apartheid was ending. Had it been two minutes? Five, perhaps? It had been no more than a lingering moment, yes, but I had witnessed first hand *Tata*, my grandfather, losing his faculties.

I saw a big man reduced to a child. It was in the way his eyes became blank, fumbling at the emptiness in front of him. In how his eyes shifted – hollow, holding his fork upside down, poking at his plate with the blunt end, the sharp prongs folded in his fist. "There-there, my dear, there …" Mama had whispered the same tender words, again and again and again, quietly turning the fork around. And in those two, five minutes, my grandfather had travelled to his North and returned from it quiet. Had my father's North been like this too?

From the time he graduated from university back in the late forties, *Tata* had been in and out of prison. First, it had been short detentions. Then there was the big arrest following the Sharpeville massacre, which saw him and his cousin on Robben Island for three years. After his release, there were long and short stints in various prisons, more detentions and banning orders, more tortures in every decade.

I pedalled slowly through St Giles, thinking of Bongani, my red dragon, my albatross letting go of my shoulders. I looked forward to returning to my normalcy. I had missed it. Climbing off my bike, I made my way into the postgraduate computer centre, and straight to my spot in the second to last row of seats. I scrabbled through my thoughts, waiting for my e-mail inbox to open.

And there it was, tucked away in the middle of my new e-mails. FROM THE GHOST OF MARECHERA, the title read. An e-mail from: <u>marechera48@hotmail.com</u>. "Things are not what they seem. Birds festoon the skies. But they all eventually end up on the dust of the ground, where they all come from."

I read it again and again, searching the emptiness, the barrenness of the floor of the e-mail. There was nothing else – not even an anonymous signature. As I worked on my thesis that day, I kept on going back to that Marechera e-mail address. Around lunchtime, I asked for assistance from the centre's IT technician, but even she could not get beyond that the address domain was in the United Kingdom. And so, I resigned myself to getting back to work. Then, as the night drew closer, I pulled on my backpack and cycled back to Summertown House to prepare for my last night out with Bongani.

•••

"Fuck my table," my Ghanaian friend hollered at me as I zipped my pants. Hovering over his counter with its assortment of hand lotions, aftershaves and cologne in the toilet at Mood, I saw his cheeks firming behind his well-trimmed beard.

"Charlie, fuck my table," he shouted, his eyes boring into me.

"No," I said, listening to the rush of water down the sink as I washed my hands.

"Charlie, I said fuck my table," he yelled over Ja Rule's hit about what had happened last night, and over a toilet flush.

"Charlie," I lowered my voice, and rolled out a paper towel, "I need to get back to my friends out there. And I'm missing my favourite number." Bottle after bottle of Thailand's Tiger lager fermented in my head over Ja Rule. I had actually begun to enjoy my last night out with Bongani, Patrick and Mkhize.

"Charlie, fuck my table," he shouted again.

"Aargh, Charlie!" I raised my voice. "I fucked your table with a fiver two weeks back, didn't I? Who has ever fucked your table with more than a quid? And I don't even use your stuff." I moved away from the door to allow two other men inside.

"Did I say fuck my table two weeks back, or fuck my table now?"

A sudden push of the door flung me forward.

"So, you fuck tables now?" Josh was staring down at me.

"Josh, my man," I cheered, throwing myself at him. "Good to see you, man."

"So, you do tables now?" he frowned.

I looked over at Charlie, smiling, and then back at Josh. "You won't understand."

"Yeah, yeah ..." Josh scoffed, the lines on his forehead becoming sharper. "That's true – there's a lot of things I don't understand about you these days, Luzuko."

"What do you mean?"

"Where have you been these past months?"

"Around. I've been around, man." I threw my hands about. "Come, let's get back inside," I said. "I'll buy you a Tiger. Oh, and I'll introduce you to my South African friends ..."

"I don't wanna meet your homies, man." I saw that bored, unmoved Josh frown. "You running around with immigrants now, I hear."

"You heard?"

"Yeah. Running around with illegal immigrants now, Luzuko. What happened? What's happening to you? How did you get to this?"

"Who told you that?"

"Everyone knows."

A silence fell over me, my mind twisted by eleven questions.

"You still working on that thesis of yours?" Josh asked.

"Yes, of course."

"If you're not hobnobbing with illegal immigrants, then you're running around with Dela's Togolese shenanigans."

"Look, Josh, I'm fine."

"Have you even confirmed your status?"

"In a few weeks."

"Whatever happened to what I've been telling you, mmh? Focus on the ball, mate. Don't lose sight of the ball. Keep your eyes on the ball." His forefinger stabbed me fast and hard on my chest.

I stumbled back, balancing against Charlie's table.

"Josh, I'm done talking to you," I said, standing straight. "You can keep your advice to yourself from now on."

"There's no from now on, Luzuko. I'm flying out to Juba tomorrow."

"South Sudan?"

"Going to practise medicine in some of the conflict regions. I'll be back in a year for graduation. I couldn't even tell you that I successfully defended my thesis three weeks ago, because you were busy bollocking with your illegal immigrant friends and Dela's Togolese nonsense."

I watched Josh turn away, heading out the door to Michael Jackson's 'Blood on the Dance Floor'.

THIRTY

I SLOWED DOWN AT THE beginning of St Giles, pedalling in reverse as I turned towards Queen Elizabeth House. I was two days from submitting my package for the confirmation of status – an introduction, a chapter on theory and theoretical analysis, as well as two substantive body chapters. The package had to be presented that way, nothing more and nothing less.

There was to be no improvisation when it came to the order of the confirmation of status package. If you didn't go through that phase, you simply could not proceed. You would not get the official go-ahead to continue with the write-up of your thesis. I supposed you could go ahead on your own and finish writing, but the confirmation of status paperwork – whether you passed or not – had to be filed at the administration offices at Wellington Square House.

There was no going about it your own way with the order of the confirmation of status package. I remembered, three semesters back, hopping on a bus from the city centre to Summertown with Bafana and his buddy Vernon from Nelspruit, Mpumalanga. He was a doctoral student in Social Work and Social Policy at Mansfield College. He was ashen faced, livid – thrown off, in complete disbelief. His confirmation of status had gone south very swiftly from the get-go of his meeting with his examiner.

We were in the back seat. Between us, Vernon – tall, well built, strikingly handsome – sat with his legs apart. Breathing hard, he thumped his neatly packaged papers. His voice raised, he went on and on about how unfair his examiner had been. He had minced his narratives in single space, he explained, and so ended up with more words on a page than was demanded.

"It's not about the word count, Vernon," Bafana had said, balancing a hand on the seat as the bus swerved. "You were not required to submit a third body chapter. The package is an introduction, theory and two body chapters. And you submitted one more body chapter. Words minced into single spacing – that doesn't mean anything. You'll have to do it all over again, Vernon. That's it."

I had not seen Josh since that night at Mood. His phone had gone dead. I had sent him three e-mails, but then recalled what he used to say: "I'm not really good with e-mails, mate." That was the Josh I missed. The Josh who found the entire concept of a bedtime read to lull him to sleep ridiculous. He simply switched off immediately when his head hit the pillow. I missed the Josh completely disconnected from literary fiction. The Josh who cut through the cobwebs of complexities that I had unnecessarily made up.

"Stuck," he had suggested, standing behind my chair in my apartment at Summertown House. I was sitting in front of my laptop, the cursor hovering over the first draft of a short story I had just completed, in need of a catchy title. Without any effort whatsoever, he had swiftly given me such a precise title, replacing the almost sentence-long one I had chosen. "'Stuck' – call it 'Stuck'. Now, let's go," he had said, rushing me to put on my shoes and coat before we missed happy hour at Mood.

I pedalled on slowly, overtaking a bus that had swooshed to a stop. I had ample time before the seminar at Queen Elizabeth House. Dela had put together a seminar on pro-democracy processes and campaigns in Togo. I guessed it was the test phase at the end of the first leg of the advocacy campaign we had been driving in Oxford.

We expected quite a crowd. Our supervisor had promised to come, and I also expected to see my Jamaican internal examiner from Harris Manchester College who had transferred my status. I had last seen her at the Ian Smith debate.

After the bus doors had shut, I heard a sweet voice behind me calling my name. Turning my head, I saw her rushing up to me, carrying a big beige leather bag. I climbed off the bike and hoisted it onto the pavement.

"Hi," Nomusa panted, fiddling with the straps of the bag around her shoulder.

"*Yebo*," I smiled at her. "So, we meet again."

"I'm on my way to my new job in Summertown." Her words came out in short bursts as she tried to catch her breath.

"The nursing job?" I wondered out loud.

"Yeah."

"Aren't you going to be late?"

"No, I still have time." Nomusa reached for my arm. "Luzuko, listen, man. I got off the bus when I saw you because I need to talk to someone."

"Yeah?"

"My mom ... she's disappeared. It's been a few days now. I mean, I can't reach her on her phone. Her number is 'unavailable' all of a sudden."

"And her place?"

"That's the problem. I don't know where she lives. And I

don't know exactly where she works. My friend, who helped her get that job, has moved to Liverpool and has changed her mobile number. And I don't have her boyfriend's number. I'm worried sick, Luzuko. I don't know what to do. And, of course, I can't go to the police."

I stared straight into her face, lost for words.

"I understand, Luzuko." She placed her hand on my forearm. "I just needed someone to talk to." She caressed my forearm. Then, suddenly, she let go, and I watched her head back to the bus stop.

I parked my bike on the rack outside Queen Elizabeth House and locked it. Loosening my backpack and slipping it off my back, I strode towards the hall. The door was open wide, and I headed straight to the podium. Slamming the backpack on the wide, mahogany table, I opened it and poured out its contents. Programme flyers and leaflets.

Walking up and down the rows of chairs, I placed a flyer on each seat. It felt like I was preparing for a funeral service.

"L-Lu-zuko Goba." I turned around to see Dela standing at the entrance. Dropping his brown leather briefcase to the floor, he took off his glasses and, breathing onto the lens, wiped them with the scarf draped around his neck.

"Dela!" My smile emerged with a sparkle.

"Ever diligent," Dela said, sliding his glasses back to his eyes. "You ... you've already started with the preparations." He walked past a row of empty chairs, lifting a flyer and then putting it straight back on the chair. We huddled around the main table as I listened to his soft, measured tone. This was a day not just for Togo, but for Africa, he started. It was a life-and-death mission. We need to learn to transcend the idea of democracy and human rights, shift it from simple academic discourse to real life. Translated to the day-and-night experiences of the ordinary man and woman of Togo, and Africa, he said. That was our duty, as scholars and activists. We have to reduce these experiences to their simplest manifestations. And then he rounded up with the Frantz Fanon quote of a generation's mission from *The Wretched of the Earth*.

Four women had walked in quietly as I listened. Anna Mwangi was there with Bernadette, her lover from Llandudno in Wales who was completing a postgraduate diploma in tourism and management at Oxford Brookes University. Dela, Vernon, Bafana, Wilson and I once spent a long, soulful night in their apartment on St Giles. In a candle-lit room, I remembered Bernadette's languid way of pouring red wine into our glasses. The allure was in the way she pulled and tossed her dark, wavy hair to her back without even knowing that she was pulling you into her.

Sprawled out on their dark Persian rug against a background of fifties' African-American women singing blues, we chatted the night away. Right up until the first glimpses of dawn, we weaved in and out of African politics, world cultures, journal publications, and who hates who and connives with who to scam which scholarly grants and funds among Oxford's Africanist scholars.

Smiling as they approached, both Anna and Bernadette waved at us. Then Donald Dudzai walked in with some British woman, his new lover. Dudzai had completed his undergraduate Theology degree at Brasenose College and, soon after, had joined Thames Valley. I stared at him, playing in my mind my last conversation with him three weeks back.

"Luzuko." Dudzai had stopped me as I bundled out of Waterstones. I suspected that lurking behind his sneaky smile was a snide remark he had restrained himself from making about me and illegal immigrants.

"Dudzai." I stood in front of him, pulling out a copy of Rachel Seiffert's novel, *The Dark Room*, as well as the recent biography of Miles Davis. "So, what are you up to these days?" I had asked him, my eyes staying on my books, slotting them carefully back into the plastic bag.

"Well, I've passed my Theology degree."

"So, are you preparing to be ordained now back in Zim?"

He let out a soft, staggering laugh. His eyes seemed bloodshot, wet and swollen. "I've just joined Thames Valley," he said, shoving one hand into the pocket of his brown chinos. Then a large British woman with a shiny, pudgy face and ponytailed hair shot up from behind him.

"This is Sarah, my fiancée." Dudzai moved his hand between Sarah and me. "Sarah, this is Luzuko, a South African doctoral student in Politics and International Relations."

"Nice to meet you, Luzuko," Sarah smiled, extending her hand to me.

"Likewise." I took her hand delicately, as if I was about to kiss it.

"Love, I'll be at Borders," said Sarah, planting a soft kiss on his cheek. We watched her walking off into Cornmarket Street.

"So, yes, where were we?" Dudzai picked up our conversation. "As I was saying, I've just joined Thames Valley. Beating the streets for now. But soon I'll join Oxfordshire's detective desk. I'm on a year-long detective training course."

"So, you're a policeman now, Dudzai?"

"Yes. Yes, I am." He shoved his hand deeper into his trouser pocket, the lines on his forehead grown thicker.

"When are you going back to Zimbabwe?"

"When Mugabe's dead."

"But you won't have democracy and human rights when the likes of you stick around here forever. You and your lot are fast becoming perpetual exiles here, there and everywhere now. You have to go home and fight for what you want. You have to go home and fight for the democracy and the human rights you want. No one is going to fight for you. And fighting for it while you're here won't have the same effect as when you're on home soil. You have to go home and fight for it there, and die there if you must, fighting for it."

"I'm not going to sacrifice my life for Zimbabwe. Never."

I watched Dudzai draw out a chair for his fiancée. She

pulled down the Mexican shawl draped over her shoulder and, sliding back on her seat, crossed her legs at the ankles. I followed him, greeting Anna and Bernadette.

Dela's voice slithered faintly into my ear. Standing next to me, both of us hovering over draft notes of his opening address, he explained how I should tuck in one paragraph, shuffle it to the beginning, bring two sentences from the end to the third paragraph. A particular phrase came out grandiloquent, another far too academic to take the crowd's breath away. "Work them out. Simplify them," he said.

I turned more purposefully to the notes as Dela moved off. I watched him biting down on his lower lip. Then his lips shifted to a tremble. Searching his face, I could not figure out what had troubled him so suddenly.

Osman stood at the entrance with what appeared to be some British chap I had never seen before. He laughed so freely, greeting a number of African students streaming through the door. His white-cream scarf was thrown carefully around his neck, his black Kennedy tie fixed neatly beneath his Adam's apple. As usual, he wore a black suit and white shirt. In a purple jersey, white shirt, and light khaki trousers, the British gentleman next to Osman smiled broadly.

I scanned the room for Dela and spotted him not far off. He had his back to me, typing a text on his phone. When he finally turned to face me, I openly hunted the plains of his face. He simply stared back at me, and then returned to his phone. By now, Osman and the British chap had gone their separate ways, the Englishman having taken a seat in the second row and Osman chatting among the crowd, smiling and laughing.

Standing behind the table, I hesitated, measuring the jostle. My eyes rushed through the throng of loud, bristling voices. Wilson had just walked in, his falsetto pitched high, running his hand over his paunch. I stared at Dela shuffling his handwritten notes. Lifting the small bell from the table, I tinkled away. Heads turned towards me, the din of voices abruptly coming to a hush.

"Ladies and gentlemen," I cleared my voice, plastering the palms of my hands on the table, "thank you ever so sincerely for taking the time to attend this seminar. Dela Owusu and I, and all the people of Oxford who love Togo, who cherish and want to nurture democracy and a culture of the good practice of human rights in Africa, thank you for taking precious time out of your busy schedules to participate. Today's discussions will focus on pro-democracy processes and activities and the practice of human rights ahead of the next elections in Togo. Dear lives, decent standards of living in Togo are at stake. So this seminar is invaluable. It hopes to contribute positively to advocating for what should be done to achieve free and sustainable multiparty democracy in Togo. And multiparty democracy in Togo is not the continuation of the Eyadéma regime in any guise. So, ladies and gentlemen, to launch this presentation with his opening address, please welcome onto the stage Togo's first stateless citizen in Oxford, Dela Owusu."

Standing to an ovation, the crowd cracked in laughter. Wilson sent out a brief, sharp whistle. Osman remained seated at the back, his ankles crossed. The British gent in the purple jersey stood up, clapping fiercely. I noticed his smile, so wide and his teeth so white.

"I ..." Dela opened his address amid a hushing crowd. "I came here by accident." His stutter had vanished, evolving into a slow, measured tone, dragging his sentences. "I was sitting in a bar in downtown Lomé as the sun set on a Thursday afternoon. I sat hunched over my quart of ice-cold Gulder, my tie slovenly skewed. I'd had a long day at the office, chasing and filing three political stories. They were to run for print, to come off fresh in the following day's morning newspaper. I had just written and published four stories on the massacre of a few weeks before. The heat and the sweat stuck against my chest. I ran my hands on the bruises on my wrists – eight-months-fresh wounds, credit to

Eyadéma's special police branch. I thought of going home to the rural areas in the south for the weekend. I wanted to go away from it all, just for a weekend.

"Before I knew it, I had floored my first quart of Gulder. I guessed that I was going to need five more of them, I remember thinking. I was not going to drive anyway. My old Beetle had, yet again, balked. I don't remember what the problem had been. It was too hot, and I was too tired to think of such details. Gearbox or piston or carburetor, I just couldn't remember. And I didn't care that *tro-tros*, the public minibus taxis, were going to run out for the night while I was in the depths of my Gulder.

"'Let's go.' I turned over my shoulder and saw my friend Leonard from the British Embassy.

"'What?' I had replied, thinking that he was whisking me away to a fancier joint patronised by diplomats. 'Let's go, right now.' I saw an edginess in his face that I had never seen before. 'Eyadéma's soldiers are looking for you. The order is that you be shot dead on the spot.'"

Slouched back on my seat with my arms folded, I smiled at the anecdote, which had clearly hit the spot. It had not been in the draft address I had seen. He had sprung it on me. And it had such a profound, individualised effect on me and the crowd. It brought a human face to the otherwise rigidly politicised and academic subject of democratisation in any country.

Dela then went on to talk about the political nature and wiles of the Eyadéma regime. Addressing first the brief history of the regime following the assassination of Sylvanus Olympio, he took us on a journey, a blow-by-blow account of the desecration of democracy and human rights in Togo. Then he talked about the importance and the plight of the opposition parties and civil society. I listened carefully to how he cascaded down to the end of his address, making a plea to Oxford to add its voice on the matter.

Dela bowed to a standing ovation. I stood up, opening

the floor for questions. The British gentleman in the purple jersey was the first to throw up his hand. Dela tugged my jacket so fast and so violently that I startled. I saw in his eyes a trace of sharp anger. But I had already pointed to the Brit.

"Thank you, Dela Owusu, for such an insightful, informative and animated address," the gentleman began. "You are surely an expert on the matter, what with your personal experiences and brushes with the Eyadéma regime. And that's exactly what I want to bring to focus here – the authenticity, the legitimacy of your political agency as a stateless exile from Togo.

"A lot of writers skip their countries and go into exile, claiming that their books and writings were seen as a threat to the stability of a rather rotten state. I admit, these states are rotten to the core. And in so many of these cases, such books, read by so few, and read by even fewer state security personnel, are, what shall we say, mildly irritating. To be perfectly honest, these writings don't drive the state to rampant killing. These writers are not important. They are not irritating enough. The writers have an insignificant reach among a population more concerned with buying staple foodstuffs than reading material. Maybe to the writers themselves, in the figment of their own imaginations, they are critically important and a nuisance to the stability of the state. But their books hardly make any impact on either the state or the masses, certainly not enough to drive the state to order the killing of writers."

At the back of the hall, Osman stood to his feet. What started briefly as a slow simmer had blown up into outburst. I ignored his hand shooting up and floating in the air.

"Chenjerai Hove!" Osman shouted from the back.

"I did not recognise your hand, Osman," I yelled to Osman.

"Chenjerai Hove," Osman continued, standing, his hand firmly on the back of the seat in front of him, "after publishing his fiction, left Zimbabwe for exile, claiming that the Zimbabwe Central Intelligence Organisation and the Zimbabwe Republic Police were after him. And yet there was no such. The Zimbabwe government even came out saying that they were not even aware that Chenjerai's books posed any threat to the stability of the Zimbabwean state. And many of these state personnel, who were astounded by Chenjerai's claims, had not even read his books. They had no idea who or what had chased Chenjerai out of the country. In fact, they were not even aware that he had left."

A loud, decidedly British voice from the middle row of seats boomed. I searched for the man, but could not pinpoint him in the simmer of the crowd that had grown warmer and louder.

"Mr Dela Owusu," Osman shouted louder, "who chased you out of Togo to exile?"

"Osman! Osman!" I shouted, pointing straight at him, and to the crowd's loud hissing and hackles.

"Or were you just a momentary itch for the Togolese government?" Osman went on without hesitating. "Did you chase yourself into exile, Dela Owusu?"

I felt Dela's grip on my jacket getting tighter. I looked down at him, watching him scribble on a piece of paper.

"Mr Chair," Anna had stood up, "we're not here to interrogate Dela's political credibility. We are here to deliberate on the state of democracy and human rights in Togo, for the benefit of the Togolese people."

"Ch-Che ..." I lowered my ear to Dela's whisper. His stutter had started up again. He wanted to say something about Chenjerai Hove. And his scribbled notes on Hove were incomplete and barely legible.

"The questions are, Dela Owusu: Who chased you into exile? To fight for who? And for what?" Osman blundered on, both his hands shoved even deeper into his trouser pockets. "A man in a throng of demonstrations is chased and beaten by the police, jailed for a day or three and then he goes into exile. Is that truly an exile? And so you left because you wanted to save yourself, as it were. No one in the state was looking to take you out, Dela. You know as well as I do that no one in the Togolese army or state was looking to take you out. There was no order that had gone out to take you out, Dela. I know that, and you know that. So, why are you stateless, Dela? Are you *really* stateless? Since your so-called fray with the police or military, or whatever, back then, for how long have you been stateless in exile, Dela? Are they still looking out for you with your little column pieces read by so few in a population that can barely afford a newspaper, let alone internet data? Were you ever chased into exile? Whose voice are you stateless for? Even when you thought you were fighting for someone back in the Togo of the early to mid-nineties, are you sure you were fighting for them? Did they recognise you as fighting for them, or was it just you who thought you were fighting for them?"

Osman hurled himself down to his seat, crossing his legs.

Dela scribbled another note. I shut my eyes, hoping it was not going to be about Chenjerai Hove. The crowd had turned louder, yelling at each other across the rows of seats. Anna had gravitated towards the back. I saw her fingers stabbing at Osman slouched on his seat, both hands rested behind his head, his feet crossed at the ankles. The din rose louder. I watched Wilson as he stomped up to Osman and Anna. I had lost control of the crowd. Dela tugged hard at my jacket and handed me a piece of paper. *Mark – MI6 / DGSE.* I looked up and into the crowd, searching for the British gentleman in the purple jersey. He had vanished. And the wind behind my sail had been stolen.

THIRTY-ONE

I clicked 'Send' and watched my confirmation of status package zoom off into cyberspace, to my supervisor. That Friday lunchtime, sitting in my Summertown apartment, I felt many things ebbing away. There was an eerie emptiness, its tentacles jerking me to a feverish chill. I sensed an unsettling silence hovering over me.

Dela told me that he was flying back to Togo. He was going back home for good. I had followed his haggard posture as we slowly walked away from Queen Elizabeth House. It's time, he had kept on saying. I had watched his skin tightening around his cheekbones. Just as on that Ian Smith night after we had been chucked out of the Oxford Union bar, we stayed away from each other's eyes.

Swiftly shifting his brown leather bag to his other hand, he had said, "Let's have our last meal this coming Sunday." I had watched the traffic lights ahead of him. "I am leaving on Monday, in the evening, via Paris." It had come out of him unhurried, without a stutter. "So, let's have our last meal this coming Sunday." And then he had vanished into the oncoming crowd at the pedestrian crossing. I had blinked away the flapping wind, and when I opened my eyes, he had gone. I sensed in the way he had pushed his feet to carry him so fast ahead of me that he had wanted to disappear without a fuss, to end our uncomfortable conversation.

Bafana had also just left, gone home for good too. He had taken up a permanent position at some scientific institute in Johannesburg. Even Vernon had left to take up a senior civil-servant position in the provincial government of Mpumalanga. Wilson had also disappeared – well, had been sent down. He left without completing his thesis. His scholarship had long lapsed, and his confirmation of status had been due a year ago. I guessed he left because he didn't want to linger longer in Oxford like Osman. Rumour had it that he had been spotted washing dishes in some fancy restaurant in North London.

Even Josh was not around. And it was him I missed the most.

And Osman? Had he really belonged half to one world, and half to another? Living on the dole? Since 1997? Who was Osman? And why had he attacked Dela so fiercely at the seminar? What was his association with that British chap in the purple jersey? Did they arrive at the seminar together? What was it that Osman had against Dela? And why did Dela become so edgy when he spotted Osman and the Brit come marching through the door? Was that Mark? Really? Was he MI6 or a French DGSE or some combination of both? The guy who had taken Dela's Catherine to bed?

I stood up from my desk and walked through to the bathroom, the sadness streaming out of Blue Mitchell's 'Mona's Mood' following me. From the bathroom cabinet high above the washbasin, I took three headache pills and popped them into my mouth. I bent down to drink water from the tap, and then up at my face thrown back at me by the mirror. I was happy that I was myself again after the Bongani madness.

I had been the last to come up to Oxford, after Bafana, Josh, Dela, Vernon. So, it was natural that I was to be the last to come down from Oxford. I smiled, reassuring myself, and headed to the big window looking out over the quad lawn and the administration offices across. All I had to do was make sure that I came down, and was not *sent* down, like Wilson, like Brandon Pillay. I had to confirm my status. Then I had to write the last four chapters of my thesis and the conclusion. And then I had to push for a date as close as possible for my *viva voce*. And I would be done.

I rested a foot on the wide, low-hanging windowsill, my elbows on my knee. I stared at the big tree outside the window. Birds shifted and flew around it. Summer had set in. By now, another sadness was wafting out, this time from the trumpet of JJ Johnson in 'It's You or Not'. Trinity term was coming to an end. At the end of summer and the beginning of Michaelmas term, my college suspension was to be lifted. But I no longer knew what it would mean to me. Although I had long forgotten about The Barney McIntosh Affair, I wasn't sure whether I had managed to put behind me the injustice of it all. Not even sure if there was any justice to be had for a minority like me in a foreign land. All I knew was that I wanted to complete my doctoral thesis and leave behind the emptiness, the hollow loneliness that was fast becoming my Oxford.

The pills were doing nothing to numb my headache. I thought of Dela. Something had unhinged us after the seminar, and I wasn't sure it would ever go back to normal. I had a sense that this was cutting me off, and I did not know if it was a good thing or not. He was going, returning home. This was the strange, elusive anguish about exile – how it tore apart, cutting off, hollowing out parts of us. The pain of exile was not in the leaving. It was in the returning. It was in the coming back, when the left-behind and the departed finally met beneath a ground that had grown so brittle, and the air around them so foreign. The left-behind had grown. The departed were not the same.

Back at my desk, I turned up the lid of an opened pack of Marlboro Reds and took out a stick. Lighting it, I returned to the window to stare at the large tree and the birds that had made their home there. The chirping and the twittering had picked up tempo. Inhaling smoke, I held it in, listening to the throb of the headache only then settling down.

I took in the brightness, the yellowness of everything. I had turned down an invitation from a former tutorial student at my old university back home who was studying in Berlin. I had also turned down an invite to see an old university friend who was working as a diplomat at our embassy in Lisbon. I was determined to spend the summer in Oxford, writing the last four chapters of my thesis. I had to complete and then submit the thesis over the summer.

And then, suddenly, Dela was back in my thoughts. I tossed the cigarette butt out the window. Did I really know Dela? Who was he really? Who was he? Was he, indeed, stateless, an exile? Or had he been a fraud all along? Were his exile and statelessness figments of his imagination? Was he his own writer, driven to exile by dangers only he had imagined? But what if he was another Chenjerai Hove? So what if his exile, his statelessness, were inventions of his own mind?

But still I felt betrayed. Why? Did I feel betrayed because what might have been his imaginings of his statelessness, of his exile, did not match my own expectations? Weren't my own of exile, of statelessness, also just figments of my imagination? And what about the people of Togo? The pills had begun to spread through my body. I felt a well of relaxation tingling in my toes. My eyelids felt droopy. I had taken two codeine and an aspirin. I turned away from the window and fell onto my bed, collapsing on my back. Closing my eyes, I was soon gone.

I hopped on the seven o'clock bus from Summertown through the city to Cowley Road. Why was I going there? Why was I seeing Bongani again? I watched the houses glide steadily by. We had parted ways at Mood that night. So why was I on my way to see him and his crew again? I had promised myself that I was never going to see that paperless immigrant world again. Watching the bus glide down St Giles, I realised that, perhaps, the paperless immigrant crowd was the only Oxford that remained with me, still with me in that lingering emptiness. It was the only Oxford left for me to hang onto. Beyond them, after the immigrants, there truly was no Oxford left for me. And that scared me.

But I still felt uncomfortable at seeing Bongani again. When I woke, I saw his text message. He wanted me to join him at a party on Leopold Street, a house where his other South African friends lived. He and his crew were hanging out there. But something kept pulling me back, telling me not to go. It was not just that I was simply not in a drinking mood that night. Not in a partying mood. I felt like working. I wanted to work on my thesis, get back to my novel, in the quietness of my apartment in Summertown House. But, in all that, I still found myself drawn to party with Bongani. I promised myself, yet again, that this would be the last time.

I climbed off the bus at the corner of Cowley Road and Leopold Street. I took in the lights as I walked, the soothing South Asian music from the passing black cabs, the rainbow of fruits and vegetables on display outside the shops. I found myself settling into a relaxed mode. And before I knew it, I was right in front of the house. Mkhize opened the door at the third knock. He gave his usual wet cough, held my hand tight, bringing me close, up to his shoulder. Bongani came up behind Mkhize, clasping a long can of Foster's.

"My brother," Bongani smiled, locking me in a tight embrace. "It's obvious that I can't get enough of you." He cackled out a loud laugh.

"How are you?" I wiggled out a smile.

"Good. Good. Come." He held my hand, squeezed it, walking me across the creaky wooden floor of the passage where a rust-orange light lingered in the air. Silhouetted against the flood of a lone light bulb, I caught a slanted reflection, a mist of dust and dirt specks. A sharp dankness rose from the carpet.

We stepped into a big room. A barrage of kwaito music bounced off the walls. And there, in the centre of the room, Big Mavis danced, softly swaying her hips. She kept on at her dance, the sensuous gyrations of her hips reflected in the large mirror in front of her. I sat on the bed next to a young man around my age. In a white tracksuit top with black stripes and faded baggy jeans, with his long and frizzled hair, he looked like a cross between a yob and an amateur rapper. His long, angular face, mouth wide open, hung on every hip sway Big Mavis tossed his way. Big Mavis flung out two quick hip sways, and he bit hard on his lip. I wondered what this lone white man was doing in that house.

Bongani stood smiling in front of me, holding a saucer with three grilled lamb chops, and an ice-cold Foster's.

"Nibble on, my brother." He shoved the saucer against my chest, and handed me the Foster's. I wasn't at all hungry, but forced the lamb down. My focus was on the man drooling over Big Mavis.

"He's Albanian." I caught Bongani's whisper in my ear above the whirl of kwaito and loud chattering. "Doesn't speak good English. I'll be back." And then he wheeled out of the room, to the kitchen.

I returned my eyes to the Albanian, catching him as he dug deep into the front pockets of his jeans. His hand swiftly returned with a wad of notes folded between his fingers. I tried to guess the amount by the thickness of the wad, but lost count in that fast move as he stretched out his hand to Big Mavis. Fiercely tapping her arm, he shoved the wad into her hand. Big Mavis turned around, her eyes peeling out, wide open, and slapped her hand back at him. Nodding her head hard and fast, Big Mavis searched anxiously around the entire room, her eyes sweeping it three times.

"Let's go." Bongani had returned and taken hold of my hand. "Let's go to JD. We're all going." The crew had already started filing out ahead of us, the loud chattering and kwaito beat following behind. A blue Toyota Corolla was parked outside. Again, I made a silent vow that I would never be part of that crowd again.

Once in the back seat, I shut my eyes as a strong wave of nausea washed over me. I felt a sneer forming on my face. I thought of taking a black cab back to Summertown House once I arrived at JD Wetherspoon's. Finally, the car jerked to a stop and Bongani opened the front passenger door. I felt dizzy, a tiredness settling on my feet. Bundling out of the car, I stood in the circle of bright light at the entrance to JD's and then followed Bongani inside.

The Burundians at the table at the entrance were on their feet, shouting. I shuffled past the East African corner table. The three ladies at the Kenyan table were holding to the jackets of their men, who were ordering drinks at the bar. I followed behind Bongani as he, too, headed for the bar, lining up his drinks order.

"Luzuko." I turned at a tap on my shoulder.

"Nomusa," I smiled at her. "What's up?"

"I still haven't heard from her."

"Really?" I moved closer when she shook her head.

"Oh, I'm so sorry, Nomusa."

"I don't know what to do now." She tapped her feet. My hand reached out for her shoulder.

"I should go." She stepped back. "Later then, Luzuko."

"Later."

I watched as she picked up pace heading for the door, hugging her chest with both arms.

Bongani was already balancing three pints of Foster's,

with Mkhize and the rest of the crew now settled at the South African table. The Zimbabwean table behind us heaved with an extra load that night. I stood at the table, my face flushed, feeling apart from everyone.

I quickly made my way to the bathroom. Flinging the door closed behind me, I went straight for the tap over the sink. Again, I stared at the reflection of my face in the mirror. I didn't know what I was looking for. Closing the tap, I picked up loud noises from the bar area. There was a franticness about them, serious, a mixture of languages being thrown around – of English, isiZulu, isiXhosa, chiShona, Kiswahili, French. And so I opened the bathroom door and walked back inside.

"Party's over, mate!" a police officer stood at the door, his thumbs tucked into his black armoured belt. "The party's over, buddy!" I recognised him immediately. Ginger Moustache. The officer who had arrested Hugo in the bus that evening.

"Come," he grunted. "Let's go, mate." He stretched out his hand. I watched the twitch of his ginger moustache, shifting first left and then right. He breathed in his tight potbelly. Behind him, far at the back, I saw Khumalo in handcuffs, bobbing his head drunkenly, his face cast down. And I knew instantly what had happened. Tata Linda's burden, his prophecy about Khumalo, had come to pass. A policewoman stood behind Khumalo, fiddling with the handcuffs. Again, the same policewoman who had taken Hugo from the bus. Mkhize stood alongside them, also buoyed in handcuffs. Through a gap between three other officers, I spotted Bongani. A policewoman held his tightly cuffed hands. But I couldn't read his face, his stare cast down at the floor.

THIRTY-TWO

NOMUSA BLINKED TWICE. She turned her head slowly to the bedside drawers on her left. The digital clock read 05:55. She was grateful that for once she had not been woken by Baby Angelina's wail. I have to get up, she thought. Social Services had visited. And then, again and again, they had come with that policewoman. On their fourth visit, the policewoman arrived with a plainclothes detective.

Dressed in blue jeans, a green shirt and grey jacket, with jet-black hair smoothed back, he had been friendly at first. His questions had been easy, going through checks and ticking boxes. By their seventh visit, his questions had been sharper. And it came to a point where she no longer knew what she had answered to what. They circled around her, the questions slowly roping her in. And then they scheduled an eighth visit.

Nomusa stumbled sleepily towards the bathroom. In her mind, she paired her answers with the questions the detective had asked. There were more holes than she had realised, answers she hadn't thought of. The rope had been wound tighter. Nomusa turned the bath taps. A rush of hot water cascaded from them as she ran a Tesco foam bath.

Baby Angelina let out a long cry, and Nomusa shuffled back to the bedroom. She picked her up, cooing while gently undressing her. Covering Angelina with a hooded towel, she returned to the bathroom, struggling to remove her gown with the baby in her arms. Gauging the temperature with her left elbow, she carefully immersed Baby Angelina in the tepid water. Ignoring the child's wails, she quickly dropped her nightdress to the floor and stepped into the bath.

Baby Angelina was quite playful after her bath. She lay on her mother's bed, the heat from the three-bar heater in the corner helping to soothe her. Quietly, Nomusa dried her and sprinkled baby powder. She fiddled around in the black gym bag and pulled out a white long-sleeved cotton vest and a pair of blue cotton leggings and, nestling Angelina back into the pillow, began dressing her.

The clock next to the bed read 06:29. Alongside sat a packed suitcase. Baby Angelina sat snugly in her blue car seat dotted with teddy bears. Nomusa stared at the *burka* neatly laid out on the bed. At 06:34, she began to panic – the cab she had called for was just ten minutes away. Lifting the *burka* with both hands, she closed her eyes and lifted it up over her head. The cab driver honked. Carrying Angelina in her car seat, Nomusa headed stealthily down the stairs, covered from head to toe in black.

THIRTY-THREE

I WATCHED THE SNAKY vapour waft up from the fried plantain on my plate. Dela's jaw ground the cooked goat meat and the Ghanaian *wache*, a dish of black-eyed beans that I also rather enjoyed. I had forgotten what he had said the soup was called. I never caught on to the West African craze over soup, rather than the meat itself. His eyes remained focused on his plate. The cubes of goat meat were modest in size and quantity, swimming in a bowl of thick green. I had barely touched the plantain. I didn't like sweet potatoes at the best of times, or any other food that looked like potatoes that tasted sweet. That mouldy smell, the stiffness in the air that came with much West African cooking choked me. I scooped up the *wache*. I had banked on it, as well as the goat meat, to fill me up.

Dela folded his arms and pushed his spectacles farther up the bridge of his nose, and I wondered if I really cared what was going through his mind. My eyes kept sliding to the gym bag behind him. The zip at the end seemed locked. There was a decisiveness in his uprooting. Dela was leaving. Dela was truly leaving Oxford, for good. The tightness of the zip at the clasp said it all. He was not coming back. It had come to this. It had all come to this end, that swaying to old homes and to exiles not so new. It had finally come to that sway end.

Sylvanus Olympio had left the small table too, gone from the wall next to the window in the kitchen. He had probably been slid into some far corner of the gym bag. I had grown so used to his generous smile and his neatly parted hairline. His son, Gilchrist Olympio, had also been removed from the passage wall, his pudgy face and drained eyes most likely also hidden somewhere in that gym bag. They were all going back to Togo, via Paris.

Via Paris. It was in the way Dela mouthed it. *Via Paris* became a standalone sentence. It wasn't simply a matter of flying straight back to Togo, so that we get back to Togo quickly. No. It was *via Paris*. There was a sense of prestige attached to the stopover in Paris. As if the trip itself would not be important, not worth talking about if the plane did not stop over in Paris.

I finally plucked up the courage to shove the plate away, folding my arms against my chest. The force of my push took even me by surprise. The fork and knife clanged together in a tight clank-clank. There wasn't any time to squat over the carcass and slice it out, bit by bit.

"You barely touched the plantain?" Dela's tone was measured and slow.

"I hate sweet potatoes."

"They are not sweet ..."

"Whatever, man."

I looked away. Dela dropped the fork on his plate and turned the window. The sharp sweet fragrance of his Givenchy cologne drifted out of his beige turtleneck. He finished chewing, and I watched the last morsel groaning down his throat. Standing up, he pushed the chair back under the table, and slowly made his way over to the fridge. He plonked a one-litre Coca-Cola in the centre of the table, and then a bottle of red wine next to the Coke. This time there was no jazz to serenade us. For the first time in this apartment, there was no Miles, no Coltrane, no Charlie Mingus, no Hugh Masekela, no JJ Johnson and no Chet Baker. Just the two of us and the stiffness in the air.

I poured the Coke into a glass, measuring every question, every statement, every phrase, each word said in anger, all the betrayals, every wonder, this and that shock, every humiliation.

"I ... I ..." Dela started, "requested my supervisor to arrange a date for my *viva voce* three months from now." I listened to the squelchy-squelch dance of the wine bottle as the cork was eked from its neck until, finally, it popped out.

"I reckon ..." Dela went on, pouring the wine, "I reckon I would be ready to return briefly to Oxford then. For maybe a month or so. That would give me all the time I need to defend my thesis, effect revisions, if any, since every chapter of it is groundbreaking." He let out a soft laugh. But he laughed alone. He took a sip and then, coming up for air from his wine glass, there was another solitary laugh. Returning his eyes to me, he went on. "Then I'll consult with some Togolese exiles in Brixton and in Paris." He paused, putting the glass down. "Dr Owusu. Dr Dela Owusu." He hustled it out of his mouth, smacking his lips. He craned his neck, smiling, slipping another gulp of red wine down his throat. And then his eyes released a smudge of wetness.

"And how are they going to let you into the country?" I asked, already tense.

"Mmh?"

"Via Paris, how are they going to let you into Togo?" I forced the question out of me, pushing back the chair, lapping one leg over my knee.

Dela stared at me, sliding his fingers around the stem of the glass.

"So, Dela, just like that, Eyadéma's government has decided that you are, again, a Togolese citizen? Just like that? When did that happen?"

"Luzuko …"

"They've taken you off the *persona non-grata* list?"

"You are l-le-letting w-what what … You're letting Osman get into your head, mmh. Mmh? Kind of yes! Yes!" The stutter had returned. And the pots and pans in my head clanked loudly.

"I guess I am."

"Why? Why, Luzuko? D-do you … do you … think I am another Che-Chenj—"

"Forget Chenjerai Hove for once, for crying out loud!"

"Are y-you you … going to allow a DPhil dropout to tell you who is exile and stateless, and who is not?"

"Eyadéma's government hasn't changed. And his government has decided to give you back your Togolese citizenship after all these years? One minute they want you dead. And the next they want you back in Togo. How, Dela? How?"

"Eyadéma, the son, is in power. Things have changed."

"A son of a goat is a goat! Remember?"

Dela looked away, holding the half-empty glass of wine to his lips.

"Were you ever on the list, Dela? Were you ever *persona non-grata*, Dela?" I stared at the ceiling, my arms resting on my thighs.

His fist came crashing down on the table, sending the wine glass smashing to the floor. My glass tipped over with a clunk, pouring its contents out onto the table.

"How the fuck can you even ask me that question?"

"Or did you send yourself into exile?"

"Fuck you, Luzuko! Fuck you."

"It's happened before, Dela."

"What, I made myself stateless? I sent myself into exile?"

"No one chased you out of Togo, Dela."

"Fuck you!"

"It happens all the time. Exilic consciousness. It's all in your head. It was all in your head, Dela, to make yourself politically relevant."

"Are you calling me a fraud?"

"No. But you're suffering from delusions of grandeur."

"I've worked so hard for the Togolese people while here in exile, stateless. I've sacrificed so much for my people."

"Just like all these exiled charlatans, those so-called revolutionaries churning out one wordy and meaningless manifesto after another on pavement cafés in the capitals of Europe while sipping on espressos."

"Luzuko …"

"Why did you get so edgy when you spotted that British chap and Osman coming through the door at the seminar? Mmh?"

"Because … because …"

"Because he's the spy who took Catherine to bed, to break your political strategy. Right?"

"He's MI6, DGSE. He's a spy."

"You betrayed me, Dela."

"Then where are the scars from?"

"I'm sure there are countless other Delas with those wounds who remained in Togo, who are still inside Togo. They never made it to the 'stateless' and *persona non-grata* list like you did, because they dared not put themselves on imaginary stateless lists."

"You insult me, Luzuko."

"How could you betray me like this, Dela?" I turned my back on him, walking to the door. "And what about all those big books you promised we were going to write?" I asked him, feeling my lips wobble and my voice quiver.

Two swollen tears sat on the bags below my eyes. I stopped at the door, listening to the slow, heavy breathing behind me. I turned the doorknob, and stepped back into my Oxford, my Oxford, fast becoming lonelier and lonelier.

THIRTY-FOUR

Wagner's 'The Valkyrie' sounded out. "Damn!" Nomusa hissed, the oil sputtering from the pan, a spat landing just under her right eye. "Dammit!" she hurled out again. With a wet dishcloth, she quickly wiped away the spat of oil. Wagner hummed on from her phone. PRIVATE NUMBER, the screen read.

"Hello."

"Hi, hi, hello." A male voice rattled jerkily on the other end of the line.

"Yes." Nomusa answered.

"Eh ... eh ..."

"Jasmine here, how can I help you?"

"Nomusa."

"No, Jasmine. This is Jasmine. Who's this? Who am I talking to? I think you have the wrong number, mister."

Silence.

"Can I help you, mister?"

"Nomusa, it's Eddie. Eddie McKenzie."

"Eddie ..." Nomusa choked back a gasp and stumbled back into a chair. "Eddie McKenzie?"

"I know where you are, Nomusa. How the hell did I get your number, then? Let's not play hide and seek here, please, Nomusa."

Silence.

Nomusa breathed heavily, eyes tightly shut.

"I have bad news, I'm afraid."

Another silence.

"I'm not ratting you out," Eddie went on. "I haven't told anyone where you are. It's none of my business. I just want to relay the news."

"What?" Nomusa whispered. "What news?"

"Your mother ... she's passed on."

"What?" Nomusa stood up. "Say what?"

"Your mother has died. Grace is no more."

She felt the blood drain from her.

"I'm so sorry ... so sorry, Nomusa."

Nomusa stared around the kitchen.

"Hello? Hello?" Eddie raised his voice.

"Yes, I'm here."

"Three weeks ago. She collapsed in the bus, on her way home from work. Hypertension, I'm afraid. I've been trying to get hold of you ever since."

Another silence.

"The state says that if no one claims her body, she'll be given a pauper's burial."

Not a sound.

"So, are you coming back to Oxford? To claim her body?"

Silence. She wanted to ask what he meant, what a pauper's burial was. But no words came out.

THIRTY-FIVE

Bongani lifted Noel Mostert's book to his face, slowly running his eyes over the title, *Frontiers: The Epic of South Africa's Creation and the Tragedy of the Xhosa People.* Turning the flap of the hardcover, he flicked through the pages until he came across a slip of paper wedged between the pages as a bookmark. He stopped at the pictures, wondering at the background of the country's orange, the brown and green earthy colours of the frontiers. How the refugees had made the clothes on their backs from hides and wools of wild animals. They seemed always in trek, knapsacks on their shoulders.

The first time he had picked up Mostert's book from the library, all the ambience of the frontier had come to him – wild, dirty, shifty, earthy, deadly. Bongani studied the medium-height man in the picture. His body was not exactly slight, but certainly taut. The body of a man shaped by the endlessness of the trek – scorched by the sun. Was that Luzuko's forefather? Bongani had asked himself. Time and again, he had pored over the picture, running his finger over the brim of the man's hat with protruding feathers, perhaps made from the pelt of a skunk. He ran his finger from the skunk hat down to his jacket, from the skin and fur of a jackal maybe. Shutting his eyes, he felt the orange from the skin. A fox? Wild dog? The man's knees were bent, that ready, forward bend of the trek. Bongani had wondered where exactly in KwaZulu-Natal the man had come from.

And where was mine? Bongani huffed, shifting Mostert's half-open book a little farther from his eyes. Where was my forefather? Had he remained behind in KwaZulu-Natal? Poking two fingers into the far ends of his eyes, he strained them. Where was my forefather in all that trekking? Round purple-black hazes formed in front of his eyes, thin shafts of light filtering through as the piercing whistles from the prison warden became sharper. He shut his eyes again, to the loud clank of the warden's baton stringing against the steel rails of cell gates. A *'voetsek'* and a 'fuck you' echoed around.

Bongani closed Mostert as the prison warden sauntered past his prison cell. First came his potbelly, round and tight behind a clean brown jersey. Then the slow heaves of his breathing, pulling in and pushing out. Bongani hauled himself up, his eyes fixed on the opened door of his cell. He stretched and reached for James Whyle's *The Book of War* on the floor, carefully slipping Mostert underneath it.

The Book of War left him wondering. Mostert presented everything as cold facts. But *The Book of War* was a novel that, frighteningly, transported him to right there amid the desperation, the hopes the refugees and soldiers had taken with them and then let go. He stared at the slip of paper angled among the pages of Whyle's book, where he had left off his reading.

"Hosh." Bob bore a white grin.

"Hosh." Bongani looked up at him, watching as the

warden closed the cell gate behind him. It clanked shut, the big key jiggling and dangling from the rustiness inside the key lock.

"Sharp." Bob winked, and the key made a final clang-clang as it locked.

"Sharp?" Bongani stood up, smudging the palm of his hands against the orange overall.

"You got my stuff?" Bob tasted his upper lip, his hands hidden in his pockets.

"You have my *bellas*?" Bongani looked straight into Bob's eyes.

"Of course."

"With the airtime I need?"

"Yeah." Bob looked around. "Gonna cost you ten."

"Ten, Bobby? Ten?"

"Yes."

"We agreed on six."

"Bongani, Bongani. International calls, they don't come easy."

"And *zol* doesn't come cheap inside here either."

"It's ten or nothing, Bongani."

Bongani sighed, eyeing the matted beard of Bob and his bulky biceps.

"You love *zol* so much, hey?" Bongani whispered, turning around and walking to the head of his bed.

"You know how it is." Bob heaved out a slow sigh. "More than half this stuff is for the boss and his wife."

"Yeah, yeah, yeah." Bongani ruffled through the inside of his pillowcase, slipping out a rolled snatch of a black plastic bag.

"Excellent," Bob whispered, rubbing his hands together.

"Ten sticks." Bob looked around, slowly reaching for his pocket. "Here."

Bongani snatched the phone from him.

"I think it'll last you fifteen to twenty minutes. Twenty, tops."

"That should do. Thanks." Bongani fist-pumped Bob.

Bob ambled over to his bed, unwrapping the black plastic. Bongani fluffed up the pillow behind his head. He wondered at the time. With the one-hour difference between London and Johannesburg, he knew that Luzuko would be up now, about half past seven on a Wednesday evening. Now would be a good time to call.

He stared at the phone's blank screen, lining up his questions, all the words and phrases he had picked up from Mostert. Wiping the sweat from the palms of his hands against his overalls, he turned on the phone and dialled Luzuko's number. Was he still in Oxford? It had been seven months. What if he was no longer there? This, then, would have been all for nothing.

Ten sticks of *zol* for nothing? Bongani mused, breathing heavily, hoping that Luzuko's number hadn't changed, that he was still in Oxford. Bongani had lost touch with everyone there. He hadn't seen or heard from Nomusa since that night he and the rest of them were arrested at JD Wetherspoon's. Thames Valley man go catch you. He smiled, huffing out a silent laugh, as he heard the far-off voice of Patrick's warning that drunken morning at Commonwealth House.

"Hello? Hello?" Luzuko's voice came through hurried but clear. The *zol*'s seedy, fragrant steam from Bob's corner had begun to hover over him.

"Luzuko." Bongani listened to his tone, slow, paced.

"Bongani." With a slight tremble in his voice, Luzuko appeared startled on the other end of the line. "Is that you? Is that truly you?"

"Yes, man," Bongani laughed, sinking back into the pillow. "The one and only, Bongani Benjamin Shezi. Me, BB."

"How are you? Where are you?"

"Slow down, my man." Bongani listened to Luzuko laughing. "I'm back. Here in South Africa."

"Back home?"

"In Westville. In a ... a ... correctional facility." Bongani cleared a cough.

"Jail?"

"I suppose you can call it that."

"How'd you end up in jail, man?"

"Culpable homicide."

"Murder?"

"No, man. No." There was a firmness to Bongani's voice. "They say I was responsible for this guy's death in Ballito. Said I was involved in it. That I was part of it. You know how these things go. Wrong place at the wrong time with the wrong crowd. Someone's killed. And then they put that someone's death on you. Imagine? You are far out there, outside, and someone dies right there inside a restaurant, and they say you're somehow partly responsible for his death. Imagine? And then they slap you with fifteen years. How? But, anyway, I'll be out in seven and three months, on good behaviour. Who knows, maybe even six, *inshallah*. But enough about prison and me. I didn't call for that."

"But, Bongani, I'm being serious now. Really, how did you end up in prison? I mean, one minute you're in Oxford, and the next minute you're in prison in Durban."

"Luzuko," Bongani tried to calm himself, "I have fifteen, twenty minutes, tops. Getting this phone inside here and all this airtime has cost me a lot. A lot of marijuana that's really expensive to get in this place. A lot of it. Just to call you. This can't all go to waste. I didn't call to talk about how I ended up in prison."

"Okay, okay." Luzuko breathed heavily on the other end of the line. "It's a bit much to take in, though. But I miss you here, man. Oxford is really quiet and boring without you," Luzuko went on.

"By the way, what happened to Nomusa? She still in Oxford?" Bongani asked.

"Dunno. She disappeared. Vanished out of the blue, just like that. And her number's off the grid. No one knows where she is."

Bongani shook his head.

"Anyway, Luzuko, I called to talk about the past."

"What past?"

"The past of our forefathers."

"What forefathers?"

Bongani sat upright, moving the phone to the other ear. "The Frontier Wars." He plugged his index finger into his other eardrum to dampen the noise coming from the other cells.

"You call me from a cell in Westville to talk about wars that happened almost two centuries ago? Seriously?"

"Remember what you said that one time, Luzuko? That morning after a night out at Sodom, and just before we had gone to help Hugo?"

"Nope, don't remember, man."

"You said, Luzuko, the reason you were in your shoes at Oxford, doing what you were doing, was because of the pact your forefathers made with the devil in the Frontier Wars."

"Aah! Aah! Aah!"

"Now you remember."

"The Faustian pact?"

"That one. That pact exactly."

"Damn, Bongani! What happened to you? What's gotten into you? I made that comment in passing. Even I had forgotten about it."

"I've been reading Noel Mostert and James Whyle. I've got all the time here to read and think."

"You've been reading Mostert and Whyle? You know Mostert's book is one of President Thabo Mbeki's favourites?"

"Yeah, man. And now I know why you are there and why I'm here. I know why you are there and able to do what you're doing there, and remain there legally, and why I'm here. Now I know, from Mostert."

"The Faustian pact ..." Luzuko repeated to himself.

"Well, here it goes. Almost two hundred years ago, my maternal great-great-great-grandfather, in 1834, sold his soul to the devil."

"That's it. That's it, Luzuko. I want that stuff. Tell me more."

"Well, the little that I was able to gather was that he was some intelligence chief, a chief spy, in King Shaka's army or his palace or something."

"And then?"

"The part that he was an intelligence chief is documented in the epic poem 'Emperor Shaka the Great' by Mazisi Kunene."

"And so? What happened? Out with it, my man."

"Just as many in Shaka's army got fatigued with his never-ending invasive wars, my great-great-great-grandfather fell out with the king. And, with many, in that chaos, he fled with his family to the Eastern Cape. Then, when he arrived there, fleeing from a war, he found himself in another war in another land, in the Eastern Cape. He and his family, as poor refugees with nothing, were treated like dogs."

"And so he signed that pact with the devil, your maternal great-great-great-grandfather, in 1834?" Bongani said.

"I'm sure, Bongani, you've read about the terrible, deadly things he carried out against his own people in the Frontier War of 1834 to 1835. And then there was also the Frontier War of 1850 to 1853 … What he did there during the War of Mlanjeni, the Frontier War of 1850 to 1853, was unspeakable. Killing the women and children of his own people on behalf of the British? Bongani, I don't like talking about what he did almost two centuries ago. There's so much shame in it."

"It's not about what you like or don't like, Luzuko. It's about the ripple effects of what he did that carried across centuries, for generations to come, and touched your life almost two centuries later."

Bongani stretched out his legs and once again puffed up

the pillow behind his head.

"I know, I know, I know." Luzuko breathed out in a long stream.

"Luzuko, your maternal great-great-great-grandfather and my great-great-great-grandfather were once one people in Zululand. They were, once upon a time, both amaZulu. They lived in one land. They spoke the same language. They practised the same customs and traditions."

"I know that."

"And then," Bongani continued, "in that dispute with King Shaka, my great-great-great-grandfather chose to remain behind in Zululand. And your great-great-great-grandfather chose to leave it all behind and trek to an unknown land. My point here, Luzuko, is that your forefather changed faces. He changed faces through migration. He changed faces at will. He changed his face from being Zulu to Xhosa, from Zululand to the Eastern Cape, all through migration. And mine chose to remain behind and wore the same face, the one he handed down the line to me almost two hundred years ago. That's the same damn face that I can't get rid of. My forefather chose the foolishness of patriotism. Your forefather chose the wisdom of treachery."

"That's what you call it? Wisdom? Treachery?"

"Yeah, I call it that."

"You know, Bongani, I would give anything in this world to have an unblemished, honourable past like yours. I'll do anything to have that foolishness of patriotism hanging over my history rather than this wisdom of treachery."

"And what has my history of foolishness of patriotism done for me? It's held me ransom to this jail of stagnancy and poverty. And what has your history of wisdom of treachery done for you? It has put your grandfathers and yourself where they were and where you are now – middle class, educated and privileged."

"Bongani, sometimes being honourable, upholding good principles, is all you need. Whether you live in poverty or riches doesn't matter. But being honourable to who you are, and not selling out your own people is all you need."

"I guess so, but that's easy to say if you've never been generationally hungry ... You'll never understand how this foolishness of patriotism and honour have fucked me up."

"Bongani, my forefathers down a line of two centuries changed faces over and over again through migration. In the beginning, he was a loyal servant of King Shaka Zulu. Then he turned his back on him and became a traitor and fugitive from King Shaka Zulu's authority. Then he became a refugee among the amaXhosa in the Eastern Cape. Then he became a traitor to his own amaXhosa hosts, the ones who had given him asylum. He became a lapdog of the British, joining the British Cape Mounted Riflemen. Then he became a victim of the British, a deserter from the British army, a turncoat. Then a victim of apartheid, then a jailed anti-apartheid activist."

"That, Luzuko, is the beauty of changing faces. Of changing faces through migrations. What has my forefather's foolishness to patriotism done for me almost two centuries down the line? Your forefather sold his soul to the devil. And selling your soul to the devil always comes with benefits – which he then passed on to his son, your great-great-grandfather. And then on to the next generation, your great-grandfather. And then the next generation, your grandfather. And that's why you were born bourgeoisie, middle class. That's why your grandfathers were educated and were able to give you the standard of living back when you were a child that was far above that of the township.

"That pact your great-great-great-grandfather made with the British in 1834 – to be loyal to them in exchange for some lands in the Eastern Cape and for privileged access to school and church – changed your family's fortunes up to this day. That is the beauty of migration. That is the power behind changing faces through migrations. What has the foolishness of my great-great-great-grandfather, his patriotism, done for me? Where has it gotten me? Whether I'm out there or here in Westville, the world is set on thinking that I belong in a prison. I was in prison in Oxford. And no matter how much I tried to shake the prison off of me, the world wants me in a prison, one way or form or another. And now I'm here where they think I ought to be. How I wish my great-great-great-grandfather had changed face and chosen the wisdom of treachery. How I wish they had travelled. How I wish they had migrated. How I—"

Beep-beep-beep. Bongani checked the screen smudged with sweat from his ear and cheek. *Twenty minutes, forty-five seconds*, he read through the vapour on the screen. More *zol* sticks? He pondered, looking over at Bob half hidden behind the thick swirl of weed smoke. Slouched in the corner of his bed, leaning against the wall, Bongani stared at the last snatch of the *zol* stick. Heaving it in slowly, Bob quickly dropped it as the bold red ash reached for his fingertip. Another ten sticks of *zol* for another twenty minutes with Luzuko? Bongani wiped the vapour and sweat on the screen against his overall. It's fine, Bongani assured himself. I got it out. Got it all out. But one way or another, I've got to change face.

THIRTY-SIX

I WATCHED THE TWO middle-aged gentlemen filing out of the tiny, carpeted passageway of The Eagle & Child. The tall one walked steadily behind the shorter, chubbier gentleman. At the door they caught up with each other, standing hipped together, almost minced, staring into each other's eyes. The tall one gave a staccato giggle. The other stepped out of the doorway, smiling as they turned right. Walking down St Giles, I stayed with them until they reached the neon lights of Sainsbury's.

My eyes returned to the board on the wall of the pub: The Eagle & Child. It wasn't my usual haunt. I always passed it by without giving it much thought. And I never cared much about its history, that it was the hangout for the writerly meetings of 'The Inklings' – JRR Tolkien, CS Lewis and some other fellow whose name always slipped my mind. I hadn't read them. They had never tickled my fancy. So, I couldn't care much about The Inklings.

And yet it was there that I found myself earlier that evening. I stood on the pavement of St Giles, staring at the plaque of The Eagle & Child. I felt the brushes of the evening's cool spring breeze. The cool of the shower I had just taken waved about my nostrils the sporty fragrance of my gel soap. The spicy grilled mackerel and peppers and mushrooms I had prepared for an early supper wafted on my breath, and I caught hints of the coriander, rosemary, freshly squeezed lemon, the crushed black peppercorn from the mashed potatoes.

I had even prepared the potatoes the way Josh's Estonian girlfriend had taught me: no milk, a dollop or two of margarine, coriander cut to bits, rosemary, parsley, salt and crushed black peppercorn. And, most important of all, I didn't mash the potatoes too mushy – just five, six or seven smashes, so that you left it rough. I suspect I had prepared it like this as my way of showing how I missed Josh. He hadn't responded to any of my e-mails. And hadn't called in seven months.

It was April. Easter was around the corner, and Hilary term would soon fold up. Spring was good. I welcomed the way the brightness and green of the day, the brilliance of the sun, scattered and tossed away the mounds of loneliness piling up in me each day. The Barney McIntosh Affair was over. My college suspension had been lifted a few months previously. And yet I could not return to that old self again.

I could not go back to many things. I hadn't really been back to the college premises, the dining hall, the library. As soon as the ban was lifted, I did go back – I sauntered through the porter's lodge, walked around the courtyard, climbed up to the library, went to the MCR – but it was all but gone. I could not go back to many things. And I did not return after that. I could not find myself there any longer.

When I closed the door behind Dela that day, the whiff of plantain remaining with me, I wept. I wept as my feet left the pedals of my bicycle on the steep slope down Morrell

Avenue. The wind huffed my tears back across my cheeks. I wept at the bitterness of betrayal, that tug of loss, the heaviness of the shock, the pounding of rage, anger at my foolishness and gullibility, and losing him. These all squatted on my soul. I wept.

Two days later, just after lunch, in my usual reading spot at the School of Geography's library, I packed my backpack and cycled onto the High Street, past Queen's College and past Magdalen, the vastness of the college taking up a vast slab of High Street. I pulled back, watching the wetness of the road, the black cabs whizzing past me. At the Cowley Road roundabout, I turned left to the first exit into St Clements, my chest wheezing as I struggled up to the top of Morrell Avenue until I saw the Warneford hospital gawking at me. I pedalled faster towards Dela's apartment. I left my bicycle leaning against the wall, unlocked. I could not care less about bike theft. I made my way up the stairs. Maybe he hadn't left yet, I remember thinking, my chest rising and falling. There was a new lock on the grille of the door. Peeping through the window, I scoured the kitchen table. That was where he had spilled his wine, where my Coke had fallen over. I searched through the pane of the window for the father and son, Sylvanus and Gilchrist.

I did not want to think about Dela. Of Dela. But I thought about Josh all the time. About how easy he made everything. He knew how to make Oxford bearable. I missed the Stolichnaya and the orange juice in little vodka glasses and R Kelly and Ja Rule and sessions at Mood and at The Cock & Camel. Dela was as big, searing, difficult, dreamy and glorious as Josh was easy, light, straight, honest and comforting.

I thought about how exile had robbed me. The pain of exile was not in the leaving. The anguish of exile was in the returning. And the thought of my father made my head spin. After the last time I had seen him – the first time I had ever seen him – he had vanished. He hadn't brought back the tricycle. I had seen the shifts in his eyes. "Please forgive me for not having raised you. Please forgive me. Please," he had pleaded, over and over again. And then he had disappeared. When he promised he would be in touch, the shifts in his eyes said it all. He vanished. He had turned his back on me, got into his car, and left. Just as I had turned my back on Dela and left. The agony was all in the return from exile.

My mind returned from its forays into life with Dela and Josh, back to the doorstep of The Eagle & Child. Two bookish ladies in their late twenties stood at the door, their sentences clambering over each other, pushing giggles here and there. I read the time on my wristwatch. It was three minutes after eight. Perhaps Osman had arrived much earlier, I mused. I still had no clue why he wanted to meet with me. And he hadn't told me how he had managed to get hold of my number.

I walked down the slim passageway, running my eyes over the framed black-and-white portraits of Tolkien, Lewis and the other writers. The long, carpeted passage, its narrowness, the chatty buzz of an Oxford bar, conjured the feel of a gathering in a lively 1950s' British home. At the end of the same passage was a huddle of tables and chairs, behind them another set of sofa and tables against the wall. In the middle of it all sat Osman. Alone. My eyes immediately locked onto his smile. His small head and thin hair stood out from afar, his thin lips on caramel skin stretching his well-groomed jet-black moustache. That night he wasn't wearing a tie. Perhaps this was his way of welcoming spring. But he still wore his brown tweed jacket.

As I approached, he stood up immediately, stretching out his hand. It struck me that, in all my time in Oxford, I had never had an unhurried chat with Osman. Perhaps a custom I had picked up from Dela – the misfortune of running into Osman, whose one half belonged to one world, and another half to another world.

"Luzuko, my South African friend." The mildness of

Osman's voice struck me with a tenderness I had never sensed before. In our past hurried meetings, there had always been a tinge of desperation hanging over the mildness of his tone. But this was a mildness at ease. "Please, pull up a chair and take a seat." Sitting down, he smoothed the creases in his well-ironed black trousers. "I'm having tea. What are you having? A beer? Of course, you can have alcohol. It's only *haram* for me, of course, not for you. Whiskey? Soft drink, perhaps? You can even order a meal if you want to. Anything, really."

"I wouldn't mind a bowl of soup." I shifted my chair around.

"Waiter." Osman snapped his fingers at one of the bar staff.

"Lentil soup, if you have it?" I said. The waiter nodded and scurried off, a sprightly spring in his step.

"So, Osman, how did you get my number?"

Osman coughed, lapping one leg up on his knee. "We've never really had a proper chat, have we, my South African friend?"

"In seminars, we have."

"Not by a long shot. Those were not proper chats. You and Dela avoided me as though I were a leper. But we're not there now. That's all in the past." He smiled. Hot flushes pushed through every pore of my skin.

"How much do you know of me, Luzuko?" Osman asked, gently lifting the teacup to his thin lips.

"Your name is Osman Hassan."

Osman quickly dropped the teacup on its saucer. "Hassana. Hassana. Osman Hassana. I am Hausa. Hassan is universal Arabic. Hassana is Hausa."

"And that you dropped out of your DPhil studies at St Antony's College in 1987, because you lost your doctoral thesis. You lost the floppy disc that contained a copy of your thesis."

The waiter placed the lentil soup and slices of ciabatta

with butter and crushed garlic on the table in front of me. I watched Osman's smile widen beneath his slim moustache as he poured more tea into his cup from the white china teapot.

"I see the legend stuck." Osman smiled.

"Mmh?" I hummed, scooping my first spoonful of lentils.

"You'll be amazed now, won't you, that what you thought was foolish and worn out actually worked and stuck."

"I don't follow you."

"Never mind." Osman rested the cup on its saucer. "I hear that you're defending your thesis next week?"

"How do you know?"

He waved his hand at me.

"Really, how did you find out?"

"And it makes it that much easier now that your college ban has been lifted."

"Osman." I dropped the spoon into the bowl of soup.

"Look, Luzuko, Oxford is not that big, you know ... And we Africans are a much smaller population in this city."

I stared at him, taking up a slice of ciabatta and wetting it with lentil soup.

"So, what did you call me here for?"

"Dela."

I sat back, my chewing slow.

"Dela Owusu." Osman picked up the teacup. I listened to the four slurps he made. Closing his eyes and tasting his lips, he sent the teacup back to the saucer.

He clasped his fingers together and looked around, first one way and then the other. For some reason, I found myself reaching for him halfway across the table, leaning closer.

"I know you think I was harsh on Dela at that seminar on democracy in Togo seven months ago." His eyes did another dance around the room, as if looking for something. I kept quiet. "Or rather, let me put it this way, I know that you think I destroyed Dela's political reputation with the remarks I made at that seminar."

"Dela was never the same again," I said. "It was a devastating blow. You truly rattled him, you and that British chap in the purple jersey."

"But you don't know Dela," Osman almost whispered, leaning closer to me. "Not really."

"And who was that British chap? Was that Mark, the MI6 spy or French DGSE, or a combination of both?"

Osman bolted out a grand laugh. "Is that what Dela said of him?"

"Who was that guy?"

"I don't know, Luzuko." Osman picked up his teacup, searching inside it. "I truly don't know him. I met him there on that day of the seminar, first time."

"So, why do you say I don't know Dela?"

"Dela has lost his faculties."

"Lost his faculties over what he thinks should be done in Togo?"

"Dela has lost his mind."

"So, you think that Togolese politics …"

"I said Dela has lost his mind." Osman raised his voice. I stared at him, taken aback by his tone. "Dela has gone mad. I mean, clinically mad."

"What do you mean? What are you talking about?"

"Dela is mentally unwell. He's in a mental hospital, as we speak – in Lomé, Togo."

I slouched back into my seat, folded my arms, and stared at the ceiling. At first, my mind was silent. Then throbs at the front of my ears began to thump. Osman's eyes remained fixed on me. And then he looked away, his fingers spread apart, their tips touching.

"It's been four months now," he went on, his eyes avoiding mine. "And his condition is just not getting any better."

I opened my mouth, but nothing but wind flowed out of it.

"He was found one night, sleeping on a bench in a park not far from his apartment in Lomé. And then he was spotted again and again, on the same bench. He was seen walking the streets and markets, bare feet and in tattered clothes, shouting at people, saying things that didn't make sense, talking to himself, scratching himself."

"What happened, Osman?" I almost yelled at him. "And how do you know all this?"

Osman looked away.

"He's not well?" I whispered, staring at the teapot.

The soup was getting cold, growing a slimy green skin. Osman turned his head the other way. My eyes remained on the teapot, but I could hear the tapping of Osman's fingers on the table.

"Everything went sideways for him," Osman went on. "Everything."

"What do you mean?"

"Like I said, Luzuko, you don't know who Dela was."

"Yes, but what do you *mean*, Osman?" I could no longer hide my growing impatience.

"All the things I said about Dela at the seminar are true. And all the things that British chap said are also true."

"So, you know who that British chap was?"

"Focus, Luzuko, focus." Osman raised his voice again. "Ask the right questions." Leaning closer, he thumped his index finger on the table. I sat back.

"Dela was playing many different moves on the same board all at the same time." He lowered his head, returning his eyes straight to mine. "Look me in the eyes when I talk to you." The mildness in his voice had vanished. "Dela went back to Togo to find his political space. That's all there was to it. He went back to Togo to take his political seat, for himself, for his own glory. He returned to Togo at a time ripe for political opportunities that were opening up. At least, that was what a lot of Togolese political players were banking on, both in and outside the system. The European Union wanted to broker talks for peace and reconciliation between Eyadéma's government and the opposition parties. There were hopes that the EU-brokered peace might bring some form of a unity government. That meant an opening up of a whole lot of cabinet and government and diplomatic posts, you see? That was why Dela roped you in to write those pamphlets and bulletins. That was why he convened that seminar. He did all those things to bolster his own political profile in the space of Gilchrist Olympio's opposition party, to prepare for his move, to take his political space in Togo."

Osman leaned forward in his seat, reaching for the teapot. I felt my heart thumping, the hotness of my blood seeping through the pores of my skin. Osman held the teapot with both hands. I listened to the drip-dripping into the teacup.

"This is getting cold," he said, steadying his fingers around the teapot.

"And then?"

Osman folded his fingers around the teacup.

"But then the talks didn't get anywhere." Osman took a sip. "And then Olympio found out that Dela had been playing moves with many pieces on the same board at the same time."

"Many moves?"

"I know you know about Antoine."

"Yes. His torturer. But I've never met him. He came to Oxford to try to bribe Dela in exchange for his political silence, to bring an end to his column, his writings against the Togolese government."

"And Dela took the money," Osman went on, slowly swinging the cup. "Because there was more to the deal. There was much more to it. There was also the promise of a position for him in the government if he stopped writing against the Togolese government. Dela was a very good writer."

I shook my head.

"That's not true. That cannot be true."

Osman patted a leather bag nestled against his thigh that I hadn't seen. "It's all here, documented, Luzuko. There's a paper trail, correspondence, receipts, all manner of documents. It's all on record, my South African friend." Osman sighed, resting his chin on his hand. "Dela chased three hares and caught none. That's the reality of it."

I stared at my cold soup in silence.

"And he was in talks with some Togolese exiles in Niger and Burkina Faso who were tied to a business stakeholder that financed a terrorist group that had eyes on Togo's bauxite mines. Now, Luzuko, that was Dela's biggest mistake. That was his deadly move. That's when we took him down. That's why we took him down."

"You took him down? Who are you, Osman?"

"I said focus, Luzuko, and ask the right questions."

Osman pushed his teacup aside and threw himself back into the chair.

"Things may scatter around in the air, but they always go back to where they came from." Osman's voice rustled on. My head was spinning. Buzzes in my head mashed in with the buzz at the bar. I tried to steady my mind and return my focus to the table.

"It's you." I felt the spike in my voice. "It's you, Osman. You're the one who sent that e-mail from a marechera48 username, about birds festooning the air but coming back eventually to the ground, where they came from."

"Do you think exiles fall from the sky, Luzuko?" His tone soared and his small eyes grew sharper and smaller. "Exiles come from political incumbency, and they yearn to return to the political incumbency they came from. Incumbency! Political incumbency, Luzuko! What Dela did was not new, nor was it strange. It wasn't betrayal. It was change. We all change. When we've been in the wilderness for that long, we all want change – change that benefits us. You were the one who was foolish enough to think that exiles go elsewhere other than the political incumbency they came from."

My heart went on thumping. The heat in my blood had reached my ears.

"Exile is not easy, Luzuko," Osman sighed. The mildness

in his voice returned. "Whether he was a *bona fide* exile or not, Dela was nevertheless in exile. And I really don't know what drove him to madness. Dela loves his country. He loves Togo. He loves his people. The separation from his homeland tore him apart." Now it was Osman's turn to stare up at the ceiling, folding his arms. "To be torn away from your land, and then not finding your seat when you return home can drive any man to madness."

I stared into my cold lentil soup, trying not to bring to imagination a tottering, barefoot Dela pounding the streets of Lomé.

"Do you have a job lined up for yourself once you come down from Oxford?"

"I haven't really thought that far." I listened to my lowly voice.

"Two or three of my good friends at your Department of Foreign Affairs in Pretoria can snap their fingers and make magic for you."

I looked up, but stopped myself short from asking another wrong question.

"We have a lot of NGOs and research institutes in your neighbourhood down south," Osman went on, his eyes fixed on mine. "But they give us desktop research and churn out a lot of political waffle, all in the name of political divination. We never asked for political witch-doctors now, did we?" He looked up, fluffing a finger against his thumb, and sighed. "It's quite amazing how far one can get with the basics of journalism." He returned his eyes, levelling them with mine once again. "The old five Ws and an H of journalism – what, where, when, who, why and how? – that's solid HUMINT. Foundational human intelligence. Are you keen to give it a try, Luzuko, and toss the answers back to marechera48?"

"You want me to work for the Union Jack?"

"For world peace."

I stood up. "I have to go, Osman. Thank you for the soup."

I turned my back to him, and the buzz and the hackling of the bar fully opened up to my ears.

"Dr Joshua Ajak is no more." The mildness of his tone reached up to me from my back. I did not turn to look back at him. "Shot dead three weeks ago in a cattle skirmish between two South Sudanese tribes at the border between South Sudan and Uganda. He was caught in the crossfire while treating patients. I'm sorry, Luzuko. I am truly sorry for your loss."

EPILOGUE

THE GRINDING OF WHITE pebbles followed me across the front yard of Queen Elizabeth House. I stood there, letting the warm breeze of the spring afternoon cool the beads of sweat on my face, but still I felt the smothering sweat on my throat, where the white bow tie fastened. I fingered the space between my Adam's apple and the collar of my shirt and that white bow tie. The black gown and the black suit under it took in all the heat of the day until, finally, a sudden, unexpected swipe of a fresh breeze wiped my face, soothing the stiffness of the sweat.

A stretch of a smile sat on my face. It lingered there. It was not something I could simply wipe away. Three hours and seven minutes. I had measured the time against the clock on the wall behind my internal examiner from Wadham College. I had been precise, following the exactness of the minute arm. My *viva voce* lasted three hours and seven minutes. And I came out of it Dr Luzuko Goba, DPhil (Oxon), passed with only minor corrections. Corrections would take me no more than about a week to effect, my external examiner from the University of London's School of Oriental and African Studies assured me.

I didn't know why I had thought that orally defending my doctoral thesis in front of two women academics would be much safer and more comfortable, that they would be more empathetic than men. It had been a tough defence. Particularly in the first hour, when we tussled over my theories, I sincerely thought I was not going to make it. When we moved to my empirical findings and their validity, I felt smudges of sweat behind the bow tie. The three glasses of water I had finished in the first two hours did not seem to have made a difference. They had no impact on either the heat or the splotches of sweat building up.

In those three hours and seven minutes, I managed to completely wipe from my mind all the things I was sure I would never be able to blot out. And then in the last hour, when both examiners hit me hardest on how I had applied my theories and empirical findings to my analysis, I developed the utmost confidence. I looked them in the eyes, parring all their questions. And every word, every thought I had come across in my thesis and notes – all my work – came together right before my eyes.

Outside, standing a little unsteadily on those white pebbles, I stared up at the tree towering over me, heard the rustles of its leaves. I stared ahead at the steel gate opened to the road leading farther across to the low-fenced cemetery of First World War soldiers. It was over. I drew in a fat breath, letting it hover over my shoulders. It felt unreal – that it was over, that I had changed. Beneath it all, beneath all that *subfusc* – the gown, the mortar board tucked under my arm, the black suit, the white shirt, the white bow tie – I still felt the same. And yet, yes, I had changed. My Supplication to Leave certificate was on its way from the Wellington Square administration offices – it would declare that I was free to make arrangements for my graduation ceremony with my college, traditionally convened at the Bodleian Library.

I steadied my feet over the white pebbles, listening to their grinding, watching as they scattered from beneath my shoes. I arranged in my head all the bureaucratic red tape I had to take care of. I was coming down from Oxford, I laughed to myself. It kept ringing in my head. Just as I had with the matriculation walk from college to the Bodleian Library in full *subfusc*, I felt like walking all the way farther up St Giles and Banbury Road to Summertown House.

I turned right onto St Giles, again lining up in my head all the tasks that lay ahead of me. I had one month left to wrap up everything before I headed home. After effecting corrections, I had to print out three copies of my thesis and hard bind them. Then I had to deposit one copy with the administration offices at Wellington Square, to be taken to the Bodleian Library. The second copy was for my supervisor. And the third was for myself, a personal copy, an ode to my years of hard work, slogging, of doubt, fear and confusion.

I stared at the board up ahead of an animated lamb hoisting a colourful flag. Stopping outside The Lamb & Flag, I wondered about what would have been. This was where we celebrated each other's victories on our oral thesis defences over a pint. But there was no one to celebrate with now. There was no Dela. No Josh. No Bafana. And there were no immigrants, no paperless.

I watched a middle-aged gentleman in dirty green overalls enjoying an ice-cold pint of lager with his lady. I would have sat here with Dela, plotting our books, our next journal papers, a novel and short story on the side. Perhaps he would have advised me to go for a post-doc. But, maybe, sensing that I had grown tired of academia, he would have advised me to try for a post in civil service or civil society. I needed to cool down from churning one thesis after another in a continuous stretch of ten years' study.

Of course, I would have waited for him to finish every

word he stuttered. I would have watched him take a cigarette from his ten pack of Marlboro Lights. And then I would have listened to him reminiscing about his old days of running and hiding from Eyadéma's henchmen. Even if they were lies, I would have listened to them. Even if they were tall untruths, I would have given everything, anything, to summon Dela from his madness in Togo to that bar bench at The Lamb & Flag.

Instead, throwing my backpack over my shoulder, I walked right on past. It all seemed so distant now. Such a long time since Josh and I sat in his car one drunken night, planning how we would belt out R Kelly's 'The Storm is Over' when that day of the *viva voce* came, and we had passed. We had rehearsed it in his room one night over Stolichnaya and orange juice. It seemed a far memory. But I had never had such a moment, a song, holding me so fast to such a far-off promise.

But there was no Josh any more. The man was dead. And the song had faded with him. The storm was over. There was no sweetness, none of that moist scent of a rainbow after the storm without him. And so I walked on past The Lamb & Flag, past the houses with ivy creeping up the walls. I watched my feet pounding the pavement, one sliding forward to overtake the other.

I stopped. I was going too fast. All this time, I had, quite mindlessly, been going too fast, following a straight and narrow path I had figured was the only true one. And, suddenly, a fear choked me. My Oxford had emptied out. Had I missed it? Had I missed the one and only true Oxford that had been mine in my mindlessly fast, straight, narrow route? I went back to that unsettling session I had with Osman at The Eagle & Child the previous week.

He had turned out not to have been belonging half to one world and half to another world after all. Osman was Pyle, and had been Pyle all along, the Pyle of Graham Greene's *The Quiet American*. But he was not the young, idealistic, theoretical Pyle, recruiting equally idealistic, unsuspecting agents for world peace. Osman had been the older, wrinkly Pyle, with faith in the fundamentals of the five Ws and one H of journalism to bring secure peace.

And, in a very crooked way, Osman was right. Who was I to judge Dela's exile and sense of exilic consciousness? Whether he had truly been an exile, or it had all been in his mind, it was his own exile from the Togo he loved in his own way. Who was I to say how he should have changed? There was no this way or that way. And had I missed all of that – in this Oxford, my Oxford, the Oxford I had wanted all along to be this straight way – for African students to go back to their African homelands? For illegal black South African immigrant workers to stop running the treadmill like hamsters?

Had I missed all that beauty in all the shape-shifting that was never meant to come to a definite, firmly shaped form? The beauty was in all that indetermination. Had I missed it all? What did our deputy ambassador to Russia, Dr Lufuno Mudau, say in his lecture, 'Paperless', at the Examination Hall? Our identities were always in the pottery machine. In the end, our destinations were never really reached, because they were never meant to be reached. Everything was hybrid, never formed in any cemented form. Everything was in flux. There was no final destination, and there were no finite forms in our endless walks.

I thought back to Bongani and our last conversation. It was funny how he was caught in that culpable homicide. But not funny that he was convicted. It was funny how he related the whole story of how he had been caught, framed for a murder he had been far away from and had nothing to do with. His telling had reminded me of a scene in Alex La Guma's *The Stone Country*. A convicted prisoner had relayed to another prisoner how he had been wrongly tied up in a robbery he had nothing to do with. As he stood outside a factory, someone had dropped a bag full of loot in front of him and ran away. It wasn't long before the police arrived and, finding the loot at his feet, pinned the whole robbery on him.

Anyway, what did Bongani say in our long conversation over the phone that night when he called from his cell? The need to change faces. We needed to change faces. That was what travelling offered. That was what migrations offered. That was why he had travelled. To be another person. That was why he had blamed his great-great-great-grandfather for having remained behind, while my maternal great-great-great-grandfather had instead set out on a journey of treacheries. My forefathers had changed faces many times over the past two centuries – from loyal spy for a great kingdom, to fugitive, to treasonous scoundrel, to murderer and turncoat, to jailed anti-apartheid revolutionary.

And now, in all that indeterminate shape-shifting, I feared I had missed the beauty of my Oxford. I wanted it to take a definite, straight, solid, moral form. But there were always going to be illegal immigrants, political sell-outs, perpetual revolutionaries in exile, charlatan or not. There would always be the Thames Valley man chasing after crime, fear and disorder; the statues and paintings of Cecil John Rhodes dotted all over Oxford; tales of drunken Marechera running away from being sectioned at the Warneford; the cat-and-mouse chase of yobos by the police; of that unkempt, mentally unwell woman in a Mexican shawl dragging behind her along Cowley Road empty cans tied to a string; of imams and contented gay men sharing a street. That was the Oxford I feared I had missed while searching for the straight, right, narrow Oxford that had never been, and would never be. I might have missed savouring all that, taking it for what it was. The beauty was in the mess. It had always been in the clutter and jumble of it all.

And my father ... He bequeathed me the greatest gift any parent could to a child – freedom to live the life I wanted, on my own terms. I became the man I had unfurled into because of his ultimate sacrifice – his life, his sanity. There was no other identity I could ever have wanted from him. That had to be the end of it, the closure I so wanted. The man died. And, through his death, I had lived.

I walked farther up Banbury Road, stopping at the gate of St Anne's College. From outside, it was small and nondescript. It was a women's college, and I had never had reason to venture inside. Yet Iris Murdoch, one of the most intelligent, prolific writers in England – if not the entire English-speaking world – was a past student. I marvelled at the strength and speed with which she had produced all her work, both philosophical and fictional, one book after another. I had always wanted to be like her. Dela and I had always wanted to write one big book and then the next, one after another, just as she had done. A writer's writer. Across mediums. Across forms. Across genres.

I crossed the street to the other side of Banbury, the commercial side of the street. Far ahead, I could see Marks & Spencer and the Dew Drop Inn, the pub with its quaint little garden. I had to sit down and wet my throat. I had been talking non-stop for just over three hours. And, again, the fear of having missed all that Oxford overcame me. I had to take all of that in before I got to my apartment at Summertown House.

When I reached the Dew Drop, I took the first empty seat I spotted out in the garden. And when the waiter came over, I didn't hesitate to place an order for a bowl of vanilla ice cream and a small bottle of sparkling water. Looking heavenwards, I summoned Josh for our moment, the moment we were supposed to belt out together 'The Storm is Over'. I listened to it for a while, searching the skies. An eerie silence hovered over me.

Once the waiter returned with my order, I fished from my backpack a twenty pack of Marlboro Reds and my phone. The cigarette lit, I reached for the phone. The blank screen stared back at me. There was no Bongani to call. No

Nomusa. There was no Major General. No Mkhize. No Tata Linda. They had been thrown out of Oxford, their Oxford. Some had left on their own.

My hand returned to the backpack and I trawled out of it a thick brown envelope. I felt the heaviness of my manuscript, *Ours*, in one hand. "Rewrite, rewrite, rewrite." I had gone over and beyond what the publisher's external reader had recommended for the revisions. But it all still felt dead, contrived, far fetched. A lie. An imagined story told by a mind that had not seen or felt any of the things I had written about. It was good writing, competent and well considered. But it was all an innocent untruth, all crafted out of a yearning to see my name on the spine of a book. This was not a story that came from the heart. It wasn't my story. I did not cry or laugh when I wrote it or read it. I was never shocked or moved by any of its constructions. And what did the poet Robert Frost say about the relationship between a writer, his writing and the reader? If the writer does not cry over what he has written, the reader would also not cry. If the writer did not laugh, the reader would also not laugh.

I carried it around in my backpack because I wanted to mail it to the publisher in Johannesburg the very minute I had finished defending my thesis. As I scooped my ice cream and gulped down my sparkling water, I noticed a rubbish bin not far from the table. I stood up and walked the few feet to it. I lingered there, the thick brown envelope carrying my novel dangling in my hands. And then I dropped it inside the bin, turned my back on it, and walked back to my seat.

Taking my seat, I turned to the heavens, and then it poured down on me from the sky – 'Peace Piece', the solo piano improvisation, that classical masterpiece of Bill Evans. Just as it had stumped on Bill back in 1958, like that, it had fallen into my lap. Some say Bill had walked into the studio, sat down, played 'Peace Piece' for six minutes, and then got up and left. Others claim that it was an unrehearsed piano modal composition he had recorded for his album,

Everybody Digs Bill. And yet others suggested that 'Peace Piece' was meant to be a take on Leonard Bernstein's classic, 'Some Other Time', which ended up on the album. Apparently, when he played the introduction, he had soon realised where the song was going, and summarily dismissed his bassist and drummer from accompanying him on the piano.

At first, the piano chords took off slowly. I had the sense, an expectation of a trumpet, a saxophone, percussion accompanying his piano. My eyes searched heavenwards, soaking in the chords, the spaces between the notes. And there was pain, time lost – a memory perhaps not truly appreciated for what it was when it was playing itself to its formation. And through those spaces between the four middle piano chords, two playing forward and two moving two steps back, I thought of how inattentive I had been of my Oxford while it had been playing out.

It was gone. My Oxford was gone. In 'Peace Piece', Bill Evans had worked hard to resolve the dissonant notes with those few intervening chords in the middle. There had been so much noise in my Oxford. The gusting wind had moved in chaotic directions, and I had tried to marshal it another way. I should have rather sat down and dipped myself into the chaos. The chaos that was never meant to be smoothed, the chaos of white and black and illegal Oxford. It was meant to be ridden for the very beauty of its disorder.

In 'Peace Piece', there was a grappling with a memory gone, the sadness and grief of it all, echoing the bereavement in my own song. My moment of exit. What I feared most was that I might not be able to hold onto that memory, reflect with clarity on what it truly *was*, not what it should have been. I was meant to savour its true meaning. But beyond the grief there was the promise of the beauty of peace and life.

It was not just that I was leaving my Oxford behind, but that I was stepping out of a memory I might not be able to retell for what it had truly been – tattered in its beauty. It was the story of immigrants who came with Thames Valley chasing after them. The story of African students who wanted a piece of the white pie and never returned to their Africa. It was a story of mothers who wanted to shed their past, and mothers who searched for redemption. A story of white Oxford chasing out blackness.

Sucking on a Marlboro Red, I craned my head heavenwards yet again. And, again, straight from the skies fell Miles Davis's version of 'It Never Entered My Mind'. It was the sadness of nostalgia, of loneliness, of hankering after what had been and gone. The sorrow of missing it all. Miles hadn't muted his trumpet as he so often liked. He let it all out, those long drawn-out notes – slow, pulled to the last tip of stretch. Searing. A bit dry. Chiselled. Full and round. And then those five donging piano chords. In the scattering of the trumpet notes, he pulled out long ones that cut deep to the bone. Then they dissipated, leaving behind, alone, the donging, sad and heavy chords of the piano. And the lyrics came flooding back to me, the loneliness and regret of it all.

I returned to my vanilla ice cream and sparkling water. I knew what I had to do in order to gather it all up, and then put it all out. I had to write the one true story – the one that tells that there ever was such a time as this in this Oxford with these people who never made any sense in a place that could not make any sense of them. I had no idea what I would call it. But it had to start from the beginning. And all I recalled of the beginning was that *I was on my way to see Ian Smith. For twenty pounds, I was going to see the last white prime minister of Zimbabwe.*